I0673976

# THE FEY

## SAGE ALDER

Shattered Glass
PUBLISHING

ISBN 978-1-63869-030-6 (eBook Edition)
ISBN 978-1-63869-035-1 (Paperback Edition)

The characters and events in this book are fictitious. Any similarities to real persons, living or dead, are coincidental and not intended by the author.

Editing by the Proof Posse (aka Dawn, Jackie, Heather, Roxanne, and Mirjam)
Front Cover Art by The Book Brander
Full Cover Design by Shattered Glass Publishing LLC
© Depositphotos.com

*To every reader looking to escape for a while,*
*Be careful what you wish for.*

# FOREWORD

Our history was inaccurate, and our fairy tales were skewed by history. The Fey existed but not in another dimension like our grandmothers whispered to us in bedtime stories. No, long ago, they'd come in ships, seducing humans to carry home with them. They haven't forgotten about us and have been waiting for the opportunity to approach once more.

This time, their needs are greater, and they have no plan to abandon Earth again.

# CHAPTER ONE

## STACY

PIN LAUGHED WITH HIS MEN, NOT PAYING ANY ATTENTION TO ME, AND I glanced at the knife on the counter. The same one I'd used to cut the takeout pizza they were sharing for dinner.

"No shit?" one of the guys asked, still laughing. "He actually went to the drop even after that?"

"He did," Pin said. "That kid brushed off his skinned knee like it was no big deal, wiped the blood off his face, and met the buyer at the park just like I told him. Right, Stace?"

Every eye in the room swung to me as I picked up the knife and rinsed it in the sink.

"Yep," I said, not letting a hint of my heartbreak and rage show.

"When did you say your aunt and uncle were sending him back again?" Pin asked. "I miss the runt."

One of the guys snorted.

"You mean you miss not having to pay out for the drops. Heard Jason's getting greedy," one of the guys said, saving me from answering.

"He shorted me fifty yesterday," Pin said, all humor gone from his tone.

I felt his focus on me but didn't look up as I washed the counter.

"We should get Nicky soon, Stace," Pin said. "Don't you miss him?"

The question was like a knife to my heart. I missed my six-year-old son so much that I barely slept at night. I went to the bathroom and quietly cried at least once a day.

"Sure," I said with an indifference I didn't feel. "But there's not a lot I can do about it unless I want to lose him forever."

The lie rolled off my tongue with ease. It wasn't the first one. Pin had no idea Nicky was my son. I'd introduced Nicky as my brother, who my aunt and uncle took once a year, according to our shared custody terms. That was the newest lie to explain why Nicky wasn't around.

"I want to see those custody papers," Pin said.

All side conversation died at his softly spoken words.

I stopped wiping the counter and looked up at him.

"Why are you rubbing it in? I know I messed up. I was barely twenty when I had to take over guardianship. I was thinking of fun and freedom when I signed it."

His signature smile flashed at me.

"Nothing wrong with some fun and freedom," Pin said. "Which reminds me...why don't you run to the store and pick up some more beer?"

I nodded, tossing the rag toward the sink, relieved that he wasn't pressing for papers he knew I didn't have. He thought my aunt and uncle had them.

But I didn't have an aunt or uncle. At least, none that I knew about. What I had was a dependable neighbor, who had a soft spot for my son, and the sense to play the long game. If only I had the sense to distinguish the bad guys from the good guys. If I had that, I wouldn't be where I was.

Grabbing the cash Pin held out, I started for the door, only to be caught around the waist and pulled into his lap. He kissed me roughly, using too much tongue, which he knew I hated. It was a test. Back when we'd first started dating, I'd pulled away and nicely told him that much tongue didn't do anything for me. He'd cockily said he bet it would. He hadn't done anything for days except treat me like a princess. Then, he'd done it again. That time, I'd kept my mouth shut because he'd been so good to me.

I wasn't treated like a princess anymore, but I knew better than to say anything about what he was doing. So I kissed him back and did my best to act as if I enjoyed it.

When he released me, I smiled at him, kissed him lightly on the lips, and left the house.

Once outside, I didn't pause to wipe my mouth or spit like I wanted to. There were too many eyes, even when it seemed no one was looking. Instead, I hurried my ass to the store and got the beer Pin wanted. The clock was always ticking in his mind, and he questioned every second I spent away from him now.

"Hey, Stace," the cashier said. "Manager just installed new cameras, so you should feel safer coming in after dark now." He nodded toward the camera behind him, angled toward the register, and the one on the far wall aimed at the entrance.

"I appreciate the manager's thoughtfulness," I said, taking the beer and Pin's change. "Have a good night." I gave a half-hearted wave as I left.

Pin was not going to be happy about the cameras. The convenience store was one of his favorite drop locations now that Nicky was no longer an option for drops at the park.

My fingers tightened on the case of beer as I relived the moment Pin had been telling his friends...the moment he'd tripped Nicky to punish me. I'd said no to drinking with him and the guys the night before. He hadn't made a big deal about it when I'd instead put Nicky to bed and read him a book. Pin had waited until the next day. That'd been the first time he'd used Nicky to deliver drugs and my wake-up call to how bad things really were.

I'd started cooperating after that...and planning.

No matter what it took, I'd promised myself I would remove Nicky from Pin's reach.

Now I just needed to figure a way out so I could join my son.

Lost in my thoughts, I didn't notice how quiet the guys were when I returned with the beer.

"The store has cameras," I said as I put the cans in the fridge. "The clerk pointed them out."

"Where's Nicky, Stace?" Pin asked, his voice devoid of all emotion.

A chill ran down my spine as I turned to look at him in confusion.

"What?"

Beyond Pin, the TV showed a picture of Nicky, Adriana, and another little girl. My heart froze in my chest.

"What's going on? Why's Nicky's picture on the news?" I was at the table and turning up the volume with the remote without even registering that I'd moved.

"That's what I'd like to know," Pin said.

His low tone, so close to my ear, sent another shiver down my spine before he grabbed the back of my neck.

The reporter said something about replaying the earlier broadcast in case anyone missed it. It showed Adriana, my neighbor. She was dressed in a sexy-as-hell sheer gown and had her hair done up.

"Hello, my name is Adriana Wilston. I was abducted May 15th from the Chicago area of the United States along with Lillian Elwiss and Nicky Ludridge and seventeen others."

My ears started to ring so badly that I couldn't hear what else she was saying for a moment. May 15th. That was the day I'd said goodbye to Nicky and sent him to her apartment.

The ringing cleared enough to hear her again.

"...Earth has resources that will interest more species than we can handle on our own. We're going to need help so that more people aren't taken like we were. This is an official request from two races—the Oebri and the Anrothe—to introduce themselves to our world leaders. They both went out of their way to help us. The Oebri even healed my broken hand."

The ringing spiked.

*Healed her? Where was Nicky? What happened to Nicky?*

"I hope our leaders agree to meet," she continued. "There's so much we don't know and very little time to learn it."

The reporter came back on.

"Authorities are speculating this is a large-scale hoax to extort money from—"

The blow to the side of my head knocked me off my feet. I tumbled into the storage cabinet before hitting the floor.

In a daze, I tried to lift myself. A hand fisted my hair and pulled me upright. Pin's enraged gaze held mine as he leaned close, his face inches from mine.

"I took you in. I fed you, cared for you, treated you like a queen, and you betray me like this? You think you can run a hustle without me?"

He jerked my head back, tearing hair from the roots, and hit my face repeatedly.

I couldn't catch my breath or think for the first three blows. Then fight or flight kicked in, and I tried to get away. When that didn't work, I brought my arms up to protect my face. That just gave him a new target. The blows rained down on my ribs and stomach, and when I collapsed to the floor after he released my hair, he kicked my legs and back as he yelled at me.

He swore, kicked me one last time, then started yelling at the guys. The sound of my pulse thumping in my ears almost drowned it out as I lay on the floor, unmoving.

Every inch of me hurt. Silent tears trailed to the floor. Fear and anger mixed in a toxic storm, and I thought of the knife again. Only this time, not to kill Pin. I was done. So done.

Images of Nicky popped into my mind. My reason to keep going. My reason to fight, no matter how pathetically.

I didn't open my eyes or stand. I waited until the yelling calmed and the volume on the TV went up. They listened to the reports, trying to figure out what scam I was running. I listened and tried to force my dazed thoughts into focus so I could figure out what had happened.

Apparently, while I was out on the beer run, Adriana's message had taken over every bit of technology we possessed. TVs. Radios. Computers. Phones. Everything and all at once. Even the stuff that hadn't been on. And it didn't just happen in our house. It happened worldwide.

Some people believed that it really was aliens. After all, who else could pull something off like that? More people were shouting that it was just a hoax. That some hacker had timed everything perfectly. Countries were pointing fingers at each other, and the evening crawled by in the chaos of speculation and so-called expert testimonials.

Eventually, when Pin's guys were voicing enough doubt, I carefully got up and went to the freezer for some ice. My eye was already swelling shut, but my forearms had taken so many hits that the bruising felt bone deep. I couldn't decide what needed more attention. Standing there, I switched between both until the ice melted and something else started to hurt more.

Around midnight, the news showed my picture and asked for any information regarding my whereabouts.

"Good thing I gave you a disguise for the next few days, Stace," Pin said with a chuckle.

I smiled, cracking my lip and making it bleed again.

Pin's humor faded. "We should find Nicky, don't you think?"

While lying in pain on the floor, I'd distracted myself by thinking of ways to save myself from my current hell so I could find Nicky. So I was ready with some quick answers that hopefully wouldn't earn me another beating.

Rather than continue to meet his cold gaze, I looked at the TV. "We should, but I wouldn't know where to start. If he was kidnapped from my aunt and uncle's, their place is going to be crawling with police."

"You telling me you had nothing to do with this?" he asked.

"I don't even know what this is yet," I said. "Is it a hoax? Is it a kidnapping? Was I caught on video doing a drop, and this is some far-fetched way to get me out in the open? I don't know. I could rule out the kidnapping by calling my aunt and uncle, but what if that's what they're waiting for?"

I sounded like a paranoid crazy person. But that was okay because being with Pin these last few months had taught me something very important.

People didn't fuck with crazy.

Pin nodded thoughtfully. "You're right. It'll be smart to let you lie low for a bit either way."

He left me alone for the rest of that night and the following day, which was a good thing. The pain from my beating only got worse, not better. I couldn't sit or lay down. Standing wasn't much better.

After another three days, the news channels were still talking about the hoax. The family of the little girl had been reported missing by the girl's aunt the day they were allegedly taken. The aunt gave an interview that she had no idea what happened and hoped whoever had the family would return them.

"Stace, grab me a beer," Pin said from the table.

I was finally slowly moving around with a little less pain, and my bruises were starting to fade to the ugly greens and browns from the deep purples they'd been. So I hated what I was about to say.

"Can't. We're out."

He didn't react angrily, though. He simply dug into his pocket and pulled out some bills, holding them up without even looking at me.

"Get a case."

I used the same pace to grab the money and head out the door as I had for any other task around the house, not letting my eagerness show.

Four days post-beating, I still looked like I was in a car wreck, and it wasn't yet dark out. Just before dusk, and the sun was sitting low on the horizon. So I walked a little slower outside, hoping someone would notice.

*Please let someone recognize me*, I thought. *Anyone.*

However, no one even looked twice at me as I made my way to the convenience store. I thought about running instead of going inside, but where would I go? Could I even make it to a police station before Pin caught wind? And if I did, what then? I had no idea what was going on with Nicky and the news. Would I be thrown in jail, leaving my son to fend for himself?

My nose started to tingle, and I blinked back my tears of frustration as I opened the door to the convenience store.

The clerk didn't say a word of greeting. He just looked at me and hurried back to reading his magazine. I realized then that no one would help me. Minding one's own business was the best way to stay safe in this neighborhood.

While the clerk rang me up, I stared at the camera behind the register and hoped the manager was watching the footage. There was a reward for information regarding me. Someone had to get greedy, right?

*Report me. Please.*

# CHAPTER TWO

## ALERNON

I watched the feeds from Earth and felt a surge of desperation.

After four days, Earth's leaders continued to tell the public that Adriana's message was nothing more than a hoax. They pretended to accuse one another, all while meeting in secret and exchanging data from their satellites and space stations in an attempt to verify our location. So far, they had been unable to confirm our position on the other side of the moon, but how long could I allow this to go on?

I, along with every member of my crew, knew what waited for us on that planet's surface. Females. Millions of them.

How long had we searched the systems, looking for an answer to our population crisis? How many planets had we contracted with in hopes of coming closer to a solution? Earth was an unmolested cache in the systems, now ready for harvest.

"How much longer must we wait?" Quinoll asked beside me, echoing my thoughts.

I glanced at my second in command. His ice-blue pale eyes, a trait of our race, tracked the information on the feeds. The tips of his long-pointed ears were slightly blue, showing his agitation.

"As long as it takes," I said. "Impatience will not drive progress. Summon Vegori to take over for you, and go help Aumnal."

He sent the message to Vegori and left me alone in the comms center to dwell on our current challenge. We needed to convince Earth of the danger they faced and persuade them to accept our help before it was too late. For them and for us. We needed to secure a claim on the planet's primary resource before others discovered what we had.

Earth females were not only plentiful, but they possessed another highly desirable trait for my people. While most other species' females fell to their knees before us and offered complete subjugation, Earth females could resist.

I thought of the way Adriana looked at Zarris and wondered what it would be like to be with a female who truly desired me.

Even before she had fully bonded to Zarris, Adriana had felt my emotions and chosen not to respond to them. A female with a will—one who could choose to be with me because she wanted to, not because I wanted her to—was something rare and precious.

A wave of hungry, angry need washed through me. I *wanted*. I *ached*. Closing my eyes, I focused on pulling those emotions back in.

Not only could the Earth females resist us, but based on the scan Adriana had allowed, human females had one hundred percent breeding compatibility with my race, the Oebri.

With our advanced technology, it would be so easy to take what we wanted. But without Earth's consent, we risked war with the systems. And there were too few Oebri for us to make a stand for Earth's rare resources.

Frustrated, I went back to reading the scans, looking for any hint of cooperation.

Fear-filled threats and speculation remained dominant.

"Command Alernon," I said, activating the ship's artificial

intelligence. "Expand the ship monitoring to encompass the Senwar system. Full alert for any non-Oebri ship detection. Notify me via comms for any Oebri ship detection. Notify Quinoll and Vegori for all other detections."

"Command Alernon acknowledged," the ship responded.

I turned away from the feed, ready for a break from the endless irritation of stubborn humans, when an alert started to flash.

"Facial recognition confirmed," the ship said. "Tracking human female, Stacy Ludridge, aged twenty-five solar-runs, confirmed. Location Chicago, Illinois."

Adriana hadn't been the only human we'd rescued from Anrothe. Of the two younglings with her, the female had lost her birther and donor. Only the male youngling still had a birther on the surface of this planet.

According to Adriana, his birther had abandoned him, which is why Adriana had insisted we look for her.

"Show Stacy Ludridge to me," I said, curious about the female.

The image displayed on my screen stunned me. A small blonde woman entered the trade center through a sliding door. Her loose coat and jeans hid her shape. But nothing hid her face.

With my fists clenched at my sides, I stared at the vividly colored skin of the female staring straight into the camera. She had been abused beyond measure.

"Command Alernon," I said roughly. "Summon Adriana and Zarris to the comms center immediately."

I impatiently paced before the picture of Nicky's birther, unable to look away until Adriana and Zarris arrived.

Adriana's gaze went straight to the other female's image, and she lifted a hand to her mouth.

"Oh my God," she said. "What happened?"

"I was hoping you could enlighten me. Is this level of damage common on your planet?" I asked, barely able to contain the outrage I felt.

"I mean, there are accidents. Maybe she was in one?" But doubt laced her words. "Is there more footage?"

I replayed the recording from the moment Stacy entered. She walked slowly and with a slight limp as she picked up a box of something and carried it to the counter. She exchanged paper with another person then left with the box.

"She bought beer?" Adriana said, sounding angry. "I want to smack her."

Zarris shot me a concerned look and rested his hands on Adriana's shoulders. Abusing breedable females was a crime strictly punished in the systems. However, that law assumed the abuser was male. I wasn't sure what punishment could be carried out if the abuser was female. Likely a light reprimand and permanent separation of the two females.

"I suggest we extract Stacy and question her first," I said.

"Agreed," Adriana said. "But there are two problems. How can we get her when you haven't been welcomed yet? And how do we know where she is?"

"Command Alernon," I said. "Show me all camera feeds in the nearby area with humans matching the hair and clothing of recently identified human female, Stacy Ludridge."

Three camera feeds popped up, showing Stacy walking down the sidewalk in front of various houses. I paid attention to the time stamps and pointed to the newest one. It took a bit more searching after that, but we pinpointed the probable house after doing a registry search.

"Stone Pinchas," Adriana said. "That has to be the Uncle Pin that Nicky mentioned. I'm betting she's there. Now that we have an idea where she is, how can we get her?"

"I believe it's time to give the humans the proof they need," I said. "I will collect Nicky's birther myself."

Adriana shook her head and made a face. "Birther? That's what you call a mom?"

"No, that is what we call the female who birthed the youngling. Mother is reserved for any female who raises the youngling. Likewise, we call the male who created the youngling a donor, and the father is the one who raises it."

Vegori entered the comms center.

"Perfect timing," I said. "Prepare for my transfer to the surface. Adriana, I humbly request that you remain here to respond to any concerns your leaders may raise during my absence. Vegori will be here to guide you."

"Wait," she said, catching my arm as I moved to leave. "You're going alone?"'

"I have reason to believe a breedable female and the birther to a youngling in my care is in danger, which is enough cause to allow my interference without welcome," I said. "However, if others accompany me, it could be viewed by the systems as an act of aggression rather than a rescue. I cannot risk that."

She held my gaze, and seeing her growing concern for me created a surge of yearning I couldn't contain. I wanted this—a female who worried for my safety. A female who waited for my return the prexel I left her.

However, Adriana didn't react in any way to my emotional surge, proving the depth of her bond with Zarris. I smiled and gently eased her hand from my sleeve.

"Do not fear for me," I said. "This is not my first time appearing unwelcomed on a planet."

"Telling someone not to worry doesn't stop the worry," she said. "I'll monitor the feeds if you promise that I can monitor you too."

"My time on the surface will be recorded," I said, evading a direct promise. "I should depart quickly before Stacy leaves again."

I left Vegori to deal with Adriana and hurried to the

transference bay. At my command, he sent me to the pre-identified location.

Earth's blue sky was washed in vibrant pinks, oranges, and purples when I appeared. Its beauty gave me a reason to pause as I stood outside a home whose wooden exterior showed signs of decay and rot. The glass openings were covered from the inside, blocking out the wonder of the planet's colorful sky.

I could think of no reason to cover viewing portals other than to hide whatever might happen within, which was beneficial for me in this instance.

After activating my companion orb, which would translate everything I said, I approached the entry and knocked as Adriana had told me was custom.

No one answered, but one of the window coverings beside the door moved.

"I wish to speak to Stacy Ludridge," I said, keeping my tone polite and a bit coaxing. "It's regarding her son, Nicky."

The orb relayed my words in English, this location's primary language, but the window covering did not move again. I glanced at the orb, which was recording everything.

"To finish my assessment, I will enter the home to visually confirm the female's welfare."

The door didn't open when I tried the antiquated handle, so I used force. The wood securing the latch gave way with a crack, and my peaceful thoughts fled as I stepped into the dim interior.

An unknown male had Stacy pinned to the wall by her throat. Her lip and nose bled, and her face was an unnatural red as she hit the arm holding her in place. While the male held her, he pointed a primitive weapon at me.

"Close the door, friend," he said.

I used my foot to nudge the door closed behind me, cutting off the rose-hued light filling the room.

The orb floating near my head compensated, growing brighter to illuminate the space.

The man watched me as the female, Stacy, continued to struggle for breath.

"Release her," I said, echoed by the orb. "Or, by the penalty of the systems, face death."

He laughed but let her go. She slowly slid down the wall and stayed in a crouch as her breaths wheezed in and out.

"Did you say you know her son?" the man asked.

"Are you the reason for her previous damage?" I asked.

"Damage," he echoed, glancing at her. "Nah, man. She's clumsy. I was holding her there so she'd stop falling into stuff. I'm helpful like that."

He chuckled, and I smiled, feeling no humor, only rage. He'd touched a female with the intent to harm.

"So, where's her boy?" he asked. "We've been missing him like crazy here."

My gaze shifted from him to *her*.

"Have you been missing him, Stacy? Would you like to see him again?"

She didn't lift her bowed head to look at me, but it didn't matter. I could feel her longing and need. Mine rose in response, but I quickly quelled it. If she'd felt it, she didn't react. It made me even more determined to convince the female to leave with me.

"I can take you to him," I said.

"She's not going anywhere," the man said. "I don't think you understand what's happening here. You broke into my house uninvited. That's trespassing, friend. We can shoot trespassers here." He waved his weapon at me.

"Nicky is well," I said, purposely provoking the man by ignoring him. "He's playing with his companion, Lil. They have both suffered much recently, and I believe Nicky would enjoy seeing you again."

Stacy's longing increased, as did the man's anger. He took a step toward me.

"Fuck-face, I was talking to you," he said.

Continuing to ignore him, I remained focused on the crouched female. Her breathing was starting to come a little easier, but I saw her wince when she swallowed.

"Despite everything, your neighbor, Adriana, did well protecting your son," I said. "The emotional trauma he has experienced will fade with time. Physically, he is unchanged."

The man had calmed while I spoke.

"Did you say neighbor, you cosplay freak?" he asked.

I looked at the man. "I was not speaking to you, fuck-face."

His face turned red, confirming my suspicion that the term was an insult.

"You have no idea who you're dealing with," he said a second before the weapon discharged with a muffled pop.

The orb's release of energy happened in almost the same instant, and I watched the metal projectile flatten against the energy field around me. It dropped to the floor, and the man fired several more times before he physically charged me.

"Nil," I said, dispersing the field.

I caught his fist as he attempted to swing at me and twisted it, moving with him in a defensive dance so he stood before me with his arm pinned behind his back and my other hand gripping his throat.

"You are clumsy," I said. "I will hold you here to protect you from accidentally falling and hurting yourself."

The man mumbled a few words that didn't translate but proved I was not holding him so tightly that he could not breathe.

Whatever he'd said gained Stacy's attention, though. She lifted her head and looked at him. I saw and felt the hate she harbored for this male.

Her gaze then shifted to me. The discoloration around her eyes and mouth was more vivid in person as was the pain in her gaze. It fueled my anger toward the male I held. I wanted to hurt him. I wanted him to suffer for the rest of his life for what he'd done to her.

My grip started to tighten.

The man flailed more desperately.

"Tell me you wish to come with me, female," I said. "This male has already proven unworthy of your keeping."

"Where is Nicky?" she asked in a raw rasp.

"Aboard my ship. He is with his guardian, assigned to him by Adriana. A male called Baynol. He is trustworthy and will protect Nicky with his life."

Stacy stood slowly, wincing as she did so.

"I don't think Pin can breathe," she said, not looking away from me.

"To abuse a female is punishable by death in the systems. Does he deserve death?"

Her gaze flicked to the male she called Pin, and I felt a renewed surge of her anger and hate.

"He deserves worse than death for everything he did to my son and me."

I immediately released the male. He fell to his knees and held his throat as he tried to breathe.

"He hurt the youngling?" I asked.

She didn't answer as she stared at the man.

"Then I will leave it to the systems to decide his fate," I said.

She still didn't look away from the man.

"Stacy," I said, holding out my hand. "Do you wish to see your son?"

She finally looked up at me, her yellow hair sticking to her sweaty and bloody face.

I withstood the scrutiny of her searching gaze, trying to shield the desperation I was feeling. I needed her to take my hand. To touch me. To allow me to take her from here, where she knew nothing but abuse. The need to take her into my arms and soothe her roared through me as I held still and waited.

For her.

For the female I'd been waiting for.

"Yes. I want my son," she said, and I felt every ounce of her desperation.

*I've won*, I thought, fighting not to smile.

# CHAPTER THREE

## STACY

Pin had called the man standing inside the door a cosplay freak, and I understood why. It had nothing to do with his lean, long build towering over my meager five foot four inches by a foot. It was the rest of him. From the shoulder-length black-to-white ombre hair he had to have paid top dollar for to his very pointed and realistic elfin ears, slightly tinted blue at the ends. If the hair and the ears weren't enough to give him an otherworldly sexy vibe, the eyes did.

The light blue eyes, almost to the point of icy silver, remained locked on me as I carefully skirted around Pin, who didn't make any move to stop me.

My head was still reeling from what had happened. When he had called Nicky's name through the door, it had set Pin off and earned me some new bruises. Pin would have killed me if the new guy hadn't broken in.

He obviously knew who I was if he knew Nicky was my son and not my brother. But it didn't mean I trusted him. He'd simply given me the opportunity to leave Pin.

Ignoring the beautiful man's hand, I limped out the door. The pretty sunset from earlier had faded to almost nothing, and the first stars could be seen in the twilight sky. A street light down the road was already on, which meant I could clearly see there was no car waiting.

*Where in the hell is Nicky?*

My throat hurt too much to ask.

"Command Alernon, prepare transference," the man said behind me.

Actually, he didn't say it. The glowing orb floating nearby did. The words coming out of the man's mouth sounded like another language.

A beam of light about six feet in diameter appeared in the street in front of me, and a dog started barking like mad nearby.

I looked up, trying to see the source of the light since I didn't actually believe it was from a spaceship. But the beam seemed to come out of nowhere.

How much money did he have to waste, trying to pull off a hoax of this degree? It had to be a lot. Considering the weird hovering glow-ball by his head, it wasn't unreasonable to believe he had some quiet helicopter up there shining a spotlight down at us.

In truth, his finances weren't my real worry. I wanted to know why he was looking for me, why he said he had my son, and why he was going to these lengths to convince me he was an alien.

Glancing over my shoulder at the man, I wondered if he was mentally all there. I really didn't have the energy to deal with another psycho.

He held my gaze as he spoke.

"Walk into the light," the orb translated.

"That's what people do when they die," I rasped, taking a step forward while still watching him.

My foot came down partially on the curb, and I started to fall.

He shot forward and caught me before I could hit the ground.

It hurt. The places Pin had kicked me were a long way from healed. But being caught was better than falling.

The man's arm supported my weight as he held me close, and I stared up at him, seeing his eyes clearly.

The icy blue color wasn't due to contacts. They were his real eyes. My gaze shifted to his ears. The pointed tips didn't look like plastic extensions. In fact, the blue tint was gone now.

*They were real.*

Panic wasn't new to me. Panicking because I might actually be looking at an alien that looked a lot like Legolas from Lord of the Rings was new, though. I struggled to breathe and act normally.

"Be at peace, female," he said softly.

He swung me up into his arms.

"We will go together."

Did I want him to carry me to God-knew-where? No. However, I couldn't stick around either—not after he'd blabbed about Nicky being my son and staying with my neighbor. Pin would make me pay for lying to him like I had.

So I nodded and watched the possibly alien-man walk us toward the light.

A tingle started in my middle the moment we entered the beam and spread outward. Before I could panic more, the sensation faded along with the light.

We were in a large empty room. The walls, ceiling, and floor were all an uninterrupted, uniform light grey.

I looked over the man's shoulder, not believing what I was seeing. None of it could be real, right? Had he drugged me?

I touched my face and winced. Definitely not drugged. I wouldn't feel that much pain if I was hallucinating.

Then this was real? He was real? I'd just stepped into a beam of light and appeared somewhere else?

When I looked at him, he was watching me closely.

"Where are we?" I asked. Each word hurt my raw throat.

"We're aboard my ship."

He continued to hold me and wait for a reaction.

I studied his face again and, this time, reached up to touch his ear. The tip was warm, and it felt very real. I ran my fingers through his hair to touch his scalp. It felt real too.

I withdrew my hand, my focus shifting between him and our surroundings.

"I can see your confusion. Allow me to explain on our way to a med bay, my beauty."

*My beauty?*

A spike of fear pierced through me.

"Please put me down."

He looked puzzled by my request but lowered me to my feet. As soon as I stood on my own, I retreated a few painful steps and tried to keep my rising fear in check.

"I'm not your or anyone else's beauty," I said. "Where's my son? I want to see him now."

The man's icy blue gaze was anything but cold as it swept over my face.

"He's in the entertainment area we created for the younglings. I can lead you there. However, I believe seeing you as you are will cause both younglings distress. Allow me to heal your injuries first. Please."

I didn't buy his nice act. I'd fallen for Pin's and would never fall for it again. But the rest? The rest was looking pretty fucking real, and I wasn't sure what to do about it but play along. At least until I could figure out what was going on and where I really was.

"Sure. Let's go to the med bay. Can I get ears like yours there? They're pretty cool." They had to be surgically augmented. It was the only explanation.

He tilted his head at me, a slow smile tugging at his lips. The man was devastatingly handsome. While kicking the shit out of Pin, he'd oozed bad-boy sexiness. And his one-armed catch when

I'd tripped in the street had been full-on heroic. But during those acts, his eyes hadn't held the level of smolder he now aimed at me. He was hot. Dangerously so. And he knew it.

"Genetic modifications to change a female's root species features is forbidden," he said. "And I prefer your ears the way they are."

"Right," I said, even though I had no idea what he was talking about. "What's your name?"

"Alernon."

"Why aren't you leading me to the med bay, Alernon?"

His smile grew more pronounced.

"You have a strong will, Stacy. I can feel your attraction to me, but you don't act on it. You fascinate me more than I anticipated."

"And you're still not walking," I said, not believing a word he said.

He chuckled and gestured for me to walk with him. I did my best to hide how much each step hurt.

A section of wall opened at our approach, and my mouth dropped a little in shock and amazement at the long, almost-white hall slowly curving in both directions on the other side. The orb floated along with us.

"I know you do not yet fully believe you are on a ship. Once you do, remember you are safe here. You will never again experience the pain you've endured."

I wanted to tell him I didn't need a hero or protector. I just needed my son and some cash so I could run as far away from Pin as possible. Starting over wouldn't be easy, but I'd done it before when I was pregnant with Nicky. I could do it again.

But a part of me wished I didn't have to. That soft part of me wanted someone in my life who would help shoulder some of the burdens. I wasn't dumb enough to listen to her, though. That needy bitch had screwed me over too many times.

As we continued down the hallway, I noticed the different

colored strips of light flashing in the floor moving in a pattern down the hall. I almost asked about them but realized he would use it as a way to distract me and delay admitting the truth—that he didn't have Nicky and that I wasn't in space.

"Will you allow me to carry you?" he asked when my limp grew more pronounced.

Pin had hit me in the thigh with the butt of the gun when Alernon said Nicky was my son. It hurt like a bitch then and felt like I was two steps away from cramping.

"No. I'm fine," I said.

"We still have a distance to go."

"I understand."

Alernon didn't say anything else, but I noticed how he slowed his pace to match mine.

We turned a few more corners before he stopped in the middle of the hallway and touched a panel on the wall. The wall opened, showing a room inside.

Whoever had designed the space had gone out of their way to make it sleek, with a smooth table in the center and a counter along one wall. An arm of some sort protruded from the table. A blue light on it blinked once when I stepped through the opening.

"You will need to remove your coverings," Alernon said.

Another jolt of fear coursed through me as I slowly turned to face him. The door behind him was gone. A smooth expanse of wall stretched out uninterrupted in its place.

No way out.

"I'd rather not," I said, meeting his gaze.

"Very well," Alernon said, not showing a hint of anger or annoyance, which worried me even more. Instead, he studied me for a moment. "Will you lie on the table for an exam?"

I slowly shook my head.

"You doubt my intentions," he said. "Very well. Watch." He walked around me and lay on the table.

"Prepare for species type: Oebri. Scan for injuries and make repair and health maintenance recommendations," he said.

The arm moved, positioning itself over Alernon's covered feet. A blue line of light flared to life and slowly moved up his body where the scanner lights narrowed and disappeared above his head.

"No injuries detected," a disembodied voice said in English. "Vitamin and mineral levels are normal. Fertility levels are normal for species averages. Scan complete."

He sat up, swinging his legs off the table.

"The scan will not harm you. You have my word."

He got off the table and indicated it was my turn.

"How can you understand me?" I asked, glancing at the orb. "Everything it says is in English."

He smiled slightly. "I have a translator implant that gives me access to all of Earth's languages."

"Ah." I didn't believe him for a second.

I glanced at where the door had been then moved to the table. It wasn't easy to get on it, but I didn't ask for help. As I lay down, I kept my eyes on Alernon, and I knew he'd read my mistrust when he took a few steps back.

"Prepare for species type: human," he said. "Scan for injuries and make repair and health maintenance recommendations."

Once more, the arm came to life. The light swept over me at the same pace it had with Alernon.

"External tissue damage. Recommend pain lubricant. Internal tissue damage has occurred to the left thigh. Recommend regeneration stims. Internal structural damage has occurred to three ribs. Recommend regeneration stims. External tissue irritation. Recommend pain lubricant. Vitamin and mineral deficiency. Recommend vitality stim. Fertility level: seventy-three percent. Species average fertility levels: unavailable. Insufficient data. Genetic compatibility: one hundred percent. Scan complete."

Stunned, I glanced at the arm as it retreated. My limp had obviously given away my thigh injury, but how had he known about my ribs? I turned my head to look at him.

Rather than ask about his machine, I asked, "What's a stim?"

"One piece of our healing process. Will you allow me to heal you, Stacy? Please. Your face has lost some of its color, and I am concerned."

"Sure," I said, no longer sure of anything. If this was all real, then he was an alien with a translator implant who was speaking a language I'd never heard before.

Shit.

"I will need you to remove your coverings," he and the orb said.

I held his gaze for a very long time before carefully sitting up. He moved quickly, offering a supporting arm behind my back this time, which I appreciated.

Once I was upright, he retreated again and watched from a safer distance as I unlaced my shoes. After toeing them off, I stood and stopped paying attention to him. My pants came off next, followed by my shirt.

I left both on the floor and lay on the table.

Alernon's silence grew until I gave in and looked his way.

He stood there with his eyes closed, and his hands fisted.

"If you're thinking of hitting something, please try a wall," I said. "It's more fun than people."

His eyes snapped open, and I could have sworn I felt the absolute rage I saw reflected in their depths. As quickly as it appeared, it disappeared.

"Forgive me," he said. "I didn't mean—" He took a calming breath. "Administer level 1 Oebri sedation."

It took a second for what he said to register. By the time it did, the arm had already stung my leg. A whimper escaped me.

"Apologies," he murmured, moving closer to the table.

I opened my mouth to tell him to back up, but a wave of something warm and nice rolled through me, taking away some of my aches.

"I wouldn't mind more of whatever that was," I said.

He reached the table and smoothed back my hair as he studied my face. His touch didn't offend me.

"A bit more, then," he said. "Administer level 2 Oebri sedation."

The arm didn't even hurt my thigh when it touched the next time.

"Are you ready?" he asked when it moved away.

"For what?"

"To heal."

"Sure."

"Proceed with recommendations," he said. He stood back as the arm touched my leg several more times.

"Would you like a translator as well?" he asked. "It would be painless and allow you to understand any language spoken on this ship and on your planet."

"Sure. Why not."

The arm moved to a spot just behind my ear. I felt pressure but nothing else.

When it finished, he moved away and returned with a small white container.

"To help things heal faster," he said.

I nodded and let him gently rub the salve around my bruised eye and lip. His focused attention bothered me a little. I knew that look. He was interested, and that was dangerous. But he didn't do anything more than carefully apply the medicine. Once he was done with my face, he smoothed it onto my collarbone, then above and below my bra-covered right breast.

Although I was pleasantly pain-free, whatever he'd given me hadn't fogged up my thinking. I watched him closely for any sign that he was doing anything more than helping me. However, he didn't give a single leer, acting like a perfect gentleman.

*Pin had been the same way*, I reminded myself.

After spreading the salve on my thigh, Alernon returned the container to its magically hidden spot in the wall.

"The bruising on your face should fade quickly," he said. "In another arc, it won't be visible. Will you allow me to show you to a room where you can refresh before—"

The door opened behind him, and Adriana stormed into the room with a huge beefcake trailing behind her. My gaze darted between him and the insanely sexy-gorgeous dress she was wearing.

"Oh, Stacy," she said a minute before she hugged me tightly.

"Adriana, stop. She has internal damage." Alernon moved quickly and had his hands on her shoulders, but I wrapped my arms around her and hugged her, unwilling to let him take her away.

"I'm so sorry," she whispered, cracking through my defenses.

The tears started to fall, and as I shook, she held me.

"You should have told me," she said. "I would have helped."

"You did help," I said. Then I started to sob.

"Go ahead and cry," Adriana said soothingly. "You're safe now."

I don't know how long I cried in her arms, but eventually, the fun stuff Alernon had given me started to wear off, and some of the rib pain returned. I eased out of her hold and looked around the room. We were alone.

"They're waiting in the hall," she said. "Zarris likes staying close."

She held out a bundle that looked like the same material she was wearing.

"Here. We can be twins for a while. It'll feel better on your bruises than your clothes will. Trust me."

# CHAPTER FOUR

## ALERNON

THE RESTLESS ANGER DROVE ME TO PACE THE HALL AS WE WAITED FOR the females to emerge. Seeing the full extent of the damage the male had done to Stacy had brought me to the edge of reason, and I doubted I would recover soon.

"You should have killed him," Zarris said, watching me.

"I wanted to," I said, fisting my hands angrily.

"How could a male do that?" Zarris asked. He'd witnessed the level of Stacy's abuse when he'd entered, and it had to feel just as alien for him as it felt for me. His people would never hurt a female.

Females were meant to be protected. Cherished in every way.

"Did Adriana watch the live feed as well?" I asked.

"She was insistent. Quinoll gave in the first time she folded her hands together under her chin and begged prettily."

I could imagine how quickly my second had succumbed to the female's pleading. It was what we, Oebri, did. We sought to please any female in our presence in hopes of winning her favor. Some were much easier to please than others due to our natural persuasion. Adriana seemed delightfully unaffected by it, though. As did Stacy.

"Quinoll is desperate for a female of his own," I said. "We all are."

"If news of Stacy's treatment on Earth spreads, will your crew want to remove females for their own safety?" Zarris asked.

"Quinoll knows to remain quiet. He understands we will all lose a chance at a female if that happens. Ensure Adriana and your men understand the same."

"I will. How badly damaged is Nicky's birther?"

I thought back to how she'd cowered against the wall after the male had released her and the way she'd winced when she'd stood, and again when I'd caught her. Her physical injuries filled me with anger, but it was the damage the male had likely done to her mind that truly enraged me.

"She has superficial and deep tissue damage and broken bones. I don't know how she walked to the med bay." I exhaled heavily, feeling a surge of frustration. "I offered to carry her, but she has no trust."

"She suffered at the hands of a male. Why should she believe that your hands will be any different?"

I stopped pacing and cast Zarris an annoyed glance. "I know that. Which is why I didn't press her to say yes. Understanding her rejection doesn't make watching her suffering any easier."

He clapped me on the shoulder. "Patience…my friend."

I laughed lightly as he'd intended. "Humans seem contrary, don't they? Calling me friend while threatening me with his primitive weapon."

"Adriana did not like when he called you 'fuck-face,' but she was entertained when you used it. She agreed that you should have killed him."

I sighed. "I had to honor Stacy's wish for him to suffer greater misery. Once we've established a peaceful collaboration with Earth's leaders, I will ensure her wish is granted. I'm certain

Earth's leaders will want the male punished after they watch the recording.

"Was there anything in the feeds regarding the transference to their planet?"

"The same outcries declaring it a hoax while they quietly speculated otherwise in private," Zarris said. "However, Adriana believes public belief will sway the leaders into action quickly."

"Let us hope it does not take much longer. Does Nicky know that his birther is here?"

"No. Once Adriana understood, she asked Quinoll to clear the halls and to keep quiet about Stacy's presence. She wasn't sure what Stacy's mental state would be."

The wall to the med bay opened, revealing Adriana and Stacy. They wore the same gown. Adriana looked lovely in it, as always. But Stacy stole my breath.

Even bruised with eyes red and puffy from crying, she was a vision. The material hugged her form to perfection, encasing her breasts so I could see the shape of her nipples then flowing loosely to her hips, where it molded to her again. I saw a hint of a single line of darkness at the apex of her thighs.

My hunger rose swiftly, and I glanced at Stacy's face as I reined in my desperate need.

Her soft brown eyes remained steadily fixed on my face, missing nothing.

"Thanks for the dress," she said with almost no emotion. "Where's Nicky?"

I could still feel her suspicion and mistrust. It rubbed against me like fine sand, mildly irritating me even as I enjoyed the sensation. When was the last time I'd felt anything other than lust and need from a female? I couldn't help the slight smile I gave her.

"He's playing with Lil, a little girl who was abducted with us," Adriana said. "We can take you to see him now, but you might want to reconsider meeting him like you are. He's been through a lot. They both have."

Stacy's level of suspicion increased.

"Alernon already said that. But don't you think Nicky needs to know I've been going through a lot, too, and that's why I left, rather than thinking I've been having a great time without him?"

Adriana glanced at me.

"Hiding from the truth never makes it less truthful," I said.

"Okay," she said, looking at Stacy. "You're the mom. Your call."

Stacy's cheeks reddened with the swell of shame she felt, but she didn't say anything else.

"Are you comfortable walking, or would you like—"

"I'll walk," she said, interrupting my offer.

"As you wish."

Adriana and Zarris remained with us. As we navigated the halls to the entertainment center, Adriana explained what had happened to them. Their abduction. Their time on the ship and crashing on Anrothe. It was similar to what she'd shared on Earth's news feeds but with more details regarding the hardships of the children.

It was a tale I already knew well. One that no female or youngling should suffer.

Stacy remained quiet, listening to everything.

"Thank you for taking care of Nicky," she said when Adriana finished. "I still think he was safer with you than he would have been with me."

With renewed anger, I thought of the man we'd left behind and wished she'd asked for his death.

The younglings' laughter rang in the hall before we reached the entertainment room. The door always remained open so that my crew could hear the sound.

Stacy's steps slowed. Her eyes watered.

"Maybe you're right," she said softly. "Maybe I should wait."

I caught her hand, lightly holding her fingers to gain her attention and to feel her skin against mine. I let a little of the need I felt for her slip as I spoke.

"Until you see him with your own eyes, will you believe he is well, or will you believe he is hiding the hurt of missing the female who birthed him?"

She frowned at me and tugged her hand free. "I'm feeling enough guilt without you adding to it."

"It wasn't my intention to cause you guilt," I said, wondering if she'd truly felt nothing from me.

"Wasn't it?" She stepped around me and gracefully strode into the room.

I was a few steps behind her and witnessed the youngling's shock when he saw his mother. Tears sprang to Nicky's eyes, and he wailed "Mom" pitifully. It broke my heart, as did the way Stacy rushed to him and fell to her knees despite her injuries. She wrapped him in her arms and endured his desperate hug even though I knew it had to cause her pain.

Her attempts to soothe him and tell him she was never going anywhere again filled the room.

Lil, the female youngling, watched the pair, tears filling her eyes. Her assigned guardian, Peltear, the one she called Ben, picked her up and comforted her with whispered promises to find her aunt.

So much pain and suffering. I ached to hold Stacy in my arms and whisper promises of riches and wonders she couldn't imagine. She would never again feel the anguish she felt if she were within my care. I would ensure it with my last breath.

Nicky pulled back from his mother. "I missed you so much. I'm glad you're here. I want you to meet someone." He turned in her arms to face Baynol, the youngling's guardian, who watched them from a distance. "This is Baynol. I want him to be my dad. Can you marry him?"

Stacy made a small sound.

Was it shock? Pain? Refusal?

If it was meant to be a rejection, then it should have matched the intensity of the silently roared denial raging through my mind. How had I been such a blind fool? I'd been so enamored of the slight human female before me and the prospect of a companion who wasn't under my thrall that I hadn't considered what her presence here would mean.

Every male on this ship would be vying for her affection. I should have thought of that prior to going to the planet to extract her. It would not have changed my determination to remove her from the planet, but I certainly would have prepared more.

Not only did I need to contend with every Oebri male on this ship but the Anrothe males too. Of them, Baynol would be my biggest opponent. Stacy's youngling held him in the highest regard as a possible mate for his birther.

Before I could decide the best course of action, Stacy glanced at Baynol. The warden, programmed from a lifetime of dealing with Anrothe females, bowed his head and averted his gaze.

Relieved by the disinterest in Stacy's gaze, I remained silent as she faced her youngling and affectionately patted his cheek.

"I haven't seen you in over a month, kiddo. How about you settle for just being happy to see your mom?"

Nicky nodded and hugged her again. With effort, she stood with the youngling in her arms. I took a step forward to intervene, but Adriana subtly waved me back and moved forward in my place.

"Nicky? Lil? Are you up for a snack in the galley? Why don't you two lead the way? I bet your mom is really curious about the ship."

Both younglings quickly squirmed out of their positions and raced for the hall.

Baynol and Peltear were two steps behind them while Adriana placed a hand on Stacy's arm to stop her from following.

"I know you missed Nicky, Stacy, but you're going to feel it later if you try to carry him today. Save it until you're healed, okay?"

Stacy reluctantly agreed then smiled at Nicky's insistence to "hurry up."

I trailed in the group's wake, watching her. Even damaged, she was enticing beyond measure. However, she only had eyes for her youngling as he explained what the colored lines on the floor meant and all the areas of the ship that he and Lil had already explored.

Watching the sway of her hips, the tight hold I had on my emotions faltered. How many times had I slipped already? Yet, she never showed any indication she sensed what I'd felt. It began to worry me. I hoped it was due to an innate, strong ability of her race to resist Oebri persuasion. But what if she was already bonded or, worse, was mentally damaged by the male who had abused her?

Once we reached the galley, the younglings provided a tour of the space and the different food stations. She appeared disappointed by the offerings.

"We are learning much about humans as we monitor the planet's communications," I assured her. "If there is something you would like to eat that we cannot provide, let me know, and we will acquire what's needed."

"I can't imagine there's anything you don't have," she said. "Mac and cheese? Hot dogs? I was expecting exotic, alien foods."

Adriana grinned. "The chefs have been working their tails off to accommodate us. The Oebri want us to feel welcome."

Stacy nodded, still looking slightly disappointed as Nicky called her to his side to assist with his food gathering.

Due to my distraction, I overlooked Baynol following her at a distance until she guided Nicky to a table. Baynol had also taken food but had sprinkled his with edible flower petals. I watched him place it in front of Stacy.

"For you," he said, dipping his head.

Stacy glanced from him to the food. I could see the disinterest and the mistrust in her gaze.

As much as I didn't like the attention that Baynol was attempting to give her, I didn't try to stop it. I could see that Stacy would do that on her own. As Zarris had said, she wasn't ready to see any male as a protector or potential mate.

Seeing that helped me understand what I needed to do to start gaining her interest, though.

First, I needed to ease her fears and earn her trust. Words would not be enough.

The ship's voice echoed in the galley. "Alernon, please go to the comms center. The news from Earth has changed."

Adriana looked over at me, concern furrowing her brow.

"In this case, change is good," I said. "We don't want to be labeled as a hoax indefinitely."

"You don't want to be labeled as an enemy either," she said.

Stacy glanced over her shoulder at me.

"No," I agreed, holding the pretty female's gaze. "That is the last thing I want to be."

She quickly focused on helping Nicky eat his snack.

"Do you want me to come with you?" Adriana asked.

"No need. Enjoy the food and your reunion. I've assigned the room on the other side of yours to Stacy."

Lil stopped eating to stare at me. Her eyes filled with tears for the second time that arc.

"I don't want to sleep by myself," she wailed.

"Hey-hey-hey," Adriana said quickly. "That's not what's happening. Nicky still gets to sleep with you. I promise." She shot me a look like that I had learned, during the past several arcs, meant I should unconditionally agree with her.

"I would never take Nicky from you," I said. "Nicky's mother can rest separately while she recovers and decide how she would like the sleeping arrangements changed when she's ready."

"Recovers?" Nicky asked. "What does that mean?"

"Time to go, Alernon," Adriana said, waving me toward the door.

I took my leave, knowing I'd caused the younglings distress but unsure how.

# CHAPTER FIVE

## STACY

"CAN HE PUT HIS FOOT ANY FARTHER INTO HIS MOUTH?" I MUMBLED as I turned toward Nicky. "Recover means to get better. The bruises on my face hurt, and I'm kind of worn out right now and need some time to get back to how I usually am. A lot's happened, right?"

Nicky nodded, accepting my vague explanation and resuming his eating. I watched him, trying not to feel overwhelmed by just how much things had changed in a matter of hours.

Nicky had grown, and not just physically. I could tell by the way he kept looking at Lil and how he'd acted in that playroom that he was more than attached to her. He was looking out for her, and it broke my heart.

I wasn't sure how much more that organ could take. Seeing Nicky again, happy and healthy, felt like a dream, but I knew it wasn't. No matter how much a part of me still whispered that this was a hallucination because of whatever drug Alernon had given me, I knew better. First of all, the pain creeping back into my side felt pretty real. Second, the guy with the weird eyes sitting across from me was pretty real too.

"Baynol, right?" I asked.

He dipped his head, his bright amber gaze holding mine. His intensity level had bypassed one hundred and was redlining big time in my head.

"Thanks for the food, but I'm not really hungry."

He nodded, looking a little disappointed, and took the plate away.

I glanced at Adriana, who was helping Lil with her food, while the other guy, who looked like Baynol, watched closely.

The third and final reason I'd accepted that this was all real was Adriana's explanation of what they'd gone through. The details and the way she'd looked while telling me what had happened to her and the kids had started to convince me. And paying attention to the physical differences of the men after we'd rejoined them had pushed me over the edge of being a believer.

Aliens were real.

The part of me desperately trying to cling to the remnants of my denial grew a little smaller every time I looked at one of those men with amber eyes. The Anrothe men were hulky studs that would have had me rolling my eyes if I'd seen them flexing in the gym. But, damn, they were something to look at.

So were Alernon and the members of his crew I'd glimpsed on our way here. They all had that ombre hair, which was apparently a trait for their species, and piercingly light-colored eyes. Silver-blue, and silver-violet. Each one of them was stunning.

What in the hell was I doing on a ship filled with sexy men?

When the kids finished their snacks, we left the dining space.

"So, how does that light beam work?" I asked as we walked. "Can they send us anywhere with it?"

Adriana glanced at me and the kids.

"Hey, why don't you two play with Baynol and Ben some more while I show your mom the rest of the ship and talk about some grownup stuff?" she suggested.

Nicky made a face but nodded. Lil copied him.

I kissed the top of Nicky's head and promised him I'd be back soon. They ran off in another direction than we were headed with the two Anrothe men trailing behind them.

Adriana kept her pace slow while Zarris shadowed us and waited until the kids turned down another hallway to start talking.

"I know you probably don't want to hear this, but I don't think going back is an option," she said.

"What do you mean? Have we been kidnapped?" I asked.

She smiled and shook her head.

"I don't know if you've been watching the news, but the Oebri are trying to get Earth's attention."

"Yeah, I heard your message. They want to say hi to world leaders, but everyone thinks it's a joke." Except for me. I didn't find any of it funny.

"Not everyone thinks it's a joke," she said. "Yes, the news is calling it a hoax, and the general public is debating all the possibilities. But behind the scenes, leaders all over the world are meeting in secret to decide what to do."

"They believe?" I asked.

"Most of them do. Enough that they're worried about what an alien presence means for the planet. How do you imagine they'd react to Nicky suddenly reappearing somewhere after being 'so-called abducted?' Do you think they'll just leave you both alone?"

I stopped and stared at her.

"I know," she said quickly. "Why did I have to use their names? Right? I didn't want to, but we needed everyone to believe this was real. We were taken, Stacy, along with so many other people. I'm pretty sure the kids and I are the only survivors. Earth needs protection from the kind of aliens who will take people against their will. The Oebri can offer that protection if Earth agrees. I couldn't just think of Nicky and Lil. I had to think of the millions of other kids who could be taken next, too."

Hearing her put it like that killed some of my resentment but not all of it. Why in the hell couldn't I just put myself and Nicky first? Why did we always end up on the bottom like this?

"So we're stuck here forever?" I asked, looking at the sterile, empty hallway. "I don't even know where here is yet?"

"Let me show you," she said. She led me along several hallways before we turned a corner into a huge open space half-filled with a view of the moon and the night sky.

"They turned the ship so we could see a little of everything," Adriana said. "The kids love being able to see the moon, and I like the stars."

I stood there and just took it all in for several minutes. The view. What had happened to Nicky and me? All the poor decisions that had led me to that moment.

"What are we doing, Rin?" I asked softly.

She wrapped her arm around my shoulders.

"It feels like a lifetime since I heard that nickname," she said. "So much has changed. All we can do now is live in the moment and survive while we wait to see what happens next."

"I've been living like that for months. I'm broken mentally, physically, and emotionally. I'm not sure how much more I can take."

She wrapped me in a full hug.

"You're not alone anymore," she said.

"That's the terrifying part."

I appreciated that Adriana didn't ask what I meant or try to tell me that living on a ship full of men wasn't going to be a problem. I'd been paying attention. As far as I could tell, Adriana and I were the only adult females aboard. And every single dangler trying to stay out of my sight had looked at me like I was candy.

Releasing Adriana, I gave her silent stalker a side glance. She noticed.

48

"Zarris, would you mind waiting in the hall for a bit?" she asked.

He nodded and left us alone.

"Ask," she said.

"Are they anatomically the same as humans?"

She grinned. "Zarris is. I haven't verified the Oebri and don't plan to. Why? Interested?"

I couldn't believe she could even ask that. Then again, she probably had no idea just how much I'd endured with Pin.

"After what I've been through, I have no interest in men. I was just curious why you and I seem to be the only women. Do I need to adjust my perceptions of gender to accommodate aliens, or do I need to start bracing myself for attention I don't want?"

She wrapped an arm around my waist and gave me a consoling pat. "I didn't seriously mean what I said."

"I know," I said, leaning into her comfort.

It was the core of who Adriana was. She cared about people, and that was why I'd entrusted her with Nicky. He'd fallen in front of our apartment when I'd been inside, and she'd been quick to help and comfort him.

That had been around the same time I'd started seeing Pin. Back when he'd been a "decent" guy and a "good" catch. Thankfully, Adriana hadn't been as double-sided as he'd been.

"There were a few other females on this ship, but they moved to the other one before you arrived. You might still need to adjust your gender perceptions, though. Not all aliens are as human looking as the Oebri and Anrothe."

"I was serious about living in the moment," I said after a moment. "So much has happened, Rin. I'm not sure how much more I can take. Thoughts creep in, you know? I'm not even sure how I'm going to fall asleep tonight."

She pulled back, and I knew she'd understood when I saw the worry in her expression.

"I can help with that," she said. "Come on."

The knotted ache in my thigh increased with each hallway we walked.

"Are we there yet?" She saw through my attempt at a playful whine.

"I promise this will be worth the walk," she said. "You're going to sleep like a baby."

I doubted it with the way my leg was hurting. Zarris was watching my limp from behind and had already offered to carry me twice.

"It's just ahead," she said as if reading my mind and knowing how close I was to saying that I didn't want to go wherever she was taking me.

Instead of an endless hallway, I saw a glowing section of the wall ahead. Adriana quickened her pace to reach it ahead of me and open the semi-transparent door.

I wasn't sure what I was expecting, but it wasn't the cavernous space filled with plants that I saw. Gnarly trees and thick vines with pretty, spindly flowers rose at least three stories high, almost touching the ceiling that shone like the midday sun. Fronded shrubs that grew taller than Zarris and spiked-leaf plants grew between the towering giants.

And a path led through it all.

"Welcome to the grow bay that I like to call 'sleepy-time bay.' There's a pretty zebra flower way in the back. It's a medicinal plant but one the Oebri deemed safe for the kids and me, or they wouldn't allow us in here. Honestly, they didn't know about its mild sedating qualities until two days ago. Nicky and Lil sniffed it and napped like angels for three hours. Then they woke up with enough energy to run races through the hallways."

As we walked the path, I breathed in deeply, amazed by how fresh the air smelled.

"This grow bay is one of my favorite spots," she said. "It helps me feel like we're not on the dark side of the moon but outside in a park, soaking up some sun. Which is what the ceiling simulates, so make sure you come in here at least once a day."

Ahead, I spotted a cream and black striped flower.

"Is that it?" I asked.

"Yep." She walked with me to the flower and encouraged me to smell it. "It doesn't work just breathing around it, thankfully. You need to have your nose pretty close."

I sniffed it, smelling a hint of something sweet but not overpowering.

"Why, thankfully?" I asked, sniffing again, trying to remember what the scent of the candle I'd burned at home was because it smelled exactly like that.

"Because you need someone to carry you once it knocks you on your ass," she said with a laugh as she pulled me back. "That's probably enough. I want to show you the park Alernon made for the kids before you faceplant."

She led me around the bend. I saw the twin swings hanging from a granddaddy tree's branches. The area around the tree and under the trees was covered in squishy moss.

"They love it here," she said. "But get bored pretty quickly. Alernon and his crew have been so sweet about doing whatever they can to help turn their ship into a home for the kids. And us, too."

When I glanced at her, my head swam a little.

"You sounded sad just now," I said.

"I am, a little. Zarris came from a planet that was full of trees taller than you'd imagine. I feel bad he's stuck in space with only grow bays."

"I'm not," Zarris said, tugging her back against his chest. "Wherever you are is where I belong."

I watched her smile up at him. It was obvious she had feelings for him. After how long? A month? How could she really know the person she loved in that amount of time? A month was around when Pin started gaslighting me.

The space swam before my eyes when I faced the tree again.

# CHAPTER SIX

## ALERNON

I LEFT THE COMMS CENTER AT A JOG AS SOON AS ADRIANA SUGGESTED the "zebra" flower to Stacy. Although I knew listening to their conversation had been an invasion of their privacy—a concept Adriana had explained after I'd shown her the feeds the ship was monitoring from Earth—I'd been unwilling to stop. If I wanted to win Stacy's affection, I needed to understand her thoughts as well as what she felt.

Her admission of the depth of her damage had cut me deeply, though. We had the knowledge to heal the body but not the heart and the mind. I'd watched many of my fellow Oebri slowly deteriorate from yearning for a mate of their own, despite their youth. And I feared the same fate for Stacy due to all that she'd suffered.

The flower, while a wise choice, wasn't a permanent solution to Stacy's anguish. If Stacy couldn't live in the moment as Adriana suggested, then she needed a focus. Something to do. And after reading the feeds, I had the perfect solution.

"Command Alernon, current location of human Stacy," I said.

The ship verified she'd reached the grow bay a few prexels ahead of me. Hurrying, I entered and ran along the path. The soft murmur of their conversation drifted from the next bend as I reached the flower, and I knew they'd already passed it.

I growled softly and rounded the final bend as Stacy said, "I think that flower's kicking in."

Her knees started to buckle.

I darted around Adriana and Zarris and caught Stacy in my arms before Zarris could. Straightening, I adjusted my hold on her with care. Her lips parted slightly as she settled against me.

"Where did you come from?" Adriana asked.

"The comms center," I said as I stared down at Stacy's sleep-relaxed face and tried to rein in my emotions.

"She'll appreciate the save when she wakes up," Adriana said. "I don't think she can take any more bruises."

The swelling around Stacy's eyes was already reduced from the stims she'd received and the topical cream, and as much as I'd wanted to talk to her, I knew rest would also help her heal. Seeking to make her more comfortable, I shifted her weight in my arms so her head rested against my chest. However, each of her exhales warmed my skin through my tunic, making it difficult to control the hold I had on my emotions.

"What's the word from Earth?" Adriana asked, thankfully giving me a distraction.

"Your Leaders are making preparations for an initial meeting. They're debating the best method to contact us." I started walking with Stacy, and Adriana kept pace with me.

"What kinds of preparations are they making?" she asked.

"Cages. Sedatives. Weapons."

She swore under her breath, and I felt a hint of worry from her. Since she'd bonded with Zarris, this was the first emotion I'd felt from her, which told me how strongly she was feeling it.

"Even after Pin's demonstration of how ineffective human weapons are, you're concerned?" I asked.

"Yes, because he had *one* handgun. Do you think Earth's

leaders don't have better, more advanced weapons hidden away for stuff like this?"

"They are likely as useless. However, I know not to make assumptions, which is why I won't meet with your planet's leaders on their terms. All I needed was a clear indication on the feed that they were ready to meet with me. I will appear where and when I choose for a very brief and peaceful introduction."

"And then what?" she asked.

"Most species typically respond with a litany of questions. Why are we here? What do we want? When will we leave? And those questions will lead to negotiations, which is why I was coming to speak to you and Stacy."

"Oh?"

"You said you wished to have the final say on the contract we sign with Earth. Perhaps you and Stacy would like to define terms of your own as a starting point for the negotiations?"

"You're pretty confident Earth's leaders will want to negotiate."

"I am. Once we send them a data pic containing every species we have cataloged in the systems and how advanced each species is, your leaders will understand Earth's place. No species wants to be at the bottom without protection."

She nodded thoughtfully as we left the grow bay.

"You've obviously had a lot of experience with this and probably already know what's fair. But, yes, I'd like to help define some terms as a starting point. Not sure if Stacy will be up for it, though."

I looked down at the female in my arms.

"I believe someone who hasn't had a say in how she was treated will want a say in how other females of your race will be treated," I said.

"You may be right, but I think she's going to need some time, too. Her life's been turned upside down."

I looked at Adriana.

57

"I desperately want to help her turn it right side up again."

She smiled slightly. "Yeah, I kind of got that impression from the way you've been watching her. You might want to ease up a bit. She has no reason to trust you."

I understood that, which was why I was determined to give her reasons.

Adriana's wrist comm, something I'd given her so she could communicate with the younglings at all times, chimed with a message request. She tapped the screen to accept it.

"Lil won't stop crying," Nicky's voice said. "She misses her mom too. Peltear said she needs you."

"I'll be right there, kiddo," she said back.

The comm pinged after the delivery, and Adriana exhaled heavily. "I really hope Stacy lets them keep sharing a room. Lil has gone through enough separation." She glanced at Stacy. "I'll check on her when I'm done settling the kids in."

I nodded and watched Adriana hold her breasts as she jogged away. Zarris flashed a smile at me and followed her.

Adriana had been asking for an Earth "bra" since arriving. Each time, I'd noted Zarris's slight frown, which finally vanished when I'd explained that acquiring Earth goods would only be possible after a contract was established. While she'd been annoyed with the answer, he'd barely suppressed his smile.

If he appreciated her unbound body, perhaps it was time to gift Adriana a systems dress. As beautiful as it might be, though, I doubted Adriana would embrace wearing it. When she'd explained human views regarding all the different forms of privacy, she'd noted they didn't widely embrace public nudity. The news had disappointed me, but I hoped some females might become open to it. Experience taught me that most hesitant wills could be molded eventually. And if Zarris could convince Adriana to wear a systems dress…

My gaze dipped to the sleeping beauty in my arms, and I

imagined what she would look like walking the halls wearing the links I'd crafted.

Need bolted through me.

Rather than return Stacy to her room, I found the nearest med bay.

"I need you well, my beauty," I said softly as I set her on the table.

"Prepare for species type: human. Run a full scan for comparison to the previous scan and make repair and health maintenance recommendations."

While the unit worked, I circled the table, lightly running my hand along Stacy's limbs, learning her size so I could better provide for her.

"No additional damage. Healing: five percent. Continue pain lubricant as needed for external damage. Scan complete."

"Do you hear that, my beauty? You're already healing well," I said as I removed the pain lubricant from storage. I set it on her midsection to take with us back to her room and picked her up.

While I carried her through the hallways, I considered my plan to win her for my own.

I faced several problems. The first was that, as the only unbonded, breedable female on the ship, Stacy would have the attention of every male. Competition for her favor would be fierce once she was healed. So I needed to ensure it before then.

As the ship's commander, I had a small period of opportunity where I would be the only one seeking her attention. I needed a way to keep her close once she was healed. If she agreed to help with the negotiations, she would be working with me.

However, her nearness wasn't enough. I needed to gain her trust, which was the second issue I faced in winning her favor.

Stacy trusted no male. I'd watched the way she'd looked at every crewmember who'd discreetly stayed out of her way during our tour and the way she'd looked at Zarris before Adriana sent him from the observation room. Considering the degree of damage done to her, she had no reason to ever provide an opportunity to earn her trust.

If I wanted one, I needed to find it on my own.

While I'd hoped to speak with her before she'd succumbed to the flower's effects, I wasn't overly disappointed I hadn't. It gave me a better reason for lingering at her side once I applied the pain cream.

I let myself into Stacy's assigned room and carefully sat her up on the edge of the bed.

"Let's hope you sleep soundly through this, my pet. I have no wish to see you suffer further."

Leaning her forward, I worked one arm out of the snug sleeve and then the other. The top of the dress fell to her waist, leaving her exposed. I let my gaze trail over her skin, noting each mark, and my fingers tingled in anticipation.

Carefully, I lowered her to the mattress and worked the material down her legs, taking extra care around her damaged thigh.

"There," I said, brushing her hair back and tossing the dress to a table. I opened the container of pain lubricant and began applying it to the deepest bruises first. The pleasure of caring for her superceded the pleasure of touching her. I kept my contact strictly on the areas that needed attention and didn't linger.

When I finished, I rolled her onto her side, facing the door, and checked her backside. The bruising was deeper there, so I applied a second layer before covering her completely with a blanket.

I'd finished folding her dress and setting it on the chair when the door opened, and Adriana walked in. She went straight to the bed without noticing me. I sat on Stacy's dress so Adriana wouldn't notice it.

"She's resting comfortably," I said, drawing Adriana's attention as she reached to straighten the blanket.

"Why are you still here?" she asked softly.

"After everything she's been through, there is a good chance she will wake disoriented. I didn't want her to be alone and afraid."

"That's very thoughtful. I think it would be better if I were the one who stayed."

"I'm sure Zarris would disagree," I said.

She crossed her arms and narrowed her eyes at me. "I know what you do, Alernon. She doesn't need you messing with her head."

"I don't believe I can. I've slipped a few times around her. She didn't react. Is there a chance she bonded?"

Adriana glanced down at Stacy. "I mean, maybe, but I don't think so. You said it would have to be heart, mind, and body, right? Look at what he did. She walked away way too easily to be bonded to him."

"If not him, perhaps another?"

Adriana shrugged. "That's something only she can answer."

"Yes. However, it would be wise not to ask until she's better. But regardless of whether she's bonded, she appears to be safe from my influence. I want to gain her trust, Adriana, and being here and watching over her is a way to do that, is it not?"

Adriana sighed. "Fine. I'm trusting you, Alernon. Don't make things worse for her."

"Never," I vowed.

Adriana left without touching Stacy or the blanket.

I removed the dress from under me, and smiling, I leaned back into my chair to wait. Healthy human adults had an optimal sleep rhythm of six to eight arcs. Younglings and the sick slept longer.

After five arcs, she rolled onto her back, winced, and returned to her side.

"I think that means you need more pain lubricant, my beauty," I said softly, going to her.

She didn't stir as I drew the blanket to her waist and started rubbing the pain lubricant into her skin. Already the bruising was significantly lighter.

She flinched a little when I touched her thigh and her ribs.

"Be at peace," I said. "The pain will fade quickly."

Her breathing deepened when I finished, and I guided her to her back as she'd originally wanted. She didn't wince again.

I took a moment to appreciate her beauty then covered her to her neck.

Adriana came to check on her after the eighth arc, and I quickly indicated that we should speak in the hallway.

"I can take over," Adriana said.

However, before she finished, the children came rushing into the hallway, asking for Stacy and breakfast.

"Perhaps you would be better suited to explain why they should allow her to continue to sleep," I suggested.

"Are you sure? You look tired."

"I dozed lightly while keeping watch. I will be fine."

She reluctantly allowed me to return to Stacy's room.

My beauty slept for another arc then woke with a yawn and another wince.

"Does it hurt as badly as it did before you slept?" I asked softly.

She froze for a halo-flash, sat up, and looked at me with wide eyes.

"Do you remember where you are?" I asked, trying valiantly to ignore the way she was clutching the sheet to her breasts.

"No. The last thing I remember is sniffing a flower and looking at a big tree with swings."

I smiled slightly.

"Then you know you're on my ship with your son and your neighbor and are safe."

Her eyes scanned the room, and I felt her growing fear.

"Safe? I'm naked, and you're here. How is that safe? What did you do to me while I was knocked out?"

"I applied pain lubricant to the worst of your injuries," I said, holding up the tub. "Twice. You rolled to your side midway through the night and winced. Other than that, I simply watched over you to ensure you wouldn't be alone when you woke."

"Simply?" She made a sound of disbelief. "I'm not blind. I see the way you and every other guy on this ship look at me."

"Of course. You are beautiful, Stacy."

"I'm average in every way," she said.

"Perhaps to Earth males, but not to us."

She considered me as the sharp edge of her fear faded.

"Whatever you're trying to do…it isn't going to work. I'm not interested in being anyone's plaything or punching bag."

"Plaything?" I asked, choosing to ignore the punching bag remark. She would never be that again.

"Forced fuck. Sex slave. Whatever you want to call it. I'm not interested," she clarified.

I tried to rein in the rush of angry emotions those words evoked. The last thing either of us needed was for me to lose control and experience Psy-surge right now.

"And I am not interested in breeding with an unwilling female. Ever.

"You're precious, Stacy. Too precious to abuse or force. When you come to me, I want you willing and those pretty lips speaking your wants and desires. That is the only way it would be pleasurable for both of us."

# CHAPTER SEVEN

## STACY

ALERNON'S AUDACITY STUNNED ME STUPID. I COULDN'T THINK OF A single thing to say to his ridiculous statement.

So, I laughed my ass off.

It hurt my ribs, but God, did it feel good.

When I finally quieted, he wasn't scowling at me but looked amused and still sexy as hell. It was a blatantly dangerous combination.

"Was that an alien attempt at seduction?" I asked.

His smile grew more pronounced. "No, my beauty. I know better than to attempt to seduce you now."

"Why's that?"

His humor faded as he stood and crossed the room. Damn, if my pulse didn't speed up, and not all of it was due to the predatory way he moved or the danger signals going off in my head.

"You've been mistreated and trust no one. Why would you ever give me a chance?" He lightly brushed back a strand of my hair and flashed a quick smile at me.

"The dress you wore previously is on the table. You may

choose to wear it or go without it. I assure you that nudity aboard this ship is encouraged."

I snorted lightly. "Then why are you wearing clothes?"

"Would you like me to disrobe?"

"I'd like you to get out."

He chuckled lightly as he turned on his heel and strode for the door.

"I'll await you in the hall and escort you to the galley."

The wall closed behind him, leaving me alone.

The first thing I did was touch myself to make sure nothing was sore. That flower had knocked me out cold. I couldn't remember a single thing after the tree. Not him undressing me or putting pain cream on me. Both of which would have required a lot of manhandling.

But after a pretty thorough check, nothing hurt down below, and my boobs felt fine. Actually, a lot of me felt pretty good. I was finally free and with Nicky. Pin couldn't touch us here.

Feeling better than I had in a long time, I stood and looked down at my thigh. The bruising was notably improved. And my ribs didn't hurt as much when I took a deep, testing breath. I even managed to tug yesterday's dress into place myself.

Standing there, I looked from the bed to the chair. Had Alernon really only been there to help me?

I shook my head.

"Don't even go there, you idiot," I murmured to myself.

Turning, I went to the spot in the wall where the door had been and realized I had no idea how to open it. I knocked on the wall.

"Hey, I'm done."

Nothing happened.

I hit it harder with the side of my fist.

"Hey! Open up!"

Still, nothing happened.

Rather than freak out, I started looking around the room. It wasn't huge. It had a bed and a small table and chairs against the walls.

But I didn't let that fool me. I'd seen how much the walls had stored in the med bay. In fact, touching the walls had opened compartments.

So, beginning near where I thought the door should be, I started running my hands over the surface. As soon as I ran my hand over the panel, I wondered how I'd missed it in the first place. It wasn't quite the same shade of white.

After touching it, lights danced on the surface, and water started raining down from the ceiling on the other side of the room.

"There's a shower?" I muttered in disbelief.

The water that fell didn't pool on the floor but disappeared.

"What in the space-age weirdness…"

I drifted closer to try to figure out how it worked. Tiny holes in the ceiling dripped the water out like a gentle rain, and tiny holes in the floor soaked it back up. A panel even glowed on the wall nearby. Playing with the light turned it green for cooler water and yellow for warmer water.

An opportunity to wash was too good to pass up. I quickly stripped out of my dress, tossed it to the bed, and stood under the rain. It felt so good. I ran my fingers through my hair and rubbed my arms and between my legs like I was using soap. Surprisingly, I did feel like I was cleaner by the time I finished and stepped out of the water.

It immediately shut off, and warm air started to blow where the water had been. I moved back into place and let it dry my front.

When I turned, I saw Alernon leaning against the wall near the door panel.

His expression and the way he watched me wiped away any shred of enjoyment I felt. One word echoed through my brain to describe the way he looked.

Hungry.

And the extent of it terrified me. He let out a long breath and turned his head so he stared at the table. I didn't miss the way he clenched his fists at his sides or how it took a few moments for him to speak.

"Forgive me. I grew concerned that you might not remember how to open the door and came to check."

"How long have you been standing there?" I managed to ask after a moment.

"Long enough to consider every desperate promise I could make that might sway you to cross the room and come to me." He swallowed hard. "What do you feel right now?"

"Violated. Angry." I hesitated a moment. "Afraid." I only admitted that truth to see what he'd do. Better now than later, I told myself.

His gaze found mine. Although the hunger remained, concern had tempered it. The easily faked emotion did nothing to reassure me.

"Fear is the last emotion I want you to feel for me, and I apologize for causing it. When you are finished drying, touch the circle here." He demonstrated. "And when you wish to leave or enter a room, place your hand like this."

The wall opened, and he left.

I stared at the space, replaying the encounter in my head and analyzing it from every possible angle. Had he been testing me? Had admitting fear been a mistake? He hadn't really reacted strongly one way or another. I wasn't sure what to think.

Running my fingers through my hair as the warm air continued to caress me, I considered everything he'd done since saving me. First, he'd drugged me and gave me a load of shots to heal me. Admittedly, those shots *were* working some serious space-magic. So I didn't hold any grudges over that part.

But then, he'd touched me while I was sleeping and watched me shower. Did aliens just not have any boundaries?

I thought of the dress Adriana had given me and her admission that aliens didn't believe in bras or underwear. Humans and aliens obviously had some cultural differences...and Alernon did say that nudity was fine. I'd thought it was just some crass comment at the time. But what if that really was how they vibed around here and the clothes were to accommodate us?

If that were the case, I would owe Alernon some heartfelt gratitude. Unless that was what he wanted. His comment about being willing rang in my head as I turned off the air.

It felt good to be clean again. After the beating, showering hadn't been possible. The pain in my ribs had made removing my shirt impossible. Plus, the thought of undressing around Pin had made me feel too vulnerable.

I glanced at the still-closed section of wall and went to put my dress back on. I'd felt vulnerable when I'd spotted Alernon watching me bathe but in a completely different way. Shaking my head, I mentally prepared myself for more awkwardness and went to the panel.

The door opened at my touch, and Alernon paused his pacing to look at me. His silvery gaze skimmed over my face and down my body before returning to my face again.

"You truly are beautiful, Stacy," he said. "Are you in pain?"

"Not like I was yesterday."

"Good. With your permission, I would like to run another scan. Would you prefer to do that before or after we go to the galley?"

"Let's get it done first," I said. Because once I met up with Nicky again, I didn't want to leave him.

As Alernon led me to a med bay, he talked about his ship. It had several med bays, grow bays, entertainment spaces—mostly adult ones that the kids and I did not have access to enter—the galley, the observation deck—

"Are you nervous?" I asked when it felt like he was rambling a little bit.

He smiled slightly. "No. I'm trying to put us both at ease."

Putting me at ease made sense. But why him? "Is there a reason why you're trying to put yourself at ease?"

He pressed his hand to the wall, and it opened to another med bay.

"I think there might be. Did you love that man? Pin?" Alernon asked while I walked to the exam table.

I felt defensive and angry at the question until I looked Alernon in the eyes. His gaze held no judgment. Just confusion and worry.

"I thought I did in the beginning when he treated me like you are now. Nice. Considerate. Complimentary." I managed to sit on the table on my own. "I quickly learned it was all a lie—who he was *and* what I felt for him."

Alernon's hand settled on my shoulder, and he guided me back until I lay flat.

"I must admit that you confuse me," he said.

"In what way?"

He stepped back from the table. "In many ways. Prepare scan: human. Compare to previous scan results and provide recommendations."

He studied me as the light swept me from the toes up, and I waited, wondering if he would explain.

"Every species has unique qualities," he said finally. "Qualities that the species doesn't think are unique but are simply normal to them. For example, your species' ability to birth an equal amount of male and female offspring. It truly is unique. No other species in the systems possess the same ability.

"Likewise, my people have the ability to sense emotions in others and influence them. We've learned to control it around others, but sometimes we make mistakes."

His gaze swept over my body. "My control has faltered several times since I've been near you. Yet, you've never reacted. What I've felt hasn't influenced your feelings. That typically only happens when a female is already bonded to a male."

I wasn't quite sure what to think. Was he saying he could control how I feel? I wasn't sure I could believe it. Sure, the ship was real. Aliens were apparently real. But believing he could influence how I felt about him? Nope. It seemed I'd hit my belief wall.

"Was that why you asked what I was feeling when you were watching me shower?"

I saw the hunger creep back into his gaze. "Yes. I felt your anger and fear, as you said, but none of what I was feeling."

"Ah."

"Ah? Nothing more?"

"Aliens are real. Okay. Sure, I'll believe that.

"One took me aboard his spaceship to reunite me with my abducted son. Yeah. That one's a little harder to accept, but it's kind of right in front of my eyes, isn't it?

"Now you're telling me you can make me feel what you feel, which is obviously horny and ready to fuck. Oh, wait. No. Breed. 'Cause that's so much better. Can you see what I'm trying to say here?"

"You are still in a state of disbelief, and I am overwhelming you with unnecessary information?"

I smiled as the light reached the top of my head.

"You're smarter than you look, Alernon."

"I think I should be offended by that," he said, sounding anything but.

"Be however you want to be. Feel however you want to feel. Neither one is my concern. I just want to be left alone."

"Healing: forty percent," the voice said. "Comparison shows overall increases. Recommend vitality stim."

"May I?" Alernon asked a second before he pulled my skirt up to my stomach.

It didn't matter that the immediate panic I felt made no sense. He'd obviously undressed me the night before and had admitted to applying the pain cream twice, which was more than just looking; it was touching too. All while naked.

However, being awake made the scenario completely different.

I tried to kick him away, but his hand immediately locked down on my legs, holding them in place.

I hit his arms, shoulders, and the back of his head.

"Proceed with the recommendation," he said.

The words froze me.

The arm moved and delivered a stinging shot to my thigh just below the bruised section.

As soon as it moved away, Alernon flipped my skirt down, straightening with care, then stepped back from the table.

Our gazes locked.

Mine were still wide with the panic-induced adrenaline spike.

"I understand," he said.

The sound of my ragged breathing filled the room for several moments until I had enough thought to sit up.

"I could have waited," he said, offering me a hand down. "I could have explained first. But I would rather show you who I am from the start."

He waited there, his hand outstretched.

I stared at it, hating him. But when I started to consider why, I realized it wasn't because of what he'd done. It was because of what Pin had done. I was afraid—so fucking afraid—of another Pin entering my life.

But Alernon wasn't Pin. I knew that. Whether or not he was a good or bad man, though, I didn't know. And I wouldn't know until I spent more time with him. Considering it was his ship, it made sense to learn as much as I could about the man who now had my life and the life of my son in his hands.

Giving in, I placed my hand in his and let him help me stand.

"I will ensure your health and safety, Stacy. Even if it means doing something that you may not approve of." His fingers moved over mine, maintaining contact.

"That sounds controlling," I said.

He didn't take the hint and release his hold.

"I imagine Nicky feels the same about you at times. Does that stop you from doing what's best for him even when it's difficult and will upset him?"

I thought of how I'd packed my child up to send him to Rin and slowly shook my head as I stared at Alernon. What was I supposed to think of him? Was he safe? Was he any different from Pin?

"Come," Alernon said. "You must eat."

I let Alernon lead me from the med bay while my thoughts were still whirling.

# CHAPTER EIGHT

## ALERNON

THE FEEL OF STACY'S FINGERS AGAINST MINE CONSUMED MY THOUGHTS as we walked the hall together.

*Did she realize I still held her hand?*

After her reaction to me in the med bay, I would never have believed she would allow my continued touch. Her comments about the male she'd been with had revealed much. Her mistrust ran deep, which is why I'd risked exposing her in the way I had.

Thankfully, she'd responded as I'd anticipated. Her attempts to kick free had been ineffectual, but fighting my hold in any capacity was a good sign, proving he hadn't damaged her will. It had also shown she didn't fear me. If she had, she wouldn't have fought as hard. She would have submitted.

And, submission was the last thing I wanted from Stacy.

I glanced down at our joined hands. If this wasn't a submission, what was it? Perhaps she craved a gentle touch and care from a male after all that she endured?

The thought tested my control.

I wasn't an unworthy human male, and she wasn't some weak-willed female. That was why I wanted her to remain by my side.

Adriana's words about easing up and earning Stacy's trust rang through my mind. Although I didn't want to release Stacy's hand, I did. She maintained her pace, walking at my side.

"I understand you're concerned about how you will be received if you return to Earth. Although things are unsettled now, it's our hope to come to an agreement with Earth's leaders that will eventually enable you to return to your home if you wish."

"I do," she said quickly. "Nicky's supposed to be starting school this fall. I'm sure Lil's the same. After everything they've been through, they need normal."

I smiled slightly. "After all the worlds I have visited, I've learned normal is simply perception. If you believe life aboard this ship is normal, then it is. And as for the younglings' education, they can begin immediately if you wish. We have access to all the information from Earth. Including education data pics for Nicky and Lil's ages."

Her expression shifted, becoming more concerned and indecisive.

"There is no need to decide anything now. The agreement with Earth will take time, and the younglings are content playing as they are."

She nodded with a heavy exhale.

"I don't like feeling this...lost."

I knew she didn't mean our location behind the moon but in her own life.

"I understand. Perhaps you would be interested in a distraction and would like to assist Adriana?"

"Doing what?" Stacy asked with a hint of suspicion in her voice.

"The latest news from Earth indicates that some of the leaders are open to an introduction. After we meet, negotiations will begin. Adriana expressed her wish to be involved. I believe she suspects that Earth's leaders will give up too many rights for the people who cannot speak for themselves."

"I might be interested in helping with that," Stacy said.

I smiled at the beauty beside me, pleased with her choice.

However, my triumph over gaining more of her time was cut short when we arrived at the galley and found the others still there. Nicky jumped up to pull his mother to his table.

"We already have a plate for you. Come see. Baynol made it."

Stacy left my side and joined her son, sitting across from him and beside Adriana.

With Adriana's watchful gaze on me, I didn't show my disappointment at the youngling's preference or my annoyance at Baynol's persistence. I went to my preferred food station to select my meal.

"News from Earth is promising," Raaln, our head chef, said as he watched Adriana and Stacy. "I hope the negotiations favor us with an abundance of females."

"I believe they will," I said. "The planet cannot sustain its numbers for much longer. They will need to reduce their population or lose their home world and cast themselves adrift in the systems."

"Either would benefit us," he said.

"The latter will only benefit us short-term. Think of future generations."

"You don't believe breeding with humans will increase our fertility?"

"I would be foolish to hold onto that hope without proof. And we will not have that proof until any younglings produced from a human age to maturity and start breeding, which is why we need to protect this planet. We need to ensure future generations will have a genetically unpolluted resource to continue harvesting."

A hint of despair crept into his expression. Our ship was one of many in the systems. If he hoped to gain a female quickly, I needed to secure Earth's agreement before more ships appeared.

His expression cleared. "Then I will strive to find a female in the first harvest," he said with conviction.

I smiled my approval and left to join the others.

If negotiations did not go well, I wasn't sure how long my crew would be able to endure. The next harvest anywhere in the systems was still over a solar-run away and not assigned to my ship. We needed a contract with Earth, and we needed it badly.

Adriana looked up at my approach.

"How did Stacy's scan look this morning?" she asked quietly as Nicky continued to explain to his birther the foods on her plate.

"She's healing well," I said, taking a seat beside Zarris. "Rest and time will see her fully restored."

"Good," Adriana said. "What about Earth?"

"I haven't checked the feeds yet, but I plan to visit your planet in a few flares."

"I want to monitor you," she said immediately.

"Me too," Stacy said, proving she was listening. "I'd like to be involved with whatever negotiations happen too. Even if I don't have a say, I'd like to understand what's going to happen to us."

"What do you mean?" Nicky asked.

"Nothing bad, nosey," Adriana said, reaching across the table to touch the youngling on his nose. "We're past the bad stuff. Only good stuff now, like playing all day and eating good food. I heard your last scan said you were still vitamin deficient. Not good, my friend. You know what that means."

The youngling made a face and hurried to eat more of the nutrient-rich porridge that I had told him would negate the need for another vitality stim. The younglings did not care for the stims.

"Only a minor deficiency," I said, hoping to put him at ease.

"What about me?" the female youngling asked.

"If you eat your porridge, you will escape the need for another vitality stim as well," I said.

She made a sad face.

"But I don't like it. It tastes bad."

I reached across the table and dipped my spoon into it. She laughed at the face I made, which was an honest reaction.

"You poor thing," I said, waving Raaln over. "Can you alter the taste of the porridge without reducing the nutrients?"

"Of course." He looked at the youngling. "What would you like it to taste like, my beauty?"

"Ice cream!" she said quickly.

Raaln glanced at me in question; however, I was equally clueless.

"Ice cream is a dessert," Stacy said. "Sugary and cold."

"Ah," Raaln said, still looking unsure.

"If you have any sweet fruits to add to her bowl, that'll help," Stacy said.

When the youngling made a face, Adriana reminded her of the foods they had on Anrothe that were sweet. Raaln hurried away to find something comparable.

"I will do my very best to acquire Earth foods for you as soon as possible," I said. "Until then, we will try to make our foods more to your liking. But even if they are not, you must eat if you wish to avoid the stims. Are we in agreement?"

She nodded and slowly ate a bite of her unaltered food.

"When we're done, can we go play?" Nicky asked, looking between Adriana and Stacy. At the last second, he glanced at me as well. Smart youngling. He was beginning to see who held authority on the ship.

I didn't miss the way Stacy glanced at Adriana and me, either, before asking Nicky, "Is that what you usually do after breakfast?"

"Yep," he said happily.

"Okay. Then we'll stick with that routine." Her gaze shifted to Baynol. "Would you be willing to watch Nicky for a little bit longer? I was hoping I could speak with Adriana privately again."

"Of course, Lady," Baynol said.

Stacy's brows shot up at the title, and I could sense her discomfort.

"It's a title of respect used on his planet," I assured her. "And any male would be honored to watch over these younglings. They're a rare sight in the systems."

"What does rare mean?" Nicky asked.

"It means you should eat your breakfast faster, or you're going to miss out on some play time," Stacy said.

I didn't contradict her but wondered why she gave him a false meaning. Did she believe they would find the knowledge frightening?

Raaln returned with fruit and added it to both bowls. The younglings ate much faster with the addition.

"I will have a better selection when you return," he promised the younglings as they finished.

They asked to be excused then ran from the galley with their wardens in tow.

"I have so many questions," Stacy said, moving to sit on the opposite side of the table.

I wanted to join her but forced myself to remain next to Zarris.

"First, Alernon told me about the negotiations with Earth and how you asked to help," she said, looking at Adriana. "Do you mind if I help too?"

"Not at all. I have no idea what kinds of terms they're going to set, but I've seen what happens when the US tries to pass bills. The non-related special interest items are insane."

"I agree," Stacy said. "But how much time each day do you think that'll take?"

"You determine how much time you wish to dedicate," I said, already thinking of the endless tasks I could provide to keep her with me.

"What about the kids while we're busy with that stuff?" Stacy asked, looking between Adriana and me.

"I know you probably don't want to hear this," Adriana said, "but they'd both rather hang out with Baynol and Peltear than with us. They're fun. They can keep up with the kids, do cool things like handstands, and also don't have the rules we have."

Stacy frowned, and I felt her worry.

"The children are completely safe on this ship," I said. "Even if they were to manage to escape the watchful gazes of their guardians—which is highly unlikely—the ship could immediately locate them. They cannot access anything that is dangerous, and every member of this crew would be delighted with their presence in your absence."

"Seriously, Stace," Adriana said. "Peltear and Baynol love watching the kids. And if, for some reason, they need a break, there are other wardens, men from Anrothe, who are dying to take a turn playing with them. I was worried at first about Lil being with them, but trust me. Zero concerns. They are super respectful in every way."

"Those younglings are the first we've ever seen at that age," Zarris said, drawing Stacy's attention. "My brothers and I would do anything to keep them safe and happy."

"Which is something you should never tell them," Adriana said. "They're smart and will know they can get whatever they want if you tell them how rare they are." She looked at Stacy. "The total population of Zarris's planet is about one thousand people. The kids live separately from the men, usually. Hopefully, that will change, though."

Zarris kissed Adriana's temple, and I looked down at my food to hide the surge of envy I felt.

"While I'm glad there's a ship full of people willing to watch them, I want to spend time with Nicky, too. But I also want to figure out a way for us to get home as soon as possible," Stacy said.

Ignoring the pain those words caused, I focused on the guilt in her voice. After leaving Nicky once, I understood why she would prefer not to leave her youngling in another being's care again.

Soon, she would understand that it wasn't necessary to feel guilt. Raising younglings was never the sole responsibility of the birther. If two created a new life, then eight helped tend to it. That was the way of the systems. Sharing the younglings prevented resentment and wars.

"Then perhaps we should start with the negotiations immediately," I said, standing.

"I'm ready," Adriana said.

I moved around the table before Stacy could stand, and she looked at me with suspicion.

"Did you think I didn't notice the way you winced when you switched places before? Allow me to assist you."

Her gaze studied mine for a halo-flash before she allowed me to grasp her hand. Did she know how far she'd already come toward trusting me? If I were an Anrothian, I would have silently basked in the knowledge and hoped for a future advancement when she was ready. Fortunately for both of us, I was Oebri and knew actions gained results faster than idle hope.

Before she could stand, I slipped my free arm around her waist and lifted her to her feet. The length of her side brushed my chest as I righted her, and the need to lean into the contact had me hesitating a fraction too long to release her.

She pushed away from me, her shocked gaze searching mine.

"Thank you for allowing my assistance," I said. "I would prefer not to see you wince again."

If her long stare wasn't enough to convey every bit of her suspicion, her words were.

"That wasn't the kind of help I agreed to."

Behind her, Adriana shook her head at me. I ignored her disapproval.

"Please explain the anger and fear you feel," I said, watching

Stacy. "I did not harm you; I helped you prevent further injury. I did not touch you any more than necessary, though I wanted to."

"That," she said. "That's what has me angry and afraid. The fact that you *want* to touch me more than necessary."

I understood then that her fear wasn't truly due to me but due to her fear of developing feelings for a male who might hurt her as the previous one had.

"Would you prefer me to hide what I'm truly thinking or feeling?" I asked, letting my disappointment show.

Stacy's lips parted as she stared at me, and I could feel her rising anger as she backed out of my hold completely.

"I'd prefer you feel nothing at all."

"And I would prefer that you stop fearing my interest in you. But I believe that will be as difficult for you to do as it would be for me to feel nothing when I look at you."

She huffed out a breath. "You're impossible."

"I'm quite possible. Speak your agreement, and I'll show you."

She sputtered indignantly, but the fear she'd initially felt had abated. Another step toward trust.

I leaned toward her, a slight smile tugging at my lips.

"Tell me truly. Do you prefer dishonest reactions to honest ones?"

"If I say no, you're going to do whatever you want then, and that's just as bad as pretending."

"You will find that I tend to do what I want regardless of what others request of me."

# CHAPTER NINE

## STACY

MY PULSE SKIPPED AS I STARED UP AT ALERNON.

He was too much. Too intense. Too good looking. Too tempting with the way he was leaning close like he was challenging me.

What in the hell was wrong with me? I had to have some kind of psychological disorder to be looking at another guy, even for a second, after what I'd gone through. My bruises weren't even gone.

"I guess your tendency to do what you want and disregard other people's wishes is why Adriana had the foresight to say she wanted to be a part of the negotiations," I said.

Alernon's lazy smile grew as Adriana snorted softly behind him.

"Adriana is a very smart and capable female. I have no doubt she understood the females of Earth needed her protection. Now, if you're ready, we can move to the comms center." He offered his arm like some guy from an old movie.

With a number of small things, Pin had seduced me into thinking I was special. Words of praise when I made dinner for him or when I'd given him blow jobs. But looking back, I saw it all for what it was. Subtle manipulations.

Now, I scrutinized everything by default.

But, Alernon wasn't Pin. Alernon had given me medical aid and a place to stay. Sure, I couldn't leave now, but not because of him. Adriana was the one who said I couldn't leave the ship, and she'd shared valid reasons. No, he wasn't giving to distract from what he was taking because he hadn't done anything but give, and that made me nervous as hell.

What was he *really* after? Because I wasn't buying that he was into me at first glance. Especially not with the way I looked. Bruised. Broken. *Bitchy*. But, I knew the only way to figure out his game was to play it.

So, I slipped my arm through his and looked up at his slight exhale.

"I will never mistreat you," he said with a look of absolute tenderness.

Did I believe it was real? Not for a second. But, God, I wanted to.

He set his hand over mine and guided us from the galley. It was my first time walking while holding onto a guy's arm. Alernon was considerably taller than me, but I didn't feel dwarfed. At least not in an intimidating way. It helped that Zarris and Adriana were walking beside us and in a similar fashion.

"Why does this feel like we're going to a dance instead of an empty room filled with endless streams of government messages we were never meant to read?" Adriana asked.

I glanced at her. "Secret messages? What kinds of things have you been reading?"

"You have no idea what you're in for. Bribes. Threats. Collaborations you would never have known were happening. It's insane."

"Insanely good?"

"Insanely everywhere. It's hard to keep straight who is working with whom and who's trying to kill whom. I'm kind of worried that Alernon is going to walk right into a power struggle and be used as a bargaining chip based on what I've been reading."

"And I've promised you that will not happen," Alernon said with calm assurance. When he tipped his head to look down at me, and I met his bright gaze, I felt something weird. Like I needed to protect him.

I frowned and glanced at Adriana.

He patted my arm. "Truly, I will be safe," he said. "You have nothing to fear. I will return unharmed and expeditiously to your side."

"Careful," Adriana said. "Your love of big words is showing your age."

Alernon snorted. "Hardly. Everything about your culture is still new and fascinating. I especially love your movies. Very entertaining."

"How long will your fascination last?" I asked, unable to help myself.

"A very long time," he said.

I purposely ignored the heavy insinuation and asked, "How long do you typically stay near a new world once you've discovered it?"

"Until the newly discovered race has the technology to protect themselves. Without adequate protection, Earth's vast resources will make it a desirable location for other species to raid. At a minimum, Earth would need to match Oebri technology."

"Is that going to be part of the negotiation?" Adriana asked. "Some of your technology for…Earth's resources?"

The way she'd hesitated before saying "Earth's resources" had me glancing at her. Did she think trading for technology was a bad thing?

"Perhaps," Alernon said. "There are many things we can offer."

"That's a bit vague," I said.

"It is but simply because there are too many possibilities to guess what might interest your leaders most. Oebri technology is highly valued in the systems and not matched by many. It would require Earth to offer a considerable number of resources to gain a single ship like this one, for example. And it would take fleets of them to protect this planet.

"While my people would be willing to negotiate a trade of such scale, I do not believe your people will be. However, there are more common technologies in the systems that might interest them, such as long-distance communication, sys units, and fabrication units. All of which would be easier to obtain in exchange for fewer resources.

"And without matching our technology, Earth will require protection, a task that does not come without a cost. If a species cannot raid Earth for resources, it will negotiate to join the protective alliance to gain access to its resources. The alliance will need to be large enough and strong enough to repel those that Earth rejects."

"Why would Earth reject any?"

Alernon glanced down at me. "Earth will need to decide how much of its resources it is willing to part with. Either a great number to protect itself and its resources or a slightly less exorbitant number to gain protection from other species that it needs."

"What resources will everyone be interested in?" I asked.

Alernon held my gaze for a moment.

"Earth's most precious resource is its human females. However, not all species will look at you as a potential breeder they wish to coax to their sides. Some will try to possess you, like Pin. Some will not look at you as a breeder at all but as a food source."

My steps slowed as I grasped what he was saying.

*Breeder? Food source?*

I looked at Adriana for validation and caught her glaring at Alernon.

"There are a million better ways you could have told her," she said.

"I believe she deserves the undecorated truth, just as you did."

Adriana finally looked at me. Pity filled her expression.

"Obviously, being a food source is a hard no," she said. "I can't unsee what was done to the other people who were taken with us. It's why I want to be part of the negotiation process. And Alernon's use of the word breeder makes that option sound like a rape case."

"Never," Alernon said quickly.

"But to us, that's how it sounds," she insisted.

"What does a breeder mean, then?" I asked, watching him.

"A breeder is a female physically able to create and carry young. Genetic compatibility will vary from species to species. But for those with whom she is compatible, she is protected and provided for. Cherished and coveted. Simply, breeders are the hope for all species in the systems that are slowly facing extinction."

"Extinction?" I echoed, struggling to keep up with everything he was sharing.

He watched me with compassion as if he knew I was struggling to believe what they were telling me.

"Yes," he said. "Humans are unique. They have remarkably high fertility and the perfect environment to thrive. No other species can match either. Yet, like many other species in the systems, Earth is facing potential extinction. For different reasons, though.

"Earth's population is at a tipping point. To save as many of your kind as you can, you need to find a way to remove a significant number of your kind from your home world. Your kind would be welcomed and treated well at many planets in the system, such as on Anrothe and Oebri."

We stood in silence for several seconds as I let all the information settle in my mind. Earth was in danger of being invaded by other aliens. To spare people from being taken as food, we needed to find a way to convince women to become beloved baby Pez dispensers.

"I know it's a lot to take in," Adriana said. "But Alernon's right about the Anrothians being welcoming. And their planet was very pretty...but a bit dangerous. The wildlife was a lot bigger than here."

"Most planets are like that," Alernon said. "Only on Earth is the sentient life at the top of the food chain."

"No one's going to want to leave if they know that," I said. I sure didn't want to.

"I think many females will once they understand the benefits," Alernon said confidently.

"What benefits? The only reason any of you are interested in a female is to have babies. No matter how well they're treated, every woman is still just a baby dispenser in everyone's eyes. Do you know how hard we fought to be seen as more than that in our own history? Why do you think we'd want to go back to that? We have thoughts, feelings, ideas, dreams, ambitions, too, just like any man."

Alernon studied me for a long moment.

"This is why you and Adriana are needed. Those of us without females lack the perspective to understand what you truly desire. Without it, how can we ever offer you what you need?"

The tone in his voice made it feel like the conversation had just turned personal.

"Maybe we just want to be left alone," I said.

Alernon slowly shook his head. "Abandon you to suffer a slow end alone? Never."

He reached out and ran a finger along my bruised cheek.

"You've already suffered enough," he said, proving I'd been right. "Let yourself experience what it's like to be cared for… cherished as you should be. How can you decide what's best for your people when you haven't experienced all the options?"

The idea of opening myself up again terrified me. Most women would probably jump at the chance to have what Alernon was offering. But I knew what he was asking for. A chance for me to be disappointed and hurt all over again.

"I think I'll pass on the opportunity to become a food source," I said lightly, as if he wasn't talking about us hooking up.

Heat flared in his gaze. "You know that's not what I was suggesting."

Damn him. The rough edge of his voice set my heart racing.

When he looped my arm through his again and started walking, I didn't even think to resist. Adriana and Zarris followed us instead of keeping pace beside us this time. Their observant presence helped curb another strange impulse I felt to lean into Alernon.

What in the hell was wrong with me? Had all of his talk about suffering alone gotten to me that much? He *did* have a way of making it feel like he was being authentic, but then again, so had Pin in the beginning.

The urge to lean into Alernon faded just before we reached the comms center.

The large space was already occupied by several other men like Alernon. Most of them wore their unique black and white ombre hair longer. But two wore it shorter. It was fascinating to see that their hair had the same ombre ratio even at that length. Black roots with white tips.

One of them caught me staring and slowly smiled at me.

"I could please you, my beauty," he said.

"I doubt that," I replied before thinking.

Alernon burst out laughing, and the guy smiled at me.

"It would be my pleasure to try if you would allow me the opportunity," he said, seemingly unbothered by my first rejection.

"Thanks, but I just listened to the whole cherish and protect thing in exchange for my uterus speech from this one," I said, tilting my head at Alernon. "It sounds as interesting as a poke in the eye."

More laughter filled the space.

"A poke in the eye?" Alernon said. "That's disappointing. What would make it more appealing?"

"I'm too afraid you'd actually try delivering on any suggestion I'd make, so I'll just keep quiet."

"Not me," Adriana said. "Give me a damn bra and some underwear, and I'd feel a whole lot better about the cherishing and protecting."

I felt a sudden burst of distaste.

Why would I want additional clothing? I was glorious the way I was with my natural beauty on display.

No, that wasn't right. The idea of wearing a bra and underwear wasn't repulsive. Going around without them felt weird. Granted, I didn't mind the bra part so much. But the underwear I missed. And why in the hell did I think my "natural beauty" was on display?

Frowning, I looked down at myself.

Nothing was actually on display, just the dress clinging to my curves in a sexy way.

"Are you well?" Alernon asked softly.

I noticed I had everyone's attention and shook off my thoughts.

"I'm fine. And I agree with Adriana. Taking away our underclothes isn't a way to win our trust."

His brows went up.

"I believe this is another difference of perspective. The materials you wore were replaced with materials that better suited your delicate skin as a gesture of consideration. I even designed the gown to more closely mimic the garments to which you are accustomed. If I had the freedom to clothe you as I wished, you would be wearing my chains."

Chains?

Everything went cold inside of me.

Chains. He said *chains*.

My airway tightened like Pin's hands were around my throat again, and I slowly tried to withdraw my arm from Alernon's.

"Wait, my beauty," he said softly. "It is not what you think. Before your panic consumes you, look how we show our females they are cherished."

He nodded toward another Oebri, and a 3D image of a beautiful woman with hair like theirs appeared in front of me. She wore chains all right, but not the kind I'd been thinking. They were delicate and pretty like necklace links. They loosely circled her neck with extensions that trailed down her torso, swaying over her bare skin as she moved. She wore nothing but those fine chains weighted by small discs. And she was completely beautiful. She smiled and motioned to someone I couldn't see. Then a little boy came running up and hugged her. She bent to pick him up, kissing his cheek and saying something I couldn't hear.

"Who is she?" Adriana asked.

"My birther. She sent this as a reminder to my crew that we each have a role to fill. Ours is to find more females. Hers is to continue to bring hope to our people."

"By being a breeder?" Adriana asked.

"Do you not see how she is so much more than that?" Alernon asked.

My gaze shifted from the woman and child to the other men in the comms center. They were looking at her with longing, but not in a lustful way. I realized the longing was as much for the child as the woman.

They didn't want breeders. They wanted families.

"Why do you call her 'birther' and not 'mother?'" I asked.

"She allowed another female who was unable to produce young to raise me. The youngling you see is her seventh and final offspring. Though she desires a female youngling for our people, no male will breed her again. Attempting another birth would result in her death."

"So it's not just women—breeders—you want. You want families," I said.

He gazed down at me, heat creeping into his gaze.

"Now you understand. Almost every male in the system yearns for a female of his own, and he will do anything to please her to keep her by his side."

I understood, all right. Alernon did have an agenda, but he wasn't the type to keep it secret.

He wanted me.

No, *wanted* was too tame for the future he had planned.

Alernon was determined to have me, willing, by any means necessary, and I wasn't sure how I felt about it.

# CHAPTER TEN

## ALERNON

STACY STUDIED ME, AND FOR THE FIRST TIME, IT FELT LIKE SHE WAS truly seeing me. Alernon, the person, not Alernon, the man, or Alernon, the alien.

It gave me hope, and my thoughts raced ahead to what the future of my world might look like if our efforts to come to an agreement resulted in thousands of fertile females for my people. Would the older females like my birther stop pushing themselves to breed past when it was safe? Would our city ring with the sound of younglings at play? Would the females finally allow themselves to bond with a single male and create families?

I wanted that future so badly that I could almost feel soft, feminine arms around my waist, hugging me close.

Stacy shook her head slightly. "You're right. Perspective can change how we view things. You'll need to be careful with what you say when you negotiate. Maybe instead of telling a human you want to see them in your chains, tell her you'd like to dress her in jewelry."

"Is that really what your women wear all the time?" Adriana asked.

"Yes. The more wealth the female has collected, the finer and more numerous her chains. After seven offspring, my birther is one of the wealthiest females."

"Hold up," Stacy said. "They're paid to have sex?"

I opened my mouth to answer, but Adriana's stunned expression changed what I was about to say.

"Do humans expect compensation when they labor?" I asked.

Both women shared a glance.

"You already know they do if you've been watching for weeks," Adriana said.

"Then why do humans not compensate females for growing younglings? It takes months of physical and emotional drain and more still afterward to recover."

"So your females aren't paid for sex...they're paid to grow babies?" Stacy asked, her tone now sounding more curious than offended.

"Yes and no. Typically, males attempt to entice a breeding partner with gifts. Chains. Discs. Chit. There is no expectation when giving the gifts, only the hope that the female will remember the male's wealth when she next chooses to breed. A wealthy donor ensures a better future for the youngling. In my case, my donor's wealth and his strong bond with my mother won my birther's favor."

"It sounds kind of like surrogacy, then," Stacy said. "That's actually pretty cool. I'm glad you explained it. So your birther didn't keep any of her kids?"

"She did. Her first and her seventh."

Although I wasn't close to any of my womb brothers, I saw them every solar-run during my birther's recognition celebration. As the second born, I understood how she suffered every time she sent one of her offspring away and how she rejoiced that we returned to her once a year.

Life wasn't easy for any fertile Oebri female. They would trade all the wealth in the systems to be able to keep their young. Yet, my birther understood why she needed to accept the gifts she was given. They were a tribute to the pain she endured for our people's continued existence.

"The Oebri aren't the only race to compensate females for the hope of life they might bring," I said. "Anywhere you go in the systems, males will try to sway you with their wealth."

Stacy made a face and looked at Adriana. "That could be a selling point, I guess."

"Only if it's spun right," Adriana said. "Asking for women to have alien babies in exchange for compensation is going to be a hard pass for a lot of people."

"Maybe," Stacy said. "But you know there are always those one percent of people who will jump at the chance."

One of my men made a sound of disbelief. "Earth's population is almost eight billion. One percent would be over thirty million females within breedable ages." He looked at me. "If we divide the number between the prime races—"

"Hold up," Adriana said, cutting through my wonder. "Don't get ahead of yourself."

"In order for any woman to consider you, you first need to get everyone to believe you're real," Stacy added.

"Your people are already beginning to accept the truth," Quinoll said.

The image of my birther disappeared, replaced by Earth script. Both Stacy and Adriana read the feeds in silence for several prexels. I watched the concern grow on both of their faces.

"Um, I'm not sure this is helpful. It sounds like Earth's leaders are going to try to bait you in and capture you," Adriana said.

"Believing is believing, no matter the intent," I said. "I will meet with them soon, which is why discussing negotiations now is ideal."

In truth, I preferred to wait until the species was calmer and more mentally prepared to meet. However, to preserve my crew and my people, we needed to acquire females as quickly as possible.

"So you're willing to let yourself be caught?" Stacy asked. "I thought the whole point was to prove you're peaceful and here to protect the planet. No one's going to take you seriously if you're caught and die."

Stacy's growing anger fascinated me. I could feel her outrage and, underneath that, her concern. She cared. About me. I struggled to suppress what that made me feel in return.

The small displays of trust had been promising. But this was beyond what I'd hoped for so quickly.

"You are wise to recognize we need to take care in how we are perceived, my beauty. Which is why I will not allow myself to be caught. We needed their communications to show that they were willing to meet us in order to appear before them peacefully. When and how is up to me."

"Okay. So when and how are you going to appear before them?" Stacy asked.

Her worry grew, goading me to nurture it.

"I believe now is the perfect time. Quinoll, prepare to relocate those who agreed," I said.

Stacy placed her hand on my arm. Warmth spread from the limb to my heart as I met her worried gaze.

"Try not to get hurt," she said.

She tempted me greatly. Unable to help myself, I leaned forward and pressed my lips to her brow.

"All will be well, my female."

She blinked at me then started to frown.

"No kissing," she said.

"My apologies," I said, withdrawing. I looked at Quinoll. "Watch for my comm."

Then I left the room and headed for the nearest transference bay.

Introducing ourselves to a new race took time and patience. Due to the influence my kind had over many females, we typically met with males at first. Which meant dealing with fear and suspicion.

Thoughts of capturing me to gain information forcefully were not uncommon. However, they were unnecessary. Neither I nor any of my kind found purpose in withholding our true intent. Doing so only delayed the acquisition of what we wanted.

Even with honesty, it still took several meetings before a new species was ready to listen to our true intent without fear. Which was why I was willing to set this first meeting into motion now. I feared how quickly other races would notice our presence in this system.

Entering the bay, I saw eight orbs already waiting for me. One for each Earthen leader and one for me.

"Now, Quinoll," I said, knowing he was listening.

The familiar tingle of the transfer started in my middle and spread outward, only to converge within me once more as I appeared in the middle of a grassy plain. In the distance, large grazing creatures moved slowly. The sun beat down on the dry grass, and I tipped my head back to bask in its light while I waited.

"Focus," Quinoll said.

I faced forward as seven humans appeared in a semi-circle in front of me and watched the shock in their expressions as they looked around. The recognition in their eyes as they saw each other was an essential part of this meeting. They trusted one another, and a shared experience would make it more real.

"Thank you for agreeing to a brief introduction," I said with a welcoming smile. "My name is Alernon of the Oebri."

The orbs were already positioned near their heads to translate my words into their native languages. One of the males jolted slightly when it spoke, looking between it and me.

"The translation orb near each of you is a gift. It contains information about the systems, such as Earth's location along with all the other known species."

Anger began to bloom in the gaze of another male as he understood what we'd done. That we'd moved them without their consent.

"Learning you are not alone in the systems is likely a shock, and you will need time to adjust. So I will return you to your locations with the orb until you wish to meet again."

"You have no—" The man's words were cut off as the transference beam returned him and the others to their original locations.

I breathed in the heat once more before the beam returned me to the ship.

Everyone in the comms center was silently reading the feeds when I returned.

Stacy noticed me first.

"That was impressive to watch. You definitely proved you were real and flexed your technology like crazy without making it look like a flex. They're not going to like knowing that they can be taken anywhere at any time like that. The fact that you downplayed it like it was a consideration to them was beautifully done. You showed them what a threat you were while giving them a gift that I bet shows the bigger threats."

I couldn't prevent my slow smile. "Are all females as insightful as you are?"

"If you think flattery is going to help your cause, it won't," she said.

I chuckled. "Words with little sincerity are flattery. I assure you that I am completely sincere. Bold, willful, intelligent…those types of females will have the systems at their fingertips."

She gave me a doubtful look and shifted her attention to the feeds.

"It looks like they're all on a conference call already. One of them is grilling an orb." She flinched. "You didn't warn them they would be shocked if they touched them."

"I guess that means no free technology," Adriana said with a glance at me.

"Allowing them full use of it would only give your people a false sense of security. It would take them decades to understand how it functions so they could replicate it. And that orb is thousands of solars behind the technology of this ship."

"Damn...are there really hundreds of species with the technology capable of reaching our planet?" Stacy asked.

I could see the fear in her eyes and wished I could lie to her.

"There are," I said. "Of those, eighty percent would see you as a breeder. Fifteen would see you as a food source. Five would use you as work slaves.

"If your world leaders reject our protection, your planet will be stripped of its resources in less than ten solars."

She and Adriana shared another worried glance.

"Then, we can't let that happen," Adriana said. "What do we need to do next?"

"We watch the feeds. It will give insight into what negotiations will eventually need to take place while we wait for our next invitation," I said.

It wasn't until Stacy's stomach started making sounds sometime later that I realized I'd neglected her.

"Apologies, my beauty," I said. "We can return after you've eaten."

I held out my arm for her as I asked the ship to locate the younglings.

"Human younglings located in prime galley," the ship responded.

Stacy clasped my arm and looked up at me. "That's pretty handy." She looked at Adriana when she noticed she was still reading the feeds. "Aren't you coming too?"

Adriana shook her head, not looking away from the feeds. "I'll go when you get back."

Stacy glanced at me, her uncertainty clear.

"Do not start to fear me, female. You've survived too much to give that emotion control."

"It doesn't control me; it helps keep me safe."

"Allow me to do that."

She gave me a long look before motioning toward the door. Taking the hint, I led her from the comms center and reveled in the soft touch of her hand on my arm.

Alone in the hall, I let myself imagine her slowly closing the distance between us. Her fingers would stroke through my hair as her attention remained fixed on my mouth. Her need for me would consume her. She would kiss me. Her tongue would—

"Alernon, I don't feel so good," Stacy said, stopping to press a hand to her stomach.

Concern washed away my lust, and I tipped her face up to look at her.

"Are you in pain?" I asked.

"No. I...I just feel weird. Not myself. My heart..." She swallowed hard. "It feels like it's ten degrees warmer in here. Those shots you gave me are safe, right? They're not mutating me or anything, are they?"

I considered her concern carefully. "We verified compatibility before administering them. Adriana and the younglings have had no reaction. But we should check just to be sure."

I swung her into my arms and hurried toward the nearest med bay.

"I can walk," she said, turning her head away from me.

"If you are having a reaction, time matters."

She didn't argue, and I had her on an exam table a little over a prexel later.

"Prepare for species type: human," I said. "Scan for health abnormalities and compare to the previous scan."

We both watched the light sweep up her body.

"No abnormalities. Healing: sixty percent complete. Continue pain lubricant as needed for external damage. Scan complete."

Relief coursed through me.

Stacy frowned as her gaze swept the room.

# CHAPTER ELEVEN

## STACY

THE SHIP MIGHT THINK I WAS PERFECTLY FINE, BUT I KNEW I WASN'T. What I'd felt in the hallway—the absolute need to hold Alernon close and kiss the daylights out of him—didn't make sense.

Why had my stomach dipped and my heart raced? Was I actually having a physical reaction to Alernon? I had to be insane. I was still bruised from Pin.

"What's wrong with me?" I murmured.

"You *are* healing…physically."

The tender concern in Alernon's gaze had me quickly looking away.

"You've suffered a great deal, Stacy. It is common for the mind to need time to adjust. Many find it useful to keep busy until such a time as they are ready to address what troubles them."

"Troubles?" I said in disbelief. "I wasn't troubled, Alernon. I was slowly brainwashed through subtle manipulation until I was in so deep that I had to send my son away to save him until I could figure out how to save myself. And I didn't. Instead, I was used and beaten and would have been beaten again if you hadn't shown up. That's not 'troubles.' That's fucked up, and I'm so fucking—"

I closed my eyes and struggled with the waves of anger and

frustration consuming me. I wanted to scream and hit something. But that was too close to what Pin had done, and I refused to be anything like him. So those emotions ate me alive from the inside out.

Alernon's fingers brushed my cheek before his arms wrapped around me and pulled me against his hard chest.

"Don't stop," Alernon said. "Be angry. Be sad. Feel whatever you need to feel. Let it out."

Instead of pulling away, I fisted my hands against his shoulders and let the tears I'd been trying to hold back free.

When humans comforted one another, they said things like, "Shh. It'll be okay."

Not Alernon.

He said things like, "He was a tuber whose vial should have been tossed at first detection..." and "He wouldn't be worthy of drinking urination on a drought-ridden planet..."

That one confused me a little.

"Say the word, and I will tell your world leaders we are using him to smuggle microscopic alien artifacts to Earth. He will be used as a test subject for new probing methods for the rest of his short life."

My sobbing stopped as I pulled back and looked at Alernon with a "what the fuck is wrong with you" expression.

His gaze swept over my tear-streaked face, and he pressed a quick kiss to my brow.

"Still stunningly beautiful. Now tell me how I am allowed to extract payment from that tuber for the pain he has caused. Shall we remove his prized appendage while he sleeps?"

"I can't tell if you're serious or kidding."

"Which would make you feel better?"

"Knowing that you're not a twisted psychopath would make me feel a lot better."

"Generally, I'm not. But when it comes to you, Stacy, I can be anything you need me to be."

Why did that make my heart trip? Alernon was too over the top and yet so tempting.

I eased out of his hold, eyeing him warily. "Weren't we on our way to get something to eat?"

"Is that what you wish? Do you feel well enough?"

I thought about it and realized I did feel better. And not just about the weirdness that had us detouring to the med bay. I felt better about being on the ship and the choice I'd made to protect Nicky, even though that hadn't turned out as I'd thought.

How I felt about Pin was still a ball of bad emotions, and I doubted that would be something I'd sort through any time soon. In comparison, the confusing twist of emotions I felt for Alernon wasn't nearly as heavy.

"I think food will help," I said.

Alernon assisted me from the table and kept my hand tucked in his arm as he led me out of the med bay.

"So, did the things you said in there goad me into the reaction you were hoping for?" I asked.

Alernon glanced at me. "You are a surprising creature."

"Because I could see what you were doing from a mile away?" I snorted. "It was the same thing you did with Earth's leaders, wasn't it?"

"Definitely not. I used a shift in location, a very brief introduction, and a gift to keep them peaceful while also providing irrefutable evidence that the Oebri are real." He paused. "Hmm. I can see the similarities now. I did say those things to help bring you peace. But in my mind, you are vastly different from the world leaders." He made another humming sound. "Although, you *are* both resistant to believing what I say due to fear.

"The similarities end there, though. I don't care if your leaders continue to fear me. But I very much do not want you to fear me,

Stacy. I want you to look upon me with affection. Until then, I will gratefully accept any measure of trust you grant me. Touching my arm. Allowing me to escort you alone. Speaking your mind without reservation.

"I will continue to goad you as you've said and take every reaction you throw at me until you understand I have no hidden intentions. I want to protect you, comfort you, and give you whatever you need simply because you are who you are."

"A female with a proven birth record?" I asked.

"Haven't I already said you are so much more?" He arched a brow at me then shook his head. "Ah. That's right. That tuber robbed words of their value in your mind."

"Or maybe I just forgot. How am I so much more?"

"You are my hope for a future and my reason to wake from the long slumber of my previously monotonous existence."

I studied him as I realized how out of my depths I was when it came to Alernon. He acted old-fashioned but showed me an essentially nude video of his mom. He seemed simple while saying things that were anything but simple. And when he held my gaze like he was doing now, he muddled my thinking in ways that made me feel crazy.

"Okay. Fine. I'm important, and you're trying to help me. I'll believe it until you prove otherwise."

The amused sound he made caused my heart to trip.

"No, you won't," he said. "You'll only pretend to believe it. But I'm content with that. For now."

The weird need to hug Alernon and comfort *him* returned.

Confused and still reeling from my breakdown and his comments, I took a few steps back.

"I think what I really need right now is a little time alone. I'm confident I can find my way to the galley from here."

He studied me for a moment, and my need to hold him increased.

"Please," I said. "You told me you'd be whatever I need. Right now, I need you to be absent."

He dipped his head slightly.

"As you desire, my beauty."

I listened to his retreating footsteps before glancing over my shoulder at him. Time apart would be good for both of us. I didn't know what in the hell was up with my sudden weird impulses and didn't have the emotional capacity to try to dissect them at present.

The galley was almost empty when I arrived. No one bothered me as I browsed the selections or sat by myself to eat. When I finished, one of the men appeared beside me and offered his hand to help me stand.

"I understand you were injured," he said when I gave him a suspicious look. "Please allow me to assist."

I slipped my hand in his and watched his expression change from kind helpfulness to lust-filled adoration as he helped me stand.

"Sweet female, I would spend my life worshipping at your feet if you allowed me."

Tugging my hand free, I tucked it behind my back.

"No, thank you. I'm not really into that."

He smiled, his gaze lighting with even more interest. "What are you into?"

"Distance," I said. "A lot of it. Please leave me alone."

I hurried away from him. He didn't follow me into the hall, which helped put me at ease.

Using the colored stripe on the side of the hall as a guide, I made my way to the kids' entertainment area. The sound of their cheers rang in the hallway before I reached the opening. I stopped just inside the space and watched Baynol lift his arms out from his sides. A kid dangled from each wrist.

"Higher," Nicky shouted.

"Higher," Lil echoed.

"Lady, you will fall and hurt yourself," Peltear said, standing close enough to catch her even as Baynol did what they demanded.

I leaned against the wall, my thoughts whirling as I watched the men entertain the kids.

Nicky's father had never been in the picture. How much of this kind of stuff had he missed out on? How much had he craved? At one very brief point, Pin had me believing that he would be the one to do this kind of stuff with Nicky. Obviously, that had been a lie. But seeing Nicky's face now made me realize how much he needed this.

What would happen when we had to leave?

Baynol's smile as he watched Nicky's struggles to hang on wasn't mocking or entertained like Pin's had been when he'd tripped Nicky. Baynol just looked happy. Like a dad would be.

According to Adriana, Baynol had been there for Nicky a lot during all the shit they endured. How could I even think about taking Nicky away from someone who unconditionally had Nicky's back? Everyone needed someone like that in their life. How shitty was it that I hadn't been that person for my own son?

"That looks fun," I said, drawing their attention.

Nicky's eyes lit up, and he started wiggling even more. Lil fell, but Peltear caught her easily and set her on her feet.

"Forgive me, Lady," Baynol said, immediately lowering Nicky.

Nicky let out a big "Aw!"

"What's there to forgive?" I asked. "It looked like you were both having fun. I really appreciate that you were willing to play with them."

I smoothed back Nicky's sweaty hair as he hugged me around the hips.

"Do you want to keep playing?" I asked.

"Sure." But instead of tugging my hand toward the climbing

dome in the middle of the padded mats, he released me and went to Baynol.

"Nicky," I said. "How about we let Baynol take a break and you play with me?"

Nicky froze and glanced at me. I could see how torn he was. Pick his mom who left him or the guy who was fun.

"We're on a ship, Nicky," I said. "Baynol can't hide forever."

Nicky heaved a long-suffering sigh and looked at Baynol. "Will you come back and play with me later?"

Baynol's expression was just as devastated as Nicky's as he nodded.

"You too, Peltear. I'd like to have some time with Lil too."

Lil was less reluctant. She kissed Peltear's cheek and scrambled out of his arms to hold my hand. I smiled down at the little girl. She grinned back, and I felt like I'd been hit by lightning.

Within a month, she'd been kidnapped, orphaned, and displaced. She'd suffered far more than I had, and she was still smiling.

I knelt so we were at eye level with one another.

"I'm so glad you're Nicky's friend," I said. "Can I hug you?"

She immediately threw her arms around my neck and hugged me tightly. I returned the gesture with every ounce of feeling and closed my eyes, fighting not to cry.

"Are you just going to hug the whole time?" Nicky asked, sounding annoyed.

I opened my eyes and saw him standing by himself near us. Baynol and Peltear were already gone.

"Of course not, silly," I said. Then I kissed Lil's face and released her.

After only a little encouragement on my part, they showed me how to play on the equipment. We played tag next. My ribs and leg hurt a lot sooner than I would have liked, but I didn't stop. I couldn't. I was finally doing what I'd dreamed of doing when Nicky had been missing. Just spending time with him.

When Lil asked for a snack, I led them to the galley.

Adriana found us there just after we sat.

"Hey, guys. Are you bored with the entertainment space yet?" she asked, joining us. "Alernon said they can switch up the stuff in there."

Both kids cheered.

"I heard that Baynol and Peltear are hiding somewhere on the ship. Do you think you can find them?" she asked.

"Wait," I said when both kids started to leave. "Finish your food."

They wolfed it down and ran.

"Is there a reason you chased them away?" I asked, staring after them.

"Yep. I need your help in the comms center. Earth's leaders are in full meltdown mode."

# CHAPTER TWELVE

## ALERNON

I WATCHED THE FEEDS, DEBATING THE WISDOM OF ANOTHER MEETING SO soon. Despite appearing before them and the video of our meeting they'd retrieved from the orbs, other leaders still doubted.

"Stubborn fools," Quinoll said beside me. "How much longer must they delay the inevitable?"

"Stay in peace, my friend," I said. "Allowing your impatience to rule you will not help move their beliefs. We need to think carefully."

Earth had many leaders. If each insisted on meeting me in person, it would take several flares. Flares we didn't have according to our home world.

Word was already spreading that a new sentient race would soon be coming forward. Without our protection, Earth would be open to invasion. Yet, they were fighting amongst themselves about the origin of the orbs, speaking all sorts of ridiculous theories. Newly created technology. Theatrics rather than real video.

I felt a measure of pity for the seven who'd met with me and wondered if meeting another group would help or simply cause more division.

"Backup is here," Adriana said.

I glanced over my shoulder as she entered with Stacy, and I immediately noted Stacy's exhaustion.

"You didn't rest," I said.

"Kind of hard to rest when you're playing with kids," she said, sounding happy. "Heard Earth isn't ready to accept aliens exist yet."

"Correct," Quinoll said. "Stubborn seems to be a species trait."

"Which is probably why we're so resistant to your charms," Adriana said with a smirk.

Stacy frowned slightly, glanced at me, and started reading the feeds.

"So it's the same as before. Like nothing happened," she said. "Why not take the biggest doubters and do the same meeting?"

"I considered that. However, the ones I first chose were the ones who seemed to have the most doubt."

"What if you met with the biggest doubters and broadcast the meeting to the rest of them?" Adriana asked.

"Why stop at only the leaders?" Stacy asked. "Meet with the doubters and broadcast it to the world again like they did with your message."

"I fear causing panic," I stated.

"There was nothing about the first meeting that would have caused panic," Stacy said. "Actually, watching you stun the hell out of them was pretty entertaining."

"Oh!" Adriana said. "We can wait until they're ready for bed and pull them out in their pajamas. That could be fun."

"Negotiations tend to go poorly if we've shown the leaders disrespect," I said, even though her suggestion did entertain me.

"Past experience?" Stacy asked.

I nodded.

"Okay. Then I'm going back to my previous suggestion," Adriana said. "Another brief yet respectful meeting that you broadcast to all the leaders." She glanced at Stacy. "I don't think Alernon's right that a worldwide broadcast would cause mass panic, but if people do start rioting, things will get messy. Giving the leaders a chance to organize things and announce it in a calm way not only prevents outrageous reactions, but it also shows respect."

I watched Stacy, waiting to see if she agreed.

She slowly shook her head.

"I don't think it'll be enough. I think you're going to need to put on a bigger show." She pointed to one of the feeds. "They're calling a meeting. How dangerous would it be for you to appear there?"

"It wouldn't be dangerous to me, but it could be seen as a hostile act, which would violate our agreement with the prime races."

"What if you send a message to those original seven, asking to meet with them again? If they say yes, then you're still allowed to choose where and when, and even if the rest react badly, you wouldn't be in trouble with the other races, right?"

Stacy's perception of the situation and her quick problem-solving didn't simply impress me. It made me want her more.

"Yes," Quinoll said with growing excitement when I remained silent. "We can do that. Alernon?"

"I agree," I said. "How long until the Earth leaders meet?"

"A few more arcs," he said.

"Very well." I held out my hand to Stacy. "That allows me time to take you to a med bay. I would like to run another scan and for you to rest. You look unwell."

"I'm fine," she said.

Rather than asking her a second time, I closed the distance between us and gently turned her toward the exit.

"Comm me if you need anything," I said over my shoulder.

Stacy pushed back against my guiding hand.

"You can't just make me do what you want," she said.

"Alernon," Adriana said, her tone carrying a warning.

"We meet with your world leaders in a few arcs. How will it appear to them if one of the humans in our care is not thriving? I will not yield on this. A scan is necessary."

Stacy frowned at me but stopped resisting as she looked at Adriana.

"I'll be right back," she said.

If I had my way, she would not be. But I didn't speak that aloud. Instead, I maneuvered her into the hallway and lifted her into my arms.

"This is unnecessary," she said. She didn't fight me, though. She simply crossed her arms and glared.

I wanted to smile at her growing trust in me. Instead, I studied her pale face.

"Did you suffer another pain episode?" I asked. "Is that why you look so tired?"

"No. I didn't have another episode. I was playing with the kids. It's been a while since I ran around like that. Apparently, I'm out of shape."

She made a face.

"This is uncomfortable?" I asked, changing my hold on her.

"Yes, it's uncomfortable. I'm twenty-five, not five. And I have two perfectly good legs."

"Your legs are lovely," I agreed. My gaze slid to the tempting limbs.

She jabbed an elbow into my ribs, and I grunted in surprise.

"My eyes are up here," she said.

I looked at them and felt another surge of desire for the female in my arms.

"They are very beautiful eyes. The almost grey-green ring around your irises accentuates the golden brown near the pupil. I could gaze at your eyes for arcs without growing tired of the view."

She frowned slightly and shook her head.

"Adriana said something about your charm before that reminded me of something you'd said about your people having unique qualities. How exactly do you influence people's emotions?"

I opened the med bay door and strode to the exam table as I tried to find the words to answer her question.

"That is like asking you to explain how you breathe. You could describe how your lungs work and how your brain sends signals to your lungs, but it's all subconscious. Rarely do you need to think, 'I need to inhale now.' The way I sense and manipulate others' emotions is similar. It's not something I consciously think to do. It's just there."

"So you know what I'm feeling right now?" she asked.

I shook my head as I gently set her on the table.

"With many species, I am only able to feel strong emotions without trying. The more subtle ones would require me to focus. However, most species find that invasive. So we refrain from focusing unless we are invited to do so."

"What about the manipulation part? Is that the same way where you have to try, or does it just happen?"

"It often just happens. However, we've learned to control that aspect of who we are to an extent. The best I can compare it to is holding your breath or breathing very shallowly. It's uncomfortable, but if we do that, most races can remain unaffected."

"What happens when someone's affected?"

"Prepare scan: human," I said instead of answering.

She watched me move around the table as the beam swept up from her toes.

"Not answering is worse than telling me," she said. "I can imagine some pretty gruesome scenarios."

I lifted her skirt purposely too high to expose her birthing cleft. She immediately pushed it down just enough to hide that sacred place and scowled at me.

"Stop trying to distract me, and just tell me. If you don't, I'm going to go around asking every member of your crew until I know."

The thought of her approaching my crew filled me with jealousy, which I quickly pushed away. In a female-deficient existence, such an emotion was too dangerous.

"Humans are a very tenacious species," I said, finally meeting her gaze. "I think that's why you're so resistant to our abilities." I ran my fingers lightly over her bruised thigh, watching for any sign of discomfort after the beam passed. "Adriana was the first human I met. With her, I learned I did not need to hold my breath or breathe as shallowly. With you, I seem to be able to be myself. You are unlike any female I have encountered."

Her fingers toyed with the material at her waist.

"If you learned how to suppress what you can do," she said. "Does that mean you can force it too?"

"Force? No. We call it a surge, or more precisely, a psy-surge where we allow ourselves to feel deeply. Others can feel the emotion too, then."

"So if you surged in the comms room, everyone would know?" she asked.

"Yes. However, where males of my species would only sense the emotion, females would be influenced by it. Very mildly in most cases. We believe it was originally used to help calm females during times of crisis. We didn't know until we started exploring other worlds that our emotions were doing more than mildly influencing some species."

"No additional damage," the ship intoned. "No additional stim recommendations. Scan complete."

Stacy was quick to sit up. "I was getting ready to argue about another shot."

"The sys-unit knows when you received the last one. It's too soon. We will run another scan before you rest, and it will likely recommend one then. Your bruising has improved significantly."

"Oh, is that what you were doing? Checking out my bruises? I thought you were goading me again with another sneak peek."

I grinned.

"Perhaps a little."

She swung her covered legs over the side and met my gaze.

"Since you've been forthright in sharing all the information you've shared, let me be forthright with you. It hasn't even been two days since you found me. In that time, I've had to come to terms with the fact that aliens are real. That my planet's in danger of being stripped of its valuable resources by just about every alien in what you call 'the systems.' And that the resource being coveted is women like me. Oh, but I don't need to worry. Nice aliens like *you* want to protect the female population...as long as we're willing to have their alien babies.

"I've been used enough in my life and have no desire to be used again, no matter how much some alien will dote on me. Your fancy alien chains? They don't mean wealth or power to me; they look like subjugation. Being the sole hope to prevent your species' extinction? That doesn't give me some sudden sense of purpose. Why should your hopes and needs to save your people be more important than my hopes?"

I could feel her growing agitation.

"I have no wish to subjugate you, Stacy. But would another youngling prevent you from achieving what you hope?" I asked.

"Would I be able to live on Earth with a little Oebri baby? We both know the answer to that. So why should I give up the life and world I know just to save yours?"

I looked away from her for a moment.

"Do you truly feel nothing for me?" I asked softly.

"Did you honestly expect me to fall madly in love with you in a day? You know how crazy that sounds, right?"

I couldn't hold back the surge of hurt and longing her words caused.

"I have no interest in having your instant devotion." I gripped her waist and lifted her off the table.

She frowned when I stepped back.

"I just hurt your feelings, didn't I?" she asked.

I didn't attempt to deny it.

"Because of the unique Oebri ability to influence emotions, we are seen as liars and thieves. Mistrusted. Males everywhere are desperate for females. We arrive, and the females they are attempting to persuade suddenly fall to their knees before us, begging for pleasure.

"We are not thieves. We do not want mindless devotion. We want what any male wants. A female at our side who truly wants to be there."

I exhaled heavily and gently stroked her cheek.

"Yes, I long for you, Stacy. You are not simply an available female with a proven birthing record. You are so unique. You do not fall to your knees. You've never reacted to me in any way but your own. I've felt your anger and mistrust as well as your elbow. You are real, and yes, I desperately want your affection. But only if it's true. I don't want it immediately. I actually look forward to your resistance and earning your trust slowly. It will make your affection for me more real."

She watched me as closely as I watched her, and I saw a hint of regret in her gaze.

"Now that you understand how I feel, what would you like me to do? How should I treat you?" I asked.

She shook her head slightly. "Like I have a choice."

"You always have a choice."

She snorted. "Only if I want to be a dick about it." She heaved an aggrieved breath. "Just keep being yourself, Alernon. Don't hold your breath, and don't worry about your surge. Feel what you need to feel."

I slowly smiled at those words, imagining what I would really like to feel—her front pressed against my front.

She wrinkled her nose at me. "You're going to be a pain now, aren't you?"

"Never," I vowed.

# CHAPTER THIRTEEN

## STACY

HE WAS SO WRONG. I COULD ALREADY FEEL THE OVERWHELMING NEED to rub my front against his front. And he thought I didn't react to him?

*Ha!*

I was just really good at hiding what I was thinking and feeling. The idea that he could feel my emotions was a little concerning.

"Come. I will walk you to your room," he said.

A model example of alien courtesy, he wrapped my hand around his arm and walked beside me. I was impressed with his restraint now that I understood how he really felt.

"Are all males really *that* desperate for females?" I asked.

"Males have indebted themselves just for the opportunity to feel a female's touch on their skin."

"Are we talking sex or just a touch?" I asked, needing to be sure.

"Not breeding," he said. "That's an honor given only to a select few. A touch is different. Females looking to accumulate wealth often choose to live in an Oebri bathhouse. Males from all over the systems go to these rare places and surrender large sums of chit simply to join a bathing selection, which consists of a group of males who present themselves as a bathing partner to the host female. Whomever she chooses will enjoy the pleasure of being bathed by her. It's an experience I've never undergone, but I've heard it's something a male never forgets. The feel of her hands rubbing cleansing salts into the male's skin…"

He shook his head and swallowed hard. I imagined myself standing between Alernon's legs, leaning forward, breasts swaying before his half-lidded gaze as I ran my hands over his sculpted shoulders.

My insides heated, and my pulse kicked into high gear.

Rather than dwelling on my reaction to his words and the image in my head, I focused on the words themselves.

"Does that mean you haven't been with a female yet? Sexually?" I asked.

The image and feeling instantly vanished, confirming my suspicion that it had been his.

"I've heard that females do not enjoy hearing of their lover's past experiences," he said.

"Well, you're not my lover."

"But I hope to be. I would not foolishly remove that chance by sharing what I shouldn't."

"Okay. But, after hearing how few females there are, I'm wondering if you're a virgin."

"Does it matter?" he asked.

"Kind of. If you haven't had experience, I'd probably be nicer to you."

"Then you should absolutely treat me like a virgin."

I rolled my eyes, fighting not to laugh.

"Yeah, right. I think it'd be safer to treat you like a man whore."

He made a contemplative sound. "If you wish to compensate me for breeding rights, I will most certainly agree."

"Ridiculous," I muttered.

He opened the door to my room. When I turned to thank him, he stepped around me and entered.

"What do you think you're doing?" I asked as he looked around the space.

"I'm assuring your comfort," he said. "Is there anything you wish to customize in here? Adriana and Zarris asked for a larger bed. If you would like one, I can arrange it."

"No need. My bed is the perfect size for sleeping alone."

"Hmm. You're right. A larger one is needed."

I didn't fall for his bait. Instead, I baited him. "I mean, I guess so. If Nicky ever wants to sleep with me, Baynol seems like he'd be part of that package too. If there's room for him, then—"

Alernon clapped a hand over his chest. "Cruel female. You haven't even possessed me and have already cast me aside."

"If you don't want to be cast aside, leave my bed alone." I motioned toward the door. "And let me rest."

He dropped all pretense of teasing and caught my hand. He reeled me close and pressed his lips to my forehead.

"Rest well, Stacy. I will return and wake you before I leave for the next meeting."

"Thank you," I said.

I watched the wall close behind him and turned to the bed. It was narrow and a little firmer than I liked. But I wasn't sure I was ready to start asking Alernon for anything. Our talk in the med bay had clarified a lot. More than I wanted to deal with at the moment, actually.

Sitting with a sigh, I closed my eyes and considered everything I'd learned.

After hearing how lonely every male on this ship was, I understood how tempting I might be to all of them. And, while going back to Earth might get me away from the female-hungry, lonely aliens on this ship, it would open up a whole mess of other problems. The apartment I'd been renting was gone—I'd abandoned it when I'd abandoned my kid—which meant he and I wouldn't have anywhere to go. And I didn't have a job or any money to my name to find something else. Even if I did, I was probably wanted by the government and would be picked up the moment someone ran my information.

So, staying right where I was until the world leaders made peace with the aliens was the smartest choice. Smarter still would be to find a way to earn a little cash while I was here so I wouldn't go back empty-handed because I didn't want to lean on anyone anymore. Not that I was even thinking of handing out alien bath favors. However, there was probably something else I could do.

Based on my conversations with Alernon, they were desperate for simple interactions. And considering the way everyone watched me, I agreed. Would I be an asshole to profit from their desperation, though? In my mind, yes, but in theirs, it didn't sound like it.

Now that I was free of Pin, did I really want to tempt fate by associating with desperate aliens in any way, even if I needed the money? That wasn't something I could answer.

SOMETHING TICKLED MY FACE. The sensation jerked me out of my doze, and I sat up, swatting.

"Stacy, it's me," Alernon said, withdrawing his hand. "I apologize for startling you."

I swiped a palm over my cheek. "I thought something was crawling on me."

Alernon smiled slightly. "I will remember your reaction and better control my impulse to stroke your cheek. You looked very peaceful."

"I was sleeping," I said, my tone full of annoyance.

"Apologies. However, the leaders have rallied and are ready

for another visit. I thought you would perhaps like to watch." He held out his hand, an offer to help me up.

Remembering my thoughts before I fell asleep, I watched him closely as I slipped my fingers into his. He frowned, a reaction opposite to what I'd thought I'd see.

"You look like you're expecting me to attack you," he said, smoothing his thumb over my skin. "Did my touch while you slept truly upset you? You didn't seem overly offended when I told you I'd applied medicine, so I thought it was acceptable."

"It's not that," I said, standing. While watching him, I ran my thumb over his skin like he was doing to me.

The frown vanished, and I was hit with the need to kiss him. I didn't act on it, obviously. But it was interesting that I felt it when he gave no other indication about how he felt concerning my touch.

"What does this kind of touch mean to an Oebri male?" I asked.

"Everything," Alernon said without hesitation.

"Is it dangerous? Will the male think I'm offering something more than this? Will he think I'm interested in him?"

"He'll hope you are, but that's all. No one would hurt you because of this." With his free hand, he traced the top of my cheek where I'd been bruised badly. It felt nice. Caring.

"I'm torn," I admitted. "I can't decide if giving someone that hope is cruel or kind."

His expression softened, and he moved closer to me. "Why are you questioning it?"

I released his hand and walked around him to create some distance.

"I can't remember a time that I wasn't living paycheck to paycheck. And things got harder once I had Nicky. I think that was why I fell for Pin so quickly. He made life seem easier. But not because he had money. He seemed to know how to save it."

I turned back to Alernon and found him standing really close to me.

"I never want to be that dependent on anyone again. If I were on Earth, I'd be stuck with a low-paying job because I have no higher skill set. Things are different here. But the idea of handing out back scrubs to earn a crazy amount of money doesn't appeal to me."

"You wish for wealth."

"No. I wish for independence. Wealth implies greed. I'm not greedy, Alernon. I just want to be left alone."

He nodded slowly and reclaimed my hand.

"I will help you find a way that does not involve touching males you are not interested in touching."

He brought my hand to his mouth and pressed his lips to my knuckles in an old-fashioned move. My heart skipped a beat, which I didn't like at all. But I kept my reactions to myself since he was watching me so closely.

"Is everyone waiting for you?" I asked.

"You are a delay they will understand," he said.

I rolled my eyes. "Stop messing with my hand, and get moving."

He chuckled, tucked my hand around his arm, and led me from the room.

"Do you already know who you're kidnapping this round?" I asked.

"I would prefer you not use that term when we are in the comms center. Everything will be recorded to protect my people and our interests regarding Earth. But, yes, we've already selected the delegates to greet."

"Are you going alone?" I asked, trying to keep my worry from my voice.

"Yes. New species feel less threatened when greeting only one of us."

A few Oebri passed us in the hall and nodded to me. Instead of ignoring them, I nodded back.

"Is life boring on a ship like this?" I asked.

Alernon glanced at me. "Lonely, but not boring. Hopefully, it will be less of both soon."

The comms center was a flurry of activity when I entered. Adriana was still there, biting her lip and watching the feed. Anticipation radiated from her.

"I'd kill for some popcorn," she said when she saw me.

A few of the Oebri paused what they were doing to look at her.

"It's a figure of speech," Zarris said. "She does not have the strength or heart to kill anything."

Adriana snorted. "That's why I have you."

He smiled at her.

Alernon's thumb drifted over my skin again, and I felt a surge of longing.

Clearing my throat, I asked, "What drama did I miss?"

"Over half of them believe Alernon is the real deal," Adriana said. "They're discussing what to do. Mostly suggesting ways to capture him so they can interrogate him about his intentions and find out how soon Earth's going to be under attack. The last part's good. That means they believe the data Alernon provided. Or at least, they perceived the potential threat in it."

"Then I should be on my way to alleviate their fears," Alernon asked. "Quinoll? Is everything ready?"

"It's ready," Quinoll said.

With one last brush of his thumb over my skin, Alernon left the room. I faced the feeds, which were a collection of flowing words and some images. One of them switched to the live view of a room full of people scattered around the tiered seating.

"Look at the veins on that guy's forehead," Adriana said. "Reminds me of my old boss. He's going to stroke out if he doesn't calm down."

I agreed.

"I'm ready, Quinoll," Alernon said through the ship.

Quinoll did something on his datapad, and the room on the feed lit up with seven beams of light.

The people within those beams looked around in confusion a moment before they and the beams disappeared.

"I thought he was going there," I said.

"Change of plans while you napped. I convinced him this would be safer and just as effective. Watch."

For a stunned second, no one did anything. Then people started to move. The ones closest to where the people had been stood and shuffled back. Others stood and started shouting. More just looked around in confusion.

An image appeared in the center of the large meeting room. It was a 3D image of a field. Everyone in the room was still as the lights reappeared in the image, depositing the people along with Alernon.

On another feed, we had a live view of the field and could hear Alernon when he spoke.

"Thank you for accepting a second invitation to meet. First, let me assure you that the threat to your planet is real. But it's not what you imagine. The species list I provided you isn't interested in destroying your planet. You're already slowly doing that yourself. They would simply raid your planet for its precious resources before they're gone.

"My people are also interested in Earth's resources. However, we understand that raiding your planet while it continues its slow decline is in neither of our species' best interests. My people would like to help you protect and heal your planet in exchange for first rights to any resources you wish to export."

Alernon paused this time, giving them the time and opportunity to react.

One of the men shook his head and looked around the field. I could see the disbelief slowly fade in his eyes as he reached down and touched the grass at his feet.

"Where are we?" he asked.

"A location in Africa," Alernon said.

I glanced at the first feed to gauge the reaction of the humans still in the meeting room.

"They still don't believe it's real," I said. "How can they see people disappear before their eyes, have a 3D floating image of them appear in front of them, and still not believe?"

"We are monitoring the Senwar system, which is where Earth is located, for any non-Oebri ships. However, without a signed treaty between us, my people cannot act on behalf of your people to offer protection…no matter what happens.

"You heard Adriana Wilston's recommendation to accept our help, but I believe you need to hear the full account of what she experienced to understand what your planet is truly facing. For her safety, she's chosen to remain aboard our ship. However, you're welcome to speak with her there at any time if you wish."

"You're acting like you want us to believe you're not hostile, yet you kidnapped us," a woman said angrily.

"Alernon doesn't like the K-word," I said to Adriana.

"Alernon's dealing with power-hungry toddlers," Adriana said in return.

"If you have the technology to take us," another much calmer woman said, "why remove us from the room instead of speaking to the entire assembly?" She spoke heavily accented English with fluency.

"For the same reason we did not broadcast Adriana Wilston's account of her abduction. We do not wish to cause panic."

"What is it you want from us?" another asked.

"For now, I am hopeful one among you will have the courage to meet with Adriana."

"Um, did you know you would be talking to someone?" I asked her.

"Yeah. They need to know what's out there and why we need help." She shook her head slowly. "I don't want anyone to see what I saw."

"Can I come too?" I asked.

"Sure."

# CHAPTER FOURTEEN

## ALERNON

My impatience was growing, though I did my best to hide it.

Stacy had touched me. Willingly.

No, it had been more than a touch. It had been a caress. I could still feel her finger teasing my skin, and I wanted to return to her and continue our discussion. Instead, I was stuck on the surface with humans who radiated angry fear.

Perhaps it was time to give up my position as the lead Oebri delegate on our ship and focus on winning Stacy as my own so we could settle on my home world. No more exploring the systems. No more meeting with resentful species. Just me and my female... and her younglings.

"What guarantee do we have that you'll bring us back?" one of the men asked.

"The same guarantee you have that I will return you now. I have no interest in detaining you. Detention? Interrogation? We have long since evolved beyond the need for those barbaric practices. We prefer open communication and information sharing...but only when both parties agree that is the goal. Until then, removing you from locations where my appearance might cause panic or jeopardize my well-being is my only choice."

The man's emotions surged between indignation and anger.

No race liked to be considered barbaric, and they often chose more peaceful routes when they understood how we viewed their actions.

"I'll go," the calmer female said.

I smiled at her. "Thank you for accepting our offer. The rest will be returned to their original locations. When you are finished speaking with Miss Wilston, you may choose where we return you."

She nodded and watched as the others disappeared.

"How does that work?" she asked.

"It's a complex process that I wouldn't attempt to explain in the limited time we have together. In simple terms, it's a frequency that matches our base energy and transfers that energy to another location."

A single beam appeared before us.

"Stepping into the light will take us to my ship."

Without hesitation, she walked into the beam. I followed and watched her as the light dissipated to show the transference bay.

Her gaze took in the space, and I felt a hint of her wonder.

"We do not have much time together before your people begin to fear you will not be returned. Would you like a brief tour of my ship on our way to meet Miss Wilston?" I asked.

"Please," she said. "I'm very curious."

"This way," I said, indicating the direction of the hallway.

She was fascinated by everything and asked intelligent questions, things that I'd come to expect from a first volunteer.

When we reached the younglings' play area, we paused to watch them with their guardians.

"The males watching over the younglings are from Anrothe, the planet where Adriana and the younglings were abandoned by their abductors. The younglings are aware that we are near Earth and that we are waiting to return them to their families until we can guarantee their safety."

The woman glanced at me. "You don't believe they are safe?"

"Adriana believes they will be taken into custody, examined for a length of time, and questioned thoroughly. You can ask her more about the reasons she would prefer to remain on the ship instead of returning to her home world."

The woman nodded and continued following me as I led the way to the galley. We passed a few of my crew in the halls. Enough to show there were more of us, but not enough to convey any threat.

Adriana and Stacy waited in the galley. Zarris stood behind them like the protector he was.

The woman introduced herself as Annah Bergen and held out her hand. Adriana gripped it in her own and gave a friendly smile.

My attention shifted to Stacy and her lingering bruises. I worried how listening to Adriana's detailed account might affect her now that she truly believed everything was real, but I knew not to attempt to send her away. Not only would I likely anger Stacy, but I risked giving Earth's leaders a false impression of how we viewed females.

"Please, have a seat," Adriana said after introducing Stacy and Zarris.

Adriana told her story, neither rushing nor lingering on any part, not even her time on Anrothe. Stacy listened as avidly as the Earth leader. A frown marred her brow when Adriana explained the disparity between Anrothe's two genders.

"The Anrothe people purposely chose to abandon their technology so they wouldn't attract the attention of the systems," Adriana said. "Unless Earth is willing to do the same, humans are going to be disappearing in beams of light left and right. Only the aliens taking the humans won't offer to return them like Alernon did with the kids and me."

"You're not really returned, though, are you? Alernon said you're choosing to remain on the ship. Do you believe you would be abducted a second time?" the woman, Annah, asked.

"Right now? No. That's not why I'm staying on the ship. With the way the world leaders are denying aliens exist publicly while privately talking about how to fight them, I'm afraid the kids and I would be used as some kind of political pawns. But in a few weeks, when ships of every kind start parking in Earth's orbit? You bet I believe I'd get abducted a second time.

"That garbage planet..." Adriana shook her head and let out a long breath. "Those aliens were eager and lined up for a chunk of human."

Stacy looked sick, and I motioned to Raaln to bring her something to drink.

"I admit," Annah said, "even with the information regarding the abundant life out there and the experience you've shared, I'm struggling to believe Earth is in danger."

"Don't wait until half the population is gone to start believing," Adriana said. "Until you do, I'll stay here aboard the ship and wait for the outcome of the treaty the Oebri want to propose. If it doesn't work out, I'm content to travel space with Zarris and the Oebri."

Raaln delivered a tray with drinks. I immediately handed one to Stacy.

Annah focused on her. "You're Nicky Ludridge's mother, aren't you? What happened to you? How did you get here?"

Stacy accepted the drink and met the woman's gaze.

"I was in an abusive relationship with Stone Pinchas. When Adriana's message aired, he beat me because I'd told him Nicky was with some family somewhere. I had three broken ribs and so many bruises no one would have recognized me. Since Nicky was with Adriana, Alernon and Adriana were looking for me. When they figured out where I was, Alernon came down and offered to take me to Nicky. I agreed."

She made it sound so simple when it was the opposite.

"The male, Pin, was in the process of beating her again when I arrived," I said. "He had his hand around her throat and wasn't allowing her to breathe."

Stacy looked down at her drink, and I felt her fear again.

"According to the law of the systems, I had the right to save the female from danger," I said. "Also, according to the law of the systems, he should be punished with death for the damage he inflicted upon her. Although he fired his weapon at me, I did not carry out the laws to which I am bound. Stacy asked that he be held to human laws."

As Stacy slowly sipped her drink, I watched the Earth representative's reaction. If she was appalled by what happened to Stacy or the death sentence the systems demanded for it, she didn't show it.

Instead, she looked at both females. "I am deeply sorry for what you've endured, and thank you for sharing what happened. It won't be easy for some to believe, but I'll go back and tell them what you've told me. Hopefully, we can set disagreements aside and band together to discuss what's next for our planet."

She started to stand. Stacy immediately tried to do the same and winced. I hurried to her side and wrapped an arm around her waist to help her.

"I would have an easier time convincing my fellow diplomats if you could provide a list of what resources other races are interested in."

"Our planet's most sought-after resource is its people," Adriana said.

"Ah." The woman frowned.

"I wasn't kidding when I said a man was butchered in front of me. We're livestock to some of the aliens."

The diplomat's composure faltered a little. "I'd hoped, since the Oebri had been willing to return you, another resource might have drawn them here."

"Earth has a delicate yet verdant ecosystem that we've not encountered anywhere else in the systems. Everything from the flora to the fauna...even the terra itself, has value. However, I would prefer to postpone any discussions regarding what we're interested in receiving in exchange for Earth's protection until a time when the leaders decide if our protection is welcome. But I can assure you, we are not interested in consuming your people as food."

Adriana came to stand before the woman.

"Just like we have laws we need to follow, so do the Oebri. I asked Alernon to help me find Stacy so we could reunite her with her son. When he found her, and we had reason to believe she was in danger, the laws that Alernon follows said he could go to assess the situation. If not for her relationship with Nicky, who was illegally removed from his home world, and the risk to her life when Alernon arrived, he wouldn't have been allowed to intervene and remove her.

"Even if a thousand ships suddenly showed up and started beaming humans off the surface, Alernon and his crew wouldn't be able to do a thing to stop them. Not without Earth's prior permission in an official agreement.

"If you can't convince the world leaders of anything else, at least convince them that our time to ask for help *before* other aliens show up is running out."

The woman nodded and looked at me.

I glanced down at Stacy. "I will return quickly."

"I'm fine. We're going to get the kids and come back for dinner. Go. You know where to find us."

The diplomat didn't say anything else until we reached the hallway alone.

"You seem to care a great deal about them," she said. "The women you rescued. What would you do if we demanded their return?"

"I would ask them if they wish to return," I said, even as anger and denial surged.

The diplomat stumbled a step, her fear spiking. I quickly shielded what I felt.

"Are you okay? Did you hurt yourself? We are near a med bay."

Carefully maintaining my shielding, I took her arm and guided her down the hall. I could feel her trembling under my touch.

"Command Alernon, summon Adriana and Stacy to this med bay," I said as I lifted the diplomat to the table. "Forgive me, Annah Bergen. I should have asked them to accompany us.

"Prepare for species type: human. Scan for injuries and make repair and health maintenance recommendations."

She blinked at the band of light that appeared at her feet before letting out a shaky breath and meeting my gaze.

"It's fine. I'm fine. I was disoriented for a moment but am better now."

"I can see you are not. Please allow the scan to finish. It will assure me the disorientation wasn't caused by anything else."

How we treated the first volunteer often set the tone for our negotiations. Respect and honesty were foremost. Yet, I couldn't admit that her disorientation was likely due to me. Likewise, I couldn't allow Earth's leaders to find out too soon how desperately we needed their females.

She looked down at the light. "What is it supposed to be doing? I don't feel anything."

"You shouldn't feel anything during a scan. If anything is detected, the sys-unit may make recommendations that might result in some brief discomfort. Adriana had her hand repaired. It was damaged during her landing on Anrothe. She endured the procedure well."

The light ended at the top of the woman's head.

"Abnormal growth detected. Insufficient data to provide recommendations. Scan complete."

Her eyes round. "Growth?"

"Please show the growth," I said.

An image of her reproductive organs appeared above her waist, overlaying their positions inside of her. A blue light flashed in the location of the growth.

"What is it?" she asked.

"Your species is still very new to us. Although we've learned much from the scans of our current guests, there is still much we don't know. Perhaps this data should be shared with your doctors?"

"Yes. Please," she said in agreement just as the wall opened.

She sat up quickly, disrupting the image of the growth. Stacy looked from the diplomat to me as Adriana rushed forward to help the woman off the exam table.

"What happened?" Stacy asked.

"She was disoriented for a moment," I said. "I ran a scan just to be sure she wasn't ill."

"I'm sure everything's fine," the woman said. "As you said when I arrived, we don't have a lot of time before people start to worry. I should return."

"Perhaps you could escort her, Adriana?" I asked, watching Stacy's worried gaze. "Quinoll is monitoring the transference bay.

"Of course," Adriana said.

# CHAPTER FIFTEEN

## STACY

As soon as the wall closed behind Rin and the diplomat, I looked at the image lit up over the table.

"What is that?" I asked.

"An unidentified growth," Alernon said.

"Is it bad?" I asked.

"We are still gathering vast quantities of information about your planet and people as we observe them. Although I do not believe it is life-threatening, I have offered to send it to her human doctors to review." He exhaled heavily. "There is a chance I caused her disorientation with a surge, Stacy."

His gaze swept over my face. "Your natural immunity to what I feel gave me a false sense of belief that all human females would be the same."

Guilt and regret hit me, and I knew it wasn't all my own.

"Why did you surge?" I asked.

"She asked what I would do if they demanded your return." Alernon looked away. "Adriana, the younglings, and you."

Demand? I hadn't considered that they might do that now that they knew where we were.

"Can they do that?" I asked. "Demand we go back?"

"They can demand whatever they wish. It does not mean we must comply. You and Adriana have a choice in whether or not you return to the planet."

That made me feel a lot calmer about the situation.

"And what did she feel from you when she asked that?" I asked.

"That I wasn't pleased."

"Hmm. I see. And how did she react to feeling that?"

He finally looked up again. The intensity of his gaze, paired with a wash of disbelief, was a little disconcerting.

"She stumbled," he said. "I immediately guarded what I was feeling, but she continued to shake, so I brought her here."

"I imagine feeling suddenly upset without understanding why was scary. Are you worried that she knows it was you making her feel that way?"

He slowly shook his head, still watching me like he was seeing me for the first time.

"No. I believe she doesn't know."

I wondered why he'd felt guilty then. Because he'd surged or because of something else? I chose not to ask.

"I'm sure it's fine then," I said. "I'm guessing you just need to be more careful around her?"

"Yes," he agreed.

An urge to go to him and wrap my arms around him tugged at me. It would probably feel amazing to rub my breasts against his chest and—

"Adriana and I were going to get the kids for dinner," I said, interrupting him mid-fantasy. "I should go."

"I'll accompany you," he said.

"Shouldn't you go to the comms center to monitor the reaction to her visit?"

The way his smile slowly overtook his somber expression did things to my insides.

"You wish to be alone again," he said. "Very well. I will respect your wish and leave you. For now. Farewell, my beauty."

He stole my hand for another kiss that I didn't mind and left me to walk to the entertainment bay alone.

As soon as I heard the kids' laughter, I felt some of the tension inside me ease. My first full day aboard an alien spaceship had been crazy. It still didn't feel real, but big changes were sometimes like that. Sending Nicky away hadn't felt real either at first.

Taking a calming breath, I smiled before walking into the entertainment area to see Baynol flipping into a handstand.

The kids cheered as he started walking around on his hands. So did I a little—on the inside—as his tunic bunched around his chest, showing a crazy amount of abs.

"Lady Stacy," Peltear said, spotting me.

Baynol immediately flipped onto his feet and straightened his clothes like a tween girl caught undressing. That type of reaction out of the big, buff man was pretty cute until I remembered Adriana's story from earlier about how suppressed the men from Anrothe were.

"Sorry for interrupting," I said. "I thought maybe we could all eat dinner together."

Nicky and Lil erupted in cheers. Lil grabbed Peltear's hand and started leading him from the playroom. I lifted my hand out to Nicky, but he didn't see. He took Baynol's.

It cut me deep, but it was a cut I deserved. Nicky's love for Baynol was on my shoulders. If I hadn't sent Nicky to Adriana, he would have never met the man. Yet, I didn't regret it. Baynol was a much safer choice than Pin. So I smiled at my son as I watched him tug on Baynol.

Baynol glanced from Nicky to me and back again.

"Nicky, I would like to walk your mother to dinner. Please go with Lil and Ben, okay?"

Nicky stopped tugging and stared at Baynol for a second before his expression melted into a huge smile.

"Okay!"

He ran out of the room, leaving me alone with Baynol.

"I can see how much you care for him," Baynol said. "Does it anger you that he enjoys time with me?"

"Not at all. I know that you've helped him feel safe at a time when I wasn't there, and I'm grateful for it. Oh, and that was an impressive handstand. I'm sure he's going to talk you into teaching him that move."

Baynol looked away from me. He didn't fidget, but he looked like he wanted to.

"Adriana told me a little about your planet and how the men there are treated. I just want you to know I'm nothing like that. I appreciate the time you're spending with Nicky, and if he would rather hold your hand than mine, I'm okay with that too. He's a little boy who made a new friend. Just…don't hurt him, okay?"

"Never, Lady," Baynol said with surprising force. "I would never hurt him."

I smiled and reached out to give his arm a gentle squeeze. "Thank you, Baynol."

He glanced down at my hand, and I realized how uncomfortable I was probably making him. I quickly dropped my hold and gestured to the exit. We walked slowly together.

"I heard there are more Anrothe on the ship, but I haven't seen them. What are they doing?"

"They are learning. We only know how to hunt and protect. Those skills aren't needed on this ship, and we want to be useful to the Oebri. The Oebri can teach us many things."

"So you're not planning on returning to your planet?" I asked.

Baynol shrugged slightly. "Our females may not welcome us."

"Why not?"

"After meeting females like Adriana and you, who willingly

look at us, speak to us, and touch us, how can we be content with the indifference our females have always given us? They fear we will ask for more than they are willing to give."

"It sounds like they don't give you anything."

Baynol smiled slightly. It was shy and sweet and melted my heart a little.

"I can see now that they did not," he agreed.

"Are you sad that you'll never see your home again?" I asked, trying to put myself in his place.

"If I cannot win the heart of a human female as Zarris did, I still have no reason to regret my choice to leave. I have learned much about how your planet is thriving and hope someday I will be able to return and help change the way our people live for the better, even if I am not welcome to stay."

Would I have such an idealistic outlook if I couldn't return to Earth? I doubted it. But hearing how calm Baynol was about it had me wondering if my determination to return to Earth made any sense. There were so many reasons not to. But what would I do if I was stuck on this ship forever? What would Nicky do?

"It's hard to face an unknown future," I said. "I hope I have as much courage as you do if Nicky and I can't return to Earth."

"You fear they will not welcome you?" he asked.

"Oh, I know they would, but I don't know that it would be safe for us."

"Allow me to go with you. I vow I will protect you."

I smiled at him. "That's very sweet to offer. But, even with your protection, it would be too dangerous. There are a lot of angry humans down there. I wouldn't trust them not to do something to you just because you're different." I sighed. "My home might not be my home anymore. It's hard to acknowledge, but it's true. The idea of being homeless makes me feel a little lost."

He looked away again. "There are many planets that would welcome you. You would never be without a home."

"Because I'm a female?"

"Yes."

"Would you be welcome on any planet?" I asked.

"If I were a female's companion, yes."

I nodded in understanding, feeling bad for Baynol. His whole life, he'd been unwanted and treated as such. What would happen to Baynol if Alernon actually managed to establish an agreement with Earth's leaders? Would it be possible for Baynol to meet a female then?

I glanced at Baynol's profile, seeing how handsome he was, and hoped so. Any woman with an open mind would fall for him and shower him with the attention he deserved. I was sure of it.

"I think you'd make a great companion," I said. "Once Earth realizes we need help from the Oebri and your people, I'll do everything I can to make sure you're treated like the considerate person you are."

He smiled at me again, showing so much relief and joy that I knew I'd need to do everything possible to ensure Earth's leaders signed a fair contract.

We arrived at the galley at the same time as Adriana and Zarris. I paused to talk to her while Baynol went to join Nicky.

"How is Annah?"

"She's shaken a little by the scan, but I think she'll be fine. Actually, I think what happened will work to our advantage."

I was thinking of Alernon's surge when I asked, "How so?"

"If Alernon's scan found something serious, that means he demonstrated technology that Earth might find really useful. It might help speed up their willingness to talk to Alernon."

"Unless they suspect that Alernon's scan caused the growth," I said.

Adriana's excited expression shattered. "Why would you say that?"

"You know I'm right. There will be people who think that."

She groaned. "Why do they have to be so difficult? Aliens exist. More are coming our way. Get with the program already."

I patted her arm. "This is why we're here. Since we think like humans—

"We *are* humans."

"—we can anticipate their reactions and plan accordingly," I said as if she hadn't interrupted me.

"Okay. So they'll continue to be divided," she said. "We'll just need to work on winning over the ones who believe us, right?"

"It makes the most sense," I said. "The more we have who believe us, the more they can work on convincing the others so we're not spinning our wheels."

"Human conversations are odd," Zarris said behind Adriana.

She grinned at him. "We have a lot of weird sayings. But our plans are good. Promise."

"Mom!" Nicky called. "Baynol has food for you."

"Go," Adriana said. "I'll grab something, and we can talk some more."

I went to the table and saw Baynol had made me a plate, choosing the same foods I'd eaten the night before. There was a flower on the side of the plate.

"It's for looking at, not eating," Nicky said.

"Thank you." I patted his head and smiled at Baynol as I sat. My leg didn't hurt as much this time.

That realization gave me an idea, and I looked around for Adriana.

"What are the chances my initial scan was saved?" I called.

She looked at me, but it was the chef who answered.

"All scans are saved in order to detect changes and provide health recommendations."

"We can send my scans as proof to the doubters, then," I said.

Adriana nodded. "I like it. The more evidence we can provide that their scans are real and useful, the more people we'll win over."

Smiling, I focused on my food and took a bite. Baynol was watching me, so I nodded my approval.

I hoped for both our sakes that my scans would convince the world leaders that everything Alernon said was true and that he wasn't here to invade our planet. As soon as I had that thought, I realized what I'd done. I'd started believing Alernon too. But it wasn't Alernon who'd convinced me.

I glanced at Baynol again and caught his shy look before he focused on his plate. How could aliens that shy be bad? There were a lot of women on Earth who'd love a big, buff shy guy in their lives. Baynol needed his chance.

*But then what about Alernon?* I asked myself.

# CHAPTER SIXTEEN

## ALERNON

"LET ME KNOW IF ANYTHING CHANGES," I SAID TO QUINOLL, TURNING away from the feeds.

"With the Earth leaders or with Baynol and Stacy?"

"Both," I said, leaving the comms center.

Listening to Stacy's quiet promise to keep Baynol as her protector if she was unable to return to her planet had caused a surge of jealousy. The dangerous emotion had no place on a ship with one unattached female. I knew that. We couldn't afford additional tension. And once Stacy was healed and would openly be pursued by the rest of the crew, they needed to know I wouldn't do things to prevent their suit.

Yet, I wanted to.

I paused and focused on taking a few calming breaths. I needed to use logic and not allow my emotions to rule me.

How much longer until she was fully healed? The new bruises on her throat were already mostly faded. I didn't have more than a flare, at most. I needed to be more thoughtful in my plan to win her trust.

"Quinoll," I said into my wrist comm. "Have a larger bed

moved to Stacy's sleep bay. She expressed a desire to sleep with her youngling."

"Understood," he said.

I continued down the hall, thinking about what more I could do to coax a bond with Stacy. I wanted her with a desperation that fought to suffocate me. However, her mistrust of males and her resistance to me remained obstacles.

If she wasn't so resistant to Oebri persuasion, I could have coaxed her favor that way. But then, any other Oebri would be able to do the same.

Perhaps her mistrust of males could work in my favor. I'd watched her reject the offers from other males, just as she had rejected mine. The difference was that she could send them away, whereas her assistance with the Earth issues would keep her at my side and give me more opportunities to win her favor. However, constant male attention might cause her to retreat emotionally from me as well.

I needed a way to distract the others. Any outright orders to keep their distance would see me removed from my position on this ship. Possibly even sent to a Helix Station for holding and reconditioning.

Which led to yet another obstacle—the laws that bound my people and the systems.

I'd heard what Stacy had said about leaving her planet and feeling homeless. Life on a ship wouldn't be enough for her. However, living on a planet other than my home world wasn't an option either. Due to the past mistakes of our people, Oebri males were not allowed to linger on any planets other than our home world.

The idea of returning to Oebrion filled me with dread. Once there, Stacy would be inundated with male attention. A female had the right to choose any companion she pleased. Always. And even bonded females bred with other males to increase genetic diversity in hopes of improving fertility in future generations.

But the idea of sharing Stacy troubled me. I didn't think I would be able to.

What options did that leave us? A station?

My steps slowed as the possibilities formed. Most stations were floating trash heaps unfit for female habitation. Helix stations were clean and well-kept by the Oebri, but they were places where those who enforced the laws held those who broke the laws. I didn't want Stacy around the latter.

However, anyone with the chit could build a station. My people had the chit, and with the resources on Earth, they had every reason to spend it here.

I debated contacting Oebrion immediately with the idea, then rejected it. First, I needed Earth to agree to our protection. Only then would my people agree to build a station. Once we were approved to start building, my crew would be too distracted with thoughts of future females to worry about the one aboard.

It was an ideal solution to many issues.

Stacy was almost finished with her meal when I entered the galley.

Baynol's focused gaze on her while she conversed with Adriana grated at me. It was unfortunate for me that Nicky had bonded with the warden. While I could distract my crew, there was little I could do to distract the youngling's protector.

Except for the youngling himself.

"There's the guy we need," Adriana said, noticing me.

"Need?" I echoed, glancing at Stacy. Another surge of desperation hit me.

"Yep," Stacy said. "We're trying to stay ahead of our leaders' reactions to what Annah Bergen will tell them. Especially if her doctor finds anything where your scan indicated. If something is found, we think some of the leaders will try to say that you put it there."

"They will acknowledge the truth of our existence but in a way that makes us an enemy," I said with a nod. "It often happens that way."

"But what if we send them my scans along with the footage of me in the convenience store?" Stacy asked. "The footage would be proof that I was hurt on Earth. The first scan would confirm the injuries. And all the other ones would show how my healing progressed."

"And it would emphasize how beneficial your technology is," Adriana said.

Baynol stood, likely to get Stacy more food, and I took his seat across from her.

"It is a good plan," I said. "As soon as your leaders publicly announce our existence, we can also broadcast the benefits of our healing technology."

"There are a lot of people who'd want access to your sys-units," Adriana said. "If you can heal sick kids, the public will be on your side."

"And so will those younglings when they're grown," I said with approval. I looked at Stacy as Baynol started back to the table. "If you're not yet tired, would you be willing to return to the comms center?"

She frowned slightly. "Why?"

"You both have useful insight. However, Adriana has already spent the majority of her flare there."

Understanding lit Stacy's face. "And I got to take a nap. Sure. I'll take a turn then." She glanced at Adriana. "Are you okay with the kids?"

"Absolutely," Adriana said. "Let me know if anything big happens while I'm not there."

Stacy looked at Nicky. "Have Adriana let me know when you're ready for bed, and I'll come read you a book, okay?"

Nicky nodded, looking a little sad as he glanced at Baynol. The youngling understood very well that the warden was attempting to woo his mother.

I stood and offered Stacy my hand. "Shall we?"

She stood on her own without touching me. "My leg's already feeling better."

Behind her, Baynol slowed and looked down at the food he held.

"I'm relieved it's no longer causing you pain," I said. I took her hand in mine and tucked it around my arm, ignoring the slight resistance she offered.

"Have fun, you two," Adriana called as I led Stacy away.

Fun would not involve watching the feed together. It would involve less clothing and more—

Stacy pinched the inside of my bicep. I grunted and looked down at her as she tugged her hand from my hold.

"I don't like a bully, Alernon, and that's how you're feeling right now."

"Apologies," I said, truly feeling regret. "I saw Baynol was fetching you another selection meal and thought it would be in your best interest to remove you before he could ask to join you in your sleep bay next rest cycle."

Stacy blinked up at me. "What?"

"I'm uncertain which part you're questioning. Baynol's intentions or mine?"

"All of it. What's a selection meal, and do you mean you think he's going to ask to sleep with me?"

"A selection meal is a meal prepared by a male Anrothe to favorably influence a female into selecting him for breeding. Did Adriana not explain the selection process on their planet?

Typically, after a female eats the meal the male provides, she breeds with him. If you choose to allow him to sleep with you after breeding him, he would also welcome that."

Stacy studied me closely for a prexel.

"Thank you for letting me know. After hearing how bad the Anrothe had it on their planet, I don't have the heart to ignore Baynol. He's too sweet for that. But I don't want to mislead him either. I'll be sure to let him know that I have no intention of breeding or sleeping with anyone for the foreseeable future."

I understood very well that her words were as much for me as for any other male.

"Focusing on Earth's treaty will take much of your time," I said as if agreeing with her.

She smiled slightly. "The treaty is important, but so is my son. And I've neglected him enough already. When Adriana contacts me, I plan to read him a story, Alernon. Instead of worrying about how I'm spending my time, focus on the treaty yourself."

Without taking my arm again, she started walking.

I stared after her, reveling in the fact that she'd just told me to mind my own matters. When was the last time a female proved this difficult? Never.

Need consumed me as a slow smile parted my lips.

Several arcs later, I struggled to find the humor in her willful resistance as she left the comms center to read to her youngling. Though she'd spent time beside me, I'd made little progress in winning her affection. Her focus had solely remained on the feeds.

"How is her healing progressing?" Quinoll asked, also watching after her.

"I expect she will be fully healed after her next rest cycle," I said.

"That is good news."

For the crew, perhaps. But not for me.

"She told me that she has no intention of breeding with any

male for the foreseeable future. Let the crew know to approach her with care. Although she is physically healed, I worry the previous male has left scars in her mind."

Quinoll made a tormented sound. "You should have ended the tuber's life and brought her peace."

"You saw the vid. I do not believe it would have brought her any peace."

"What will you do?" Quinoll asked.

Quinoll knew me well. He wasn't asking about my pursuit of her but how I, as the ship's delegate, would provide her the peace she needed long-term.

"No matter which male she chooses, I believe Stacy will never agree to return to our planet. If we can contract with Earth's leaders for first rights to their resources in exchange for protection, I believe our home world would be willing to build a sanctioned trade station in proximity to Earth."

I glanced at Quinoll. "Transition your duties and rest. You've been awake too long again."

He nodded and turned away to send a message to Vegori, third in command.

I left the comms center and headed to my sleep bay, having neglected my own sleep cycle. However, my steps slowed when I entered the space, and my mind immediately went to Stacy.

The chains I'd spent solar-runs collecting hung on the wall. Clear bins of mineral discs hung in a row beside them. I had enough of both to create several gowns for a female.

If I had one.

I went to the chains and ran my fingers down their lengths. Hopelessness... Loneliness... Emptiness... I felt all three deeply.

Stacy wanted nothing to do with males. Yet, every male on this ship, except Zarris, would give anything for any scrap of her attention.

The systems needed more females. Badly. I only hoped that the humans would not react in fear as most new worlds did when they learned of our needs.

Not wanting to stay near the reminders of my empty life, I left my sleep bay. My yearning drew me to the hall that held the hope for our future. While Stacy could bring peace to one of us if she consented, Stacy and Adriana together could help establish a trade agreement that could bring peace to many.

I couldn't lose sight of that in my pursuit of her.

"Command Alernon, locate human Stacy," I said softly.

"Human Stacy is located in the assigned sleep bay."

I continued to her bay and requested entry. Nothing happened. Telling myself I was only worried that she'd forgotten how to use the panel, I let myself in.

She was already sleeping. She lay on her side, facing me, with a hand tucked under her cheek and the other resting on the mattress. The larger bed covering was pulled up to her shoulder, but I could see she still wore her dress.

"Stacy," I called softly.

She didn't stir.

Unable to force myself to leave, I moved closer to her bed.

Due to my role on the ship, I'd been in the presence of numerous females. None of them had drawn me the way Stacy did. Males from all over the systems craved females. I knew I was no different. Yet, it felt different.

As I watched her sleep, I thought of taking the space behind her and wrapping my arms around her. What would it feel like to hold her like that? To fall asleep with her in my arms? I wanted it so badly that I shuffled another step forward.

She shifted in her sleep.

"What's wrong?" she mumbled without opening her eyes.

"I don't want to sleep alone."

She made a soft sound and lifted the blanket in invitation.

My heart beat painfully in my chest as I closed the distance between us.

# CHAPTER SEVENTEEN

## STACY

I YAWNED BUT DIDN'T OPEN MY EYES AS MY MIND DRIFTED TOWARD awake. Thoughts of Pin swam to the surface, along with regret, anger, and fear, until I remembered he was gone.

No, I was gone. Untouchable by him or anyone else on the planet.

The thought brought me fully awake. I opened my eyes and looked around my dimly lit room on the ship. The sparsely furnished and rather sterile place didn't feel homey. Yet, it somehow felt safe despite knowing exactly why I was there.

I pushed those thoughts aside and thought of Nicky. Something tickled the back of my mind. A memory or a dream. I couldn't be sure. He'd come to me because he hadn't wanted to sleep alone, and I'd snuggled him. No, that wasn't right, I thought with a frown. He'd been grown and had snuggled me, making me feel safe.

Definitely a dream, then. A weird and slightly disturbing one.

Rubbing a hand over my face, I acknowledged how messed up that was. A mom dreaming of protection from her son? It was supposed to be the other way around. Maybe I was subconsciously trying to deal with the fact that I'd failed to protect him.

In fact, if not for Adriana, he wouldn't be here with me. If not for Nicky, I wouldn't be here either. My son had saved me…just by being my son. That epiphany hit me hard.

I sat up without a hint of pain and looked at the empty space beside me. Was that why I'd had that dream?

The door to my room made a sound, and I turned to watch it open. Alernon strode in and stopped short when he saw me sitting up.

A wave of need to wrap him in my arms and press a kiss to his forehead flowed into me.

"Um…good morning?" I said in an attempt to distract us both from what he was feeling.

"Apologies," he said, shaking his head slightly. "I presumed you would still be resting. Did you sleep well?"

"I did," I said. Other than the weird dream, I'd slept deeply. "Actually, I feel almost normal again."

"I'm relieved to hear that. The younglings are already awake and in the galley. I brought you a clean dress if you would like to shower and change before joining them."

He placed the dress he was carrying on the table.

"Thanks. I won't take long," I said, standing.

He didn't move to leave, and I felt a surge of intense longing.

"I'm not showering with you watching again. Out in the hall." I pointed for emphasis.

He didn't exactly frown, but the way his expression shifted ever so slightly hinted that he wanted to. After another moment, he nodded and left the room.

This time, I washed facing the door. I needed to find out if there was a way to lock it.

Twenty minutes later, I interrupted Alernon pacing in the hallway. The second he saw me, he stilled, and his gaze swept over me. I wasn't sure what he was looking for. The dress was pretty much the same as the other one. Just in a soft blue-purple shade.

"Sorry," I said. "My hair takes longer to dry. Do you have any kind of shower cap? Showering would go faster then since I don't need to wash it every day."

"I will find what you need," he said, offering his arm.

The need to take it wrapped around me. I knew it was his urge, not my own, but I wondered what harm there was in giving him this when I'd done it several times already. He'd done so much for me, and it was only a simple touch.

I took his arm and smiled up at him.

"Thank you. I appreciate everything you're doing to help me."

The need that slammed into me didn't show on his face. Not even a little.

"How many private rooms does this ship have that are unoccupied?" I asked to distract him.

"Eighty-nine. We keep spare accommodations for any females who may wish to join us. Why do you ask?"

"I'm wondering if I'll see you again once the ship is filled with the females you're hoping for. Eighty-nine is a lot. How many crew members do you have?"

"More than eighty-nine," he said. "And never fear losing sight of me. I will always watch over you."

The urge to slowly remove my dress and rub up against his front tingled down my spine.

"Seems silly to watch over me when I'm not interested in what you want. But I'm sure there's a female who will want to shower naked for you and fulfill every fantasy you have."

He walked us down the hall and shook his head.

"A female who gives in too easily doesn't interest me," he said smoothly. "I want one who will resist me when I'm in the wrong. One who will demand things from me instead of accommodating my every wish. I want a female who will challenge me and make me think about how I can please her. I want to earn my female."

Adriana had told me about the video she'd watched. The one

where the women had fallen to their knees in front of the Oebri—not Alernon—and had begged for sex.

"It makes sense," I said. "After having so many fall to their knees, I suppose the ones who resist you are more appealing. But I'm not resisting you to lead you on, Alernon. I just want to be left alone."

He looked down at the floor for a moment and took a long, deep breath.

"My crew has left you alone while you heal. They understand you've suffered mistreatment. But now that you're physically healed, I cannot order them to keep their distance while still maintaining peace on this ship. Although no male here will force you in any way, each one will seek your favor." He turned his head to meet my gaze. "We are desperate, Stacy. While you wish to be left alone to forget what has happened to you, every male wishes for a word or a look from you to forget the future that waits for them. A lifetime filled with loneliness."

"Why do their needs take precedence over mine?" I asked, annoyed. "I'm sorry your race doesn't have females. But harassing me isn't the solution."

"I understand. Truly, I do. But as I said, I cannot order them away from you. If I attempted to, I would likely be removed from my position. And although I am willing to sacrifice my place on this ship for you, being sent away wouldn't save you from anything. You would still find yourself in the same situation.

"The only solution I can offer you is that you show favor to a single male and attempt to bond with him. All reasonable males respect a female's bond and leave them alone unless they are invited to breed."

My feet slowed, and I stared at Alernon.

"Wait. I'm not sure I'm understanding you correctly. When you say bonded, what does that mean?"

"Bonding means you belong to another in your mind, heart,

and body. Once you've committed to another with all three, we Oebri sense it and cannot influence you."

"But you said you can't influence me anyway."

"I cannot, which is why I'd asked if you were bonded to Pin."

I decided to ignore that part for now. "So if I can't be influenced, what's the point of your crew bothering me."

"You are more desirable because you cannot be influenced, Stacy."

I considered what he was saying and how I felt about it. At my core, I believed I was a nice person. When I saw an elderly person struggling, I offered my help. If someone needed a favor that was within my means to grant, I stepped up. But that didn't mean I was a doormat to everyone else's wishes.

Despite the shitshow my life had become because of my blindness to Pin, I'd never been a doormat. I had a mean streak, just like any other pissed-off woman, but I used it judiciously.

In this instance, though, I couldn't decide if the Oebri deserved my temper once they started bothering me. Trying to have a conversation with me, while it might be annoying, wasn't—

I shook my head.

"I'm trying to justify their behavior preemptively," I said. "I'm not okay with this. At all. This is how manipulation starts. Making someone feel guilty like they owe you.

"You've accommodated me. I understand that. But I didn't ask you to, and I don't owe you anything. Not even my time if I don't want to give it."

Alernon studied me for a moment. "Think back. Have I ever lingered past when you welcome me?"

I didn't have to think long on it to know that he hadn't. Every time I'd asked him to leave, he'd left. Granted, he always seemed to return.

"You're one person. It's going to get very tiresome if I have to send your crew away one at a time. I want safe spaces where they can't interrupt me. Like when I'm in the play area with Nicky. He's the reason I'm here, not for your crew."

"I will let them know."

"And when I'm in my room. Actually, is there a way I can just lock my door?"

"Of course. I will show you how after you've eaten."

"Thanks. I appreciate it. I know you were only worried about me the first time, but turning around and finding you watching me was creepy, and I'd prefer not to have it happen again."

"I understand," he said.

It wasn't his accepting, pleasant tone that had me feeling a wave of guilt and hurt. It was from him. And underneath what he was feeling, I felt a hint of my own guilt.

Why, dammit? I had nothing to feel guilty for.

"So, did anything interesting happen last night while I was sleeping?" I asked, masking my frustration.

I was blasted with a storm of conflicting emotions. Contentment, lust, and guilt were the biggest players. Worry wasn't far behind.

"Are the leaders claiming you made her sick like we thought they would?"

"Ah." His relief flooded me. "The representative's doctors were able to find cancer in the location we specified. However, thanks to another exam she had recently undergone, there is proof that it existed before our arrival. They discussed treatment options, but she's refused them all for now."

"And the rest of the world leaders? What are they saying about it?"

"More have acknowledged we exist and have been meeting with Annah Bergen separately. They are studying the information we provided on all the systems' races to assess the level of threat Earth will soon face." He patted my hand and started walking with me again. "They are beginning to panic and debate what resources they are willing to give in exchange for protection. However, the majority is still resisting the truth and the need for protection."

"Resistance seems to be humanity's theme."

"Resistance and survival," Alernon said. "I believe they will make the right choice."

We entered the galley. Nicky saw me right away and started waving for me to join him.

"After you're done spending time with the younglings, ask Adriana to come to the comms center with you."

He released his hold on my hand and left.

A niggling sense of longing went with him.

As soon as I sat beside Nicky at the table, I saw he had a covered plate waiting for me. He removed the lid with a flourish.

"Baynol made it. It's like the meals he used to make for the Ladies. Try it."

I smiled at Nicky and quickly cut a bite of steak.

"It's delicious. Thank you, Baynol," I said. "You'll have to teach me how you did this so I can cook for myself in the future."

Some of the joy left the big guy's face as he nodded.

"What's everyone up to today?" I asked.

"The wardens found a grow bay with a pond in it. They're going to learn how to care for the animals there. Can I go help?" Nicky asked.

"Me too?" Lil asked.

"Is it a grow bay you have access to?" Adriana asked.

Nicky's pout came out.

"You know what?" I said, "You're right. You're just the right age to learn new things. Alernon said he has access to all the school work needed for your age if you're ready to learn instead of play."

"No-no-no," Nicky said quickly. "I think Lil and I should play again today. She's still not used to the ship yet."

Lil nodded, playing along with Nicky's desperate attempt to avoid school.

"Okay, but remember last year? You had a lot of fun coloring, didn't you?"

Nicky considered it. "Can we just do that stuff?"

"I bet Baynol and Peltear—heck, all the wardens—would like to learn Earth's ABCs and 123s," Adriana said. "It'll be easier for them to get married to an Earth girl then."

I knew Adriana and I had won when Nicky glanced at Baynol.

"Okay. We'll do school stuff. But we get to take breaks to play," Nicky said, skillfully negotiating.

"Deal," I agreed. "We'll start tomorrow. I'll get what we need from Alernon."

# CHAPTER EIGHTEEN

## ALERNON

THE INFORMATION FLASHING ACROSS THE FEEDS DIDN'T REGISTER AS I stared. My thoughts were on the night I'd spent holding Stacy and breathing in her scent. I'd loved every prexel of it.

While I'd given my word to tell the rest of my crew to leave her alone when she was with her youngling, I was grateful she hadn't pressed for my word to keep all males from her sleep bay. I was already thinking about the next rest cycle and joining her again.

But if I did, I would risk everything.

She'd clearly let me know how she'd felt about me entering her sleep bay without her permission. If that hadn't been enough to let me know that she would not appreciate me joining her rest cycle, her request to show her how to work the lock would have been.

Was it wrong of me to show her how to use the lock and allow her to believe it would keep everyone out? In her mind, it would be. I knew that. But in my mind, I knew my ability to enter would not harm her.

"You look rested," Quinoll said, drawing my attention. I glanced at my second and noted the dark circles under his eyes.

"And you do not. Did you go to the entertainment zone?"

"No. There's no point. I don't want to watch immersive vids. I want the real thing." He looked down and took a calming breath as he stared at his datapad. "I regret leaving her behind."

I knew he was referring to the Lady from Anrothe.

"If you had kept her, you would have come to regret that as well," I said compassionately. "The news from Earth is promising. It won't take much longer before they enter into negotiations with us."

Quinoll's hand trembled as he reached up to rub a thumb over his bottom lip.

"I am desperate, Alernon," he said.

"We all are."

"And yet you're rested," he said, throwing his datapad. "I tire of this endless search for females and rejection. What point is there to living when—"

He stopped abruptly, his rage evaporating between one beat and the next.

I turned and looked at Adriana and Stacy, who stood just within the comms center.

"We can come back," Adriana said.

"No," Quinoll said. "I apologize. I will remove myself and quietly reflect on my purpose."

He strode toward them, and when he would have passed Stacy, she reached out and caught his arm.

"Don't reflect on anything right now," she said. "Just breathe and exist. Time might seem like your enemy, but it's actually your friend. Everything changes with time. Even how you're feeling right now."

He looked down at her hand. She slowly removed it.

"When Nicky was gone and I hurt the worst, I asked myself that same question. What point was there to living? But I'm glad I'm still here. I get to be a part of something that might change the lives of millions of people. Hopefully for the better.

"Patience isn't easy when you feel like there's nothing left for you, but as long as you're still breathing, there's hope. So, for now, just breathe and exist, Quinoll. Don't think about anything else."

"Thank you," he said softly. Then he left the comms center.

Stacy looked at me. "Is he going to be okay?"

"He will. Thank you for encouraging him."

"Encouraging? I was just trying to back him away from the ledge."

"I'd say you nailed it, then," Adriana said. "Right, Alernon?"

I made a non-committal sound. Humans had such interesting sayings. Most of them didn't make much sense, though.

"Anything interesting from Earth since last night?" Adriana asked.

"I was still reviewing the feeds. You're welcome to join me."

Adriana and Zarris moved to one side, leaving room for Stacy to stand next to me.

I tried to inhale her scent subtly as she neared. The need to wrap my arms around her nearly overwhelmed me.

"Is everyone struggling like he is?" she asked softly.

"Yes," I said in complete honesty. "And not only the males on this ship. There are many desperate Oebri on ships like this one throughout the systems. Those with females aboard have slightly better crew morale. But not by much. We need Earth to agree quickly."

She nodded and started reading. I tried to do the same.

It appeared that the delegates from around the world were unequally split with the majority still against working with us in any way. However, many had stated that they would welcome the opportunity to speak with us in more detail.

"The biggest source of contention is what you want," Stacy said. "Resources is too ambiguous. They want to know what and how many. Have you given any thought to what you'd ask for?"

"Typically, we request ten percent of the female population every growth cycle," I said. "A harvest of that size does not jeopardize a species' numbers. However, given how populated your planet is, it would be safer for your planet to ask for twenty percent."

"What's a growth cycle?" Adriana asked as Stacy frowned.

"The number of solar-runs it takes for a youngling to reach maturity," I said. "While sexual maturity seems to occur at thirteen solar-runs for humans, we take mental and emotional maturity into account as well. We estimated Earth's growth cycle at twenty solar-runs."

"You're going to ask Earth's leaders for four hundred million females every twenty years?" Adriana asked.

Stacy's expression reflected her disbelief as she shook her head.

"They're never going to agree to that. It doesn't matter if Earth needs protection or if it's overpopulated. Our leaders will know they'll never get that many volunteers. And forcing people to leave —tearing families apart—will start wars."

"We do large-scale harvests because our presence isn't typically welcome for an extended period of time. However, considering the resistance both of you have shown to our persuasion, perhaps we could negotiate smaller, ongoing harvests."

"No matter how you break down the number, the number is still a problem, Alernon," Stacy said.

"What if I asked for ten thousand females every Earth week— which is less than three percent? Surely, that number spread out across the globe will not send anyone into a panic."

Stacy and Adriana shared a look.

"We have a saying," Adriana said. "You can attract more flies with honey than vinegar. It means you want to be polite rather than rude or demanding. So, what if, instead of asking for ten thousand a week, which is going to set people off, ask for a thousand volunteers globally."

"With the understanding that you're willing to accept more volunteers if more come forward," Stacy said.

"And if we do some kind of broadcast showing how the volunteers are treated, you *will* get more people to volunteer," Adriana said.

Acquainted with the planet's numbers, I knew one thousand a week wasn't enough to save it. Yet, I could feel the swell of their concern. If the two females who believed our intentions felt like this, I knew their world leaders would react unfavorably as they suggested.

"Very well," I said. "We will negotiate for one thousand each week. However, we need to add to the contract that we will help their scientists with environmental assessments over time so they understand the danger of Earth's current population."

"Agreed," Adriana said.

Stacy nodded. "And when we negotiate, we need to make sure where these volunteers are coming from is fair. One or two countries can't come up with all the volunteers."

"The number of volunteers from each country can be determined based on the population," I said. "We can run the calculations and include that in the initial proposal. And if a country's numbers change significantly, we can adjust."

"That's smart thinking," Stacy said. "It will prevent people from moving to avoid being voluntold."

"Do you believe your leaders will agree to these conditions as well?" I asked.

"I'll let you know if it'll work once we have a draft of what you want to say and how you want to say it," Adriana said.

The next several arcs were almost as perfect as sleeping with Stacy in my arms. The four of us sequestered in one of the private spaces off the main comms center. Stacy sat beside me, her arm occasionally brushing against mine whenever she needed to reach to point out a mistake on the display as I wrote the proposal.

I made many mistakes.

Zarris knew. I caught his slightly amused glance several times. It didn't stop me from continuing though.

"Seriously, Alernon, just let me type," Adriana said. "It used to be part of my job."

"These aren't characters you would recognize. The system is translating them as I type." I could have changed it to English characters, but I wasn't one to deprive myself when there was no reason.

"I guess the mistakes make sense, then," Stacy said. "I think we're almost done anyway."

Adriana stretched and leaned into Zarris. His hand settled on the back of her neck, and whatever he did caused her to moan.

"I think you just key-mashed," Stacy said to me. "None of that makes sense."

"Apologies," I mumbled, trying to focus.

Had a female ever moaned for me at such a simple touch?

I glanced at Stacy as she leaned forward to watch what I was entering. Would she moan?

"Perhaps we should take a break to move and eat," Zarris said.

The fleker's expression was filled with humor. He understood my torment.

"I wouldn't mind a break," Adriana said. "Or a nap." She yawned behind her hand. "I'm going to bed early tonight."

"Don't worry about the kids," Stacy said. "I'll handle bedtime. And I agree with the break. My stomach's been growling for a while."

Feeling like a tuber for not realizing and putting my wants before her needs, I stood and offered my hand to her.

"Forgive me for not noticing," I said.

"We were focused on something important. I didn't notice either right away. But a break is good. We can come back and read the agreement with fresh eyes. Who are you going to send it to first? Annah Bergen?"

"I fear that using a single point of contact will cause more mistrust," I said as she accepted my assistance to stand.

Zarris opened the door for Adriana.

"I'd recommend sending it to someone who'll read it with at least somewhat of an open mind," she said.

We followed Zarris and Adriana from the room, and I nodded to Vegori.

"Open more minds before you send it," Zarris said. "No matter who you send it to, with the majority against your presence, your requests will not be received well."

"What do you suggest?" I asked.

"Annah was grateful that you found her illness. Heal more humans."

Stacy's expression lit up at Zarris's words. "Not just anyone. Help people who are close to the leaders and already known to be sick. They can't refute it then."

"Agreed," Adriana said. "Hey, I think I'm going to lie down first. I'll swing by and send the kids your way if they haven't eaten yet."

"Are you feeling unwell?" I asked. "Perhaps we should run a scan."

She waved away my concern. "I was up too late last night. I'll be fine after a quick nap."

They left us to continue to the galley alone.

"You look worried," Stacy said, glancing up at me.

"I am. Every female is precious."

She looked ahead. "Yeah. I'm getting that message loud and clear after working on your proposal for hours. Do you really think your people are going to build what's essentially a small floating planet for the women who leave Earth?"

"Yes," I said without reservation. "We will do everything in our power to ensure every female taken from your planet transitions into her new life smoothly. If that means staying close to the place she finds familiar and giving her time to acclimate, then why wouldn't we? It's a reasonable consideration for what we're receiving in return."

"Yeah, I guess I didn't think of it that way. I'm used to people taking, not giving."

"This is a bit of both, don't you agree?"

She nodded. "How long will it take to build it?"

"It depends on how quickly we receive the resources we need. The station will be habitable within a lunar, easily."

"That fast?"

"Stations that experience heavy commerce expand with time, so it may never be fully complete. However, based on the build for initial capacity numbers, a lunar should suffice."

"And all those women are just going to live there with their, um…what do you call them? Mates?"

"Every species is different. We call them mates–or bonded mates if the male is fortunate. And few families would choose to live permanently on the station."

"Why?"

I hesitated to give her the truth since I hoped she would be one of the few females to live on the station permanently. But when she glanced at me with concern in her gaze, I could withhold nothing.

"Many races have found their younglings don't thrive as well on a station as they do on a planet. Although the atmosphere and gravity would be regulated to match a planet, it is not the same in some way we haven't yet been able to identify. But it is not the case with all races.

"In addition to that, there's the possibility of sickness. Having any significant number of females and younglings in one accessible place will draw attention from all over the systems. Inevitably, sickness will arrive. It's the nature of numbers. While the chance of serious illness would be low, most parents prefer not to expose their younglings to that risk.

"Or the risk of abduction."

"Abduction?"

I hesitated to say more then decided it was better for Stacy to know the truth from the start.

"Whether on the trade station or Earth, there will always be a risk of abduction. The more races who travel to your system, the higher the risk.

"While most planets have closed trading, which means they know who will be approaching their planet and when to prevent potential raids for resources, it still happens. Which is why Earth needs more protection.

"And to decrease the risks from growing, we will add to the contract for Earth's protection as well, stating that no foreign species should be allowed to inhabit your planet under any circumstances."

Understanding filled Stacy's gaze, and I hated the despair that accompanied it.

# CHAPTER NINETEEN

## STACY

"So none of them will have a choice, then? They'll have to go to some other planet, live with a complete stranger, and deal with rules and norms they don't understand?" I asked.

The hopelessness I felt wasn't for these faceless women who could make informed decisions when they volunteered. No, it was for Nicky and me.

When Alernon first mentioned the station, it had sounded like a perfect alternative to going back to Earth where I was only qualified for menial jobs. On this ship, though, I was creating a contract for trade between aliens and the whole planet. Alernon saw my value, and I knew the people on the station would too.

But now, knowing that Nicky could get sick or kidnapped... again? I couldn't do it. That meant a one-way ticket back to Earth and poverty. Or volunteering to be shipped off to an alien planet.

"You're upset," Alernon said.

"A little. Living on the station actually sounded like it could be a dream come true for Nicky and me. I know I could have found a way to be useful. Even if it wasn't for a paycheck, a place to live where I didn't need to worry about bills sounds magical. But you're right. I won't risk Nicky like that. I can't. Not again."

Alernon steered me into the galley. "The risk of sickness is when there are many living there, which we won't allow. And, if you wish to stay, I would ensure you and Nicky are safe. No one will ever take you."

I felt a rush of desperate wanting as I imagined myself in a lush set of rooms, lounging on a fluffy square that was either a bed or a huge pillow, as I read a book to Nicky. My stomach would be round with Alernon's child. It would kick, and he would be there, his large hand warming me and making me—

"Wow, I am hungrier than I realized," I said, releasing his arm.

I rushed to the counter I liked and started piling food onto one of their rimmed plates.

"Would you like to try the pizza I attempted?" the chef asked. "I researched the process and believe I found suitable replacements based on nutrition density."

"Nutrition density? People don't eat pizza because it's nutritious," I said. "We eat it because it tastes good."

I held out my plate for a piece and started to regret it when I saw the color of the "cheese" topping. Flecked with a bright green that stood out against its dull tan, it didn't look appetizing. The smell wasn't horrible, though. The base was thick and had a solid peachy-pink skin color. And hadn't I been initially disappointed that there weren't a bunch of alien food options? This was my chance.

"What pizza is this supposed to be like?" I asked.

"Pepperoni," he said. "Let me know how close it comes in flavor."

I nodded and took the sad slice of not-even-close-to-pizza to a table. Alernon joined me a moment later.

"That doesn't look like Earth food," he said.

"Nope. It's a chef's special. He's hoping it's like pizza. If it is, the kids will love him for life."

A wave of disapproval washed over me. Was it because the chef made me something special?

"Do you want to try a bite?" I asked, hopefully.

"I don't know how a pizza should taste," he said. I caught the hint of revulsion in his gaze.

Telling myself to be brave, I took a bite. It was as absolutely disgusting as it looked, and I only barely managed to swallow the mass without spitting it everywhere. I couldn't suppress the shiver, though.

"Not to your satisfaction?" Alernon asked. Although his tone didn't carry it, I could feel the humor rolling off him.

"It's very satisfying," I lied. "You should try a bite."

I had the pizza in one hand and reached over the table to grab his chin with another. His eyes widened as I shoved the end of the slice into his mouth.

"Eat it, Alernon. This is what those women are going to deal with when they have to move to strange new worlds. Feel their pain."

His humor intensified until he bit down resolutely and chewed. I could feel the revulsion and the need to spit it out, along with the desire for me to feed him another bite. Based on the way he maintained eye contact and swallowed it down like a champ, I knew the desire was winning.

*Twisted weirdo,* I thought. But there was no malice in it. Only amusement.

"We need to add provisions to part of the trade agreement," he said. "Favorite foods from the countries the women come from should be available when they arrive. And once they are matched with a male, he can slowly introduce her to his home world's foods here."

"That will help, hopefully." I set the slice aside. "How many different types of, um, people will approach Earth and offer their help?"

While working on the draft of the agreement, we had already added a clause about how the females would be distributed. Although the females would always have a choice, they would be presented to each species for consideration in a predefined order based on the number of that species actively offering its protection. It was a wordy chunk of the negotiation clause but necessary.

"Hundreds will offer their assistance simply to gain access to human females. How many Earth's leaders accept is up to them. Likely, it will be just enough to protect the planet from raids and no more."

"That's going to upset some people, won't it?" I said, better understanding his previous warning about abductions.

"It will," he agreed. "But having the station nearby will help dissuade any direct attacks."

I toyed with my food but didn't dare to take another bite. "This all just seems so much bigger than I expected."

An unexpected wave of lust hit me, and I rolled my eyes at him. "Why do all men twist things so they're sexual? I'm not talking about whatever's between your legs."

The lust abruptly cut off, and Alernon stared at me.

I realized what I'd done and quickly masked my panic with a playful eyeroll.

"Don't even pretend like you weren't thinking like that. I could see it in your eyes."

He continued to look at me, and I felt another wave of unchecked desire. I continued to stare right back, not giving any indication I could feel him.

"I'm sorry I rolled my eyes at you," I said after a moment. "I didn't stop to think that you might find it offensive."

"I don't." The lust doubled, and this time I didn't just feel the emotion. I could feel him touching me.

My pulse picked up and I looked down at my food. "You're

making me nervous and a little afraid." Both were completely true. "Please stop staring at me like that."

"Apologies," he said. The lust pulsed through me until I could think of nothing else but crawling over the table and straddling his lap.

I dropped my hands to my lap and fisted them, fighting the urge to meet his gaze. My stomach gave a sudden gurgling roil. My middle cramped.

"I don't feel so good," I said a second before I heaved like I was trying to barf up my own intestines.

It was so violent that I couldn't even feel any relief that the lust had vanished.

"Ugh," I panted, trying to catch my breath before it happened again.

An oversized bowl appeared in front of my face. I used it.

As the retching calmed, I became aware of a hand rubbing my bare back in long soothing strokes.

"Are you well enough for me to move you to the med bay?" Alernon asked.

My stomach gave a roll, but the threatening intestinal gurgle had me nodding.

"Go fast," I managed between my heavy breaths.

He carefully lifted me into his arms, and a clean dish settled on my stomach. He moved quickly, his long stride carrying us out of the galley and into the hall. I closed my eyes and leaned my head against his shoulder. My insides gurgled again.

"I think it's what I ate," I murmured.

"I agree."

"Make sure the kids don't eat it."

"They won't."

Neither of us spoke until after he had me on the table, the scan completed, and I had another thigh shot.

"It will work quickly to calm your reaction," Alernon said, brushing my hair from my sweaty brow.

And he wasn't exaggerating. Within minutes, the gurgling stopped. I took a cleansing breath and opened my eyes.

Alernon stood beside the exam table. He didn't stop stroking my head as he watched me with a concerned gaze.

"I desperately want a mate of my own," he said. "But I'm not certain I have the strength to endure the fear I felt when you were ill."

That fear was still there, worming its way into my mind. I caught his hand in my mine and held it.

"That's part of caring about someone. You have to take the good with the bad."

The fear ebbed, and a thread of tender affection flowed in.

"Thank you for taking care of me, Alernon. You did good."

He smiled. "You are the one who suffered, yet you are comforting me?"

"You looked like you could use a little reassurance. You didn't break me. Humans are fairly sturdy."

"That is relieving news. Would you like to return to your sleep bay to cleanse and rest?"

I looked down at myself and saw I hadn't escaped the mess.

Wrinkling my nose, I regretfully shook my head.

"I should probably clean up the galley first. No point in making more clothes dirty."

"It's already done," Alernon assured me. "Allow me to take you to your sleep bay."

I started to sit up, and he was right there with an arm around my back. What I thought was support turned into a pick-up. Once again in his arms, I tiredly rested my head on his shoulder.

"Looks like you didn't escape my stomach's wrath," I said, noting the small spots on his tunic.

"I would have gladly taken all of its wrath to spare you from the suffering you endured."

Something brushed the top of my head. "I will contact Annah Bergen and ask for provisions while also offering our help to any other delegates."

I nodded, not really caring about any of that at the moment. I just wanted a shower and my bed.

He didn't make it weird when we reached my room. After ensuring I was good on my own, he left to fetch clean clothes.

Everything was shaky as I stripped out of my dirty dress and kicked it to the side where a section of wall opened up to vacuum it away. I stood under the hot spray of the shower and let it soothe me before tipping my head and rinsing out my mouth. It was weird not having to brush my teeth, but the shower water really did clean everything.

I could have stayed there forever, but I didn't want to tempt fate and have Alernon barge in again. So, I turned on the air dryer and ran my fingers through my hair until all of me was dry. It wasn't until I shut off the warm breeze that I realized it didn't matter when Alernon returned. I had no clothes.

# CHAPTER TWENTY

## ALERNON

I wasn't angry. Mistakes had been made. Those occasionally happened even with my experienced crew. So instead of anger, I only felt fear as I left the galley.

The younglings were eating happily with their guardians, who now knew what to do if either of the younglings ever got sick as Stacy had. I tried to suppress my worry for her. Due to the effects of the stim, she would be resting comfortably in her room. Yet, I wanted to check on her before I informed Zarris and Adriana of the potential reaction humans may have to some of our foods.

I slowed by Stacy's door and looked at the dress in my hands. Once I went inside, I knew I wouldn't want to leave again. So, I continued to Adriana's room and requested access.

The wall parted, and Zarris stepped into the hall with me.

"She is sleeping," he said with a slight scowl.

"Apologies for disturbing you. Stacy had a reaction to something she ate. It was a mix of foods from the systems that had a similar nutritional composition to the pizza the younglings mentioned. It shouldn't have caused any reaction, but it did. I took Stacy to a med bay where she received treatment to stop the reaction.

"The younglings are eating safe foods with Baynol and Peltear, and the wardens know what to do if the younglings ever show any type of reaction in the future. If anything like that happens to Adriana, place her on the exam table and say, 'Command Alernon, start scan for human species.' It will administer whatever is necessary to alleviate the symptoms."

Zarris nodded then asked, "Is Stacy well?"

"I left her to cleanse and rest while I ensured the younglings' safety, but I will return to her now. She needs a fresh gown." I paused, looking at the garment. "It was very violent, Zarris. Make a note of everything Adriana eats. We should create a list of foods that are approved for humans. The younglings should avoid everything not already on the list."

"I understand," Zarris said. "Thank you."

I left him and returned to Stacy's room. The door wasn't locked, and I realized I hadn't yet shown her how as I let myself in.

She was in bed, sleeping soundly. Her blonde hair spread across her pillow in a loosely twisted coil. Wisps of it teased the perimeter of her face, and her bare shoulder peeked out from the blanket. The sight drew me closer.

"Beauty, you tempt me like no other female," I said softly as I resisted the urge to stroke a finger over that curve of bare skin.

I thought back to our conversation in the galley. When she'd spoken of things seeming bigger than she'd expected, my mind had wandered to my feelings for her and how quickly my affection and desire for her had grown...so much larger than I'd anticipated.

Somehow, she'd sensed my desire. That was the only explanation for the way she'd suddenly made such a reference to me thinking with my breeding shaft. I knew it hadn't shown in my expression as she'd insisted.

What if she could feel me?

Watching Stacy closely, I imagined myself stripping and joining her in bed. The image of how I would touch her filled my mind, and my desire for it surged through me. Each caress over her soft skin, where I'd kiss, and how she'd respond played out in my fantasy.

I grew painfully hard as I allowed myself to envision what I wished to do with her.

She continued to sleep soundly until I pictured my mouth closing over her nipple. Her breathing hitched, and she rolled to her back as my tongue toyed with the peak.

Enthralled, I pressed harder at her resistance, adding imagined suction as I caressed lower to her breeding sheath. Her legs shifted under the covers, opening slightly in her sleep, and her face slowly flushed a pretty pink. The sweet response fanned my need.

In my mind, I parted her folds with my fingers and found that special place that reportedly heightened the human female's pleasure. Stacy made a sound at the direct pressure and turned her head away.

Fascinated, I changed the vision in my head. Rather than my fingers, I circled the little nub with my tongue.

Her lips parted, and a raspy moan emerged.

Her eyes flew open, and her wide gaze found me several steps away from the bed.

She swallowed hard and took a calming breath. The flush didn't fade from her skin, though.

"What are you doing?" she asked.

"You feel me, don't you?" I asked, still picturing myself gently licking between her legs.

Her foot twitched, and she closed her eyes.

"Please leave, Alernon."

"I've told you about the history of my people. Our desire for mates and revulsion at the idea they are not truly willing. We know nothing about a human's resistance to us. Help me understand. Please. Do you feel me?"

She swallowed hard again as I mentally explored her breeding sheath with my fingers.

"Yes, I feel you. And it's invasive. Please stop."

I immediately shielded what I was thinking and feeling. She let out a shaky breath and opened her eyes to look at me as she sat up, clutching the blanket to her chest.

"You told me a female always had a choice. It doesn't matter that you weren't actually touching me. It felt like you were. It felt real. So, I need to know...how was that okay when I didn't choose you?"

Her words lashed my heart and filled me with shame.

"Forgive me. I—" Whether in my mind or in reality, I'd given my desires precedence over her wants. No reason I could give would make what I'd done forgivable.

"I will leave your dress on the table," I said quietly.

"I want to know why," she said when I moved to leave the garment.

"Why?" I echoed, glancing at her.

"Why did you do it? Why me? Why can't I just be left alone?" She let out a heavy breath. "I'm worn out and tired, Alernon. I feel like I'm constantly on the edge of breaking too far to fix. I don't want this."

I looked at her, feeling the surge of protectiveness. "It's not that you don't want what I've shown you. You simply don't want to be hurt anymore. I don't want that either. But you already know that. I haven't hidden my intentions from you."

She closed her eyes again. "I'm not ready."

"For what? To allow someone to care for you? To be loved unconditionally? To sleep at night knowing nothing can harm you? I think you're ready for all of that."

She wrinkled her nose. "Considering the dream I just had, I know that's not all you want to do."

"Correct. I do want more. But I don't need everything all at once. I want to earn it. Allow me to care for you, Stacy."

"Aren't you already? You make sure I'm fed and clothed." She nodded at the garment I still held. "You've given me somewhere to stay, and you've helped me when I was hurt and sick."

"That is the care I would extend to anyone on this ship. Allow me to care for you as the female who has captured my heart."

"What changes with that level of caring?"

I smiled slowly. "Agree and discover that for yourself. If you don't like it, you can tell me to stop, and I will."

"You're persistent," she said.

"I have to be with a female who is so willfully resistant to my desires."

"Maybe it's because they aren't my desires."

I chuckled and turned back to the bed, slowly closing half the distance.

"Then tell me your desires."

She considered me.

"Okay. Fine," she said with a challenging note. "I want a suite of rooms—a common living area with two bedrooms, so it feels like Nicky and I are living together again. And I want a learning space set up for the kids like a kindergarten classroom back home."

I nodded. "What else?"

"I want to be useful in a way that has nothing to do with making babies."

I frowned slightly. "Do you not see you are already that? If not for your input, we would not have an agreement that might tempt Earth's leaders."

"Right, but I want to be useful after that too."

Understanding spread heat through my chest, warming me.

"You do not want to return to Earth."

"If I can be useful here, why would I want to return there?

There's nothing but broken dreams and sleepless nights waiting for me."

I set the garment on the blanket as I sat beside her.

"I will gladly fulfill each of your desires, starting with those." I slipped my arm around her shoulders and coaxed her to lean against me. "We do have family units with the rooms you've described. They are closer to the grow bays. The children's current entertainment area has space to create a separate room for learning. I heard the younglings' protests regarding letters and numbers, so placing it near where they wish to play might be more incentive for them to cooperate."

Some of the tension in her shoulders eased.

"That's pretty smart," she said.

"And when we begin plans for the station, you will need to decide where you want your workspace."

She tipped her head back to look at me. "Workspace? For what?"

"We will have many females coming to the station daily. It will take coordination. Communication. And once they arrive, don't you believe their transition will be smoother if a fellow human female greets and guides them?"

Her gaze grew distant as she considered my words. "If we do a five-day work week like on Earth, that's two hundred females a day. You're going to need more than one greeter. Actually, you should have a staff of humans. People to greet the volunteers and go through an orientation with them. They could give a tour of the station and show them to their rooms. It's smarter to keep the groups small. They're easier to manage, especially if emotions are high."

I pressed my lips to her forehead. "I love the way your mind works. What else?"

She gave me a speculative look before continuing.

"I'll talk over my idea with Adriana and see if we can come up with the number of workers we think we'll need. But I don't think the volunteers should have to meet any aliens until they're settled. So instead of single rooms, maybe have dormitories? That way they can keep an eye on each other too. No undetected kidnappings."

"How can you possibly believe you are not already useful?" I asked.

She pulled out of my hold slightly. Her gaze searched mine. I wasn't sure why until she shifted her hold on the blanket covering her chest to one hand. With the other, she reached up and gently caressed my cheek.

The contact ripped through the tenuous shield I had on my emotions, and I *wanted*. I *needed*.

# CHAPTER TWENTY-ONE

## STACY

ALERNON PAINTED A PRETTY PICTURE OF GIVING ME EVERYTHING I wanted, but I knew better than to trust it. Yet, I could feel myself starting to hope and believe. That's why I reached for his face. If he was going to change his tune, I'd rather he do it now before I actually bought into what he was trying so hard to sell.

The raw need that rushed through me at first contact made my breath catch.

Focusing on my own emotions, I slid my fingers along his jaw until I found the back of his neck. Then, with gentle pressure, I drew his mouth toward mine.

"My female," he whispered.

He was drowning in want and hope. He wanted to taste my lips more than he wanted his next breath. And his hope that I truly wanted him was slowly being eaten by doubt.

What he was feeling immediately disappeared.

"Wait," he breathed, catching my wrist. "Who are you?"

His doubt and fear helped ease some of my own.

"I'm not your fantasy or your next wet dream," I said, gently touching his face. "My name is Stacy. I'm broken and desperate for a safe place to call home so I can heal. And I'm trying to figure out if you're it, Alernon. So let me kiss you, and let's see what happens."

I could see the indecision in his gaze a moment before he groaned and closed the distance between us. His lips brushed over mine gently at first before he nipped at my bottom lip. It was unexpected and shocking, and I jolted.

"Did I hurt you?" he asked, immediately pulling back.

"No."

"Can I try again?"

I knew I should say no. We weren't kissing to actually kiss. I'd wanted to know how he'd react to it. And I knew that now. He'd shut it down to verify my intentions. As he'd said, he'd been open about what he wanted and who he was.

However, I was still having trouble believing it.

So maybe another kiss was in order.

I nodded.

He dipped his head and brushed his lips against mine again. The kiss was nothing like what he'd done to my breast in my dream. It was gentle and sweet and questioning. His lips thoroughly explored mine at an unhurried pace. The hold he had on my wrist loosened, and his fingers began stroking the skin there.

Some crazy part of me wanted to push him further.

My tongue darted out to tease his bottom lip.

He made a pained sound and released my wrist to cup the back of my head. His hold changed the tone of our kiss. Playful exploration left the building. Desire and foreplay entered in earnest.

As quickly as the feelings had come, they vanished. Along with his mouth.

Alernon's lips brushed my forehead before he shifted his hold and held me to his chest. His pulse thundered like crazy under my ear. Mine wasn't any better.

"You're wrong," he said softly. "You are my fantasy. Please tell me you'll allow me to care for you."

Breathing heavily, I considered my next words.

"Okay. Until I say stop," I said, agreeing.

His hold on me tightened as he lifted me enough to settle me in his lap. I didn't miss what was pressing against my bare backside.

"You will be in your suite of rooms this rest cycle. And when you wake, the learning center for the younglings will be ready."

"With crayons and paper?" I asked.

"Colored wax is easy to replicate."

"Easier than pizza?"

He made an annoyed sound and gently ran his hand over my hair.

"Before we acquire the staff you suggested, we should acquire a food tester. I do not want to see another female suffer as you did."

I relaxed against him, daring to let myself feel the protection he was offering. Trusting it was real wasn't easy, though.

"I'm sure Adriana is wondering where we are. You should leave so I can get dressed."

Alernon continued to play with my hair.

"I explained what happened to Zarris. Adriana was still sleeping. She will likely want to check on your well-being once she wakes. Until then, rest."

He made no move to put me down.

"You want me to sleep in your arms?" I asked.

"More than anything."

I rolled my eyes. "But I feel wide awake now."

"Try closing your eyes."

I snorted but did.

FALLING asleep in someone's arms and waking up lying down was disorientating. I opened my eyes and looked around the room in confusion. Alernon wasn't just no longer holding me. He was completely gone. The dress he'd brought lay on the table now.

I got out of bed and quickly put it on. Then I left my room to check on Adriana. No one answered their door, though.

Guessing that it meant she wasn't napping anymore, I made my way to the entertainment area to check on the kids. They weren't there, either. However, a dozen Oebri were using machines that had arms like the med bay's exam table. As I watched, one of the arms swept over a half wall, ejecting material to add to its height.

One of the men noticed me and stopped his machine.

"My beauty," he said. "Are you recovered? I heard you had a poor reaction to a new food. Allow me to feed you something that will agree with your system."

He said it all with kindness and consideration that didn't match the surge of desperation I felt from him.

I offered him a small smile. "I appreciate the offer. Really. But I'm not sure I could stomach eating anything just yet."

He nodded in understanding, but I felt his disappointment.

"I can't believe the progress you're making already. Can I watch what you're doing for a bit?"

Each one readily agreed.

Being inundated with the emotions from so many Oebri wasn't as overwhelming as I'd thought it would be. In fact, it felt less intense than Alernon's.

After learning how they made walls, I left them to their work and went to the galley for something to drink.

The same chef from before, Raaln, was there and apologized profusely.

"Better me than the kids," I said. "And now we know."

He reluctantly agreed through the waves of regret he felt.

As I left, I considered what it would be like for any women living on the station Alernon was dreaming of. It would be overwhelming for sure. Confusing, too, since some of the images and impulses that came with the emotions felt so real. How many of them would act on those emotions?

I thought of Alernon's hesitancy when we'd kissed and his need to make sure I was acting of my own free will. We'd definitely need a place where the females could get away so they wouldn't be assailed with emotions that weren't theirs twenty-four-seven.

That thought had me frowning.

The drafted agreement stated one thousand females every week in exchange for protection. We'd outlined equal selection from countries based on size because Adriana and I knew that would be a sticking point that could slow things down if left to Earth's leaders to decide. We'd outlined the female's right to choose from the pool of Earth-approved races and how many females could go to each race based on their level of protective presence, again determined by Earth's leaders. The agreement also outlined how the females would be treated and what would happen if there was any mistreatment, which was defined in disturbing detail, thanks to Adriana's experience.

But in everything we'd outlined, we hadn't covered what would happen to a woman who didn't choose. How long should they be allowed to linger on the station now that I understood the danger of having too many females in one place?

My mind was preoccupied with that question when I walked into the comms center, so I didn't notice Quinoll until he stepped in front of me.

"Are you well, my beauty?" he asked. "You still look pale. Are you certain you don't need more rest?"

Like I did with the others, I offered him a small smile.

"I'm fine. Not ready to eat yet, but not tired enough to sleep more. Is everyone already working?" I asked, gesturing to the room our group had occupied previously.

"They have gathered. There is no need to join them. You could keep me company."

His desperation was deeper than the others I'd felt and had a darker edge to it. Not dangerous to me but to him.

"Hang in there, Quinoll," I said. "We're going to convince Earth that this contract is in their best interest and flood this ship with females. Just hang in there a little longer."

He looked at me with sad eyes and reached out, running a finger along my jaw. The images that flashed through my mind were unwelcome and lewd. But again, with that edge of dangerous desperation.

"I can feel what you want," I said calmly.

His fingers twitched against my skin.

"Yet, you do not fall to your knees."

"Nope. I don't. I've already done that for a man I didn't actually love and kind of hate myself for being the puppet I was for his needs."

Quinoll closed his eyes with a wince and dropped his hand.

"The females who come from Earth won't be interested in being anyone's puppet either. Any human who falls to their knees for you will do it because she wants to."

He nodded and went back to whatever he was doing on his datapad. When I turned toward the conference room, I saw Alernon standing there. The pulse of irritation I felt as he watched Quinoll didn't impress me.

"Is there a problem?" I asked, drawing his attention.

His gaze swept over my face. Devotion and adoration wrapped around me.

I arched a brow.

He slowly smiled at my show of annoyance.

"No problem at all," he said. "I was about to check on you.

Now that you're here, would you like to see the progress we've made?"

"Please."

They'd smoothed over the rough spots we'd been working on before lunch. With everything reading well, we focused on what else needed to be added.

Over the next few hours, we built in what to do if a female couldn't or wouldn't choose, along with what would happen when the volunteers ran out.

Alernon didn't seem too concerned about the prospect.

"It's going to happen sooner than you think," Adriana said. "We're asking them to leave their families and friends forever with this no aliens on Earth clause."

"But they can bring their families and friends with them," Alernon said. "All would be welcome."

"Those people are going to have family and friends they don't want to leave behind, too," I said. "Humans are social and connected. So, Adriana's right. It's going to be hard on a lot of people."

I felt his rush of discouragement and bumped into him.

"Hey, now. Don't get greedy." I looked at Adriana. "We should put in there that any family or friends that choose to come along count toward the tally."

"Only females count," Alernon said.

"If a female's family and friends come along with her, I think they should all count," Adriana said. "You said fertility is an issue. Humans are prolific. Who cares if a race gets a gene pool boost from a male or a female as long as it's human?"

"Males should count as half of a female," Zarris said.

I almost laughed at that.

"Agreed," Alernon said. "They would be taking away from the resources the rest of us are fighting for."

"Fine. I'll even do you one better. We'll stop counting family members at five. Everyone over that is a freebie."

Alernon quickly agreed, and I nudged Adriana's leg under the table to get her attention.

"Does this feel weird? Talking about the volunteers like this?"

"A little, especially now that we've acknowledged they won't all be volunteers," she said. "But it's necessary. Even if the Oebri would be generous enough to offer to protect Earth for nothing, they wouldn't be enough. There's a whole planet to watch over. That's going to take a lot of cooperation, and those other races aren't going to spend all their time and resources helping without compensation. They'll just take what they want. So, either way, females will be leaving Earth. Only, this way, it can be on their terms. Or at least on terms that are more favorable to them."

"And after the way Alernon removed the delegates from their meeting, I don't think the humans will need much convincing to understand how powerless they will be against being taken," Zarris said.

"Isn't that the truth," Adriana said, leaning back to stretch her arms over her head.

Zarris totally looked at her chest.

I glanced at Alernon and found him watching me instead.

"We should stop here and join the younglings for their next meal," he said.

# CHAPTER TWENTY-TWO

## ALERNON

THE COMPLEXITIES OF THE PROTECTION AGREEMENT WITH EARTH couldn't compare to the female sitting beside me. Before meeting her, I would have gladly welcomed any female capable of loving me of her own free will. After learning more about Stacy, her compassion for others, and her hardened heart, another female was no longer an option. Only Stacy existed in my eyes.

"A break sounds good," she said, standing.

She paused and glanced back at me.

"I'm not going to get poisoned again, am I?" she asked with humor dancing in her gaze.

"I am so glad I missed that," Adriana said. "My stomach is too weak from inconsistent sleep not to sympathy puke."

Stacy grinned. "Have kids. You'll get over a lot of stuff real quick."

The pair started out the door, leaving Zarris and me to follow. It gave me a unique perspective. I saw the way every member of my crew glanced at them as they conversed. While their existence represented hope, their presence gave peace. Would it be like that on a station filled with thousands of females at any given time?

"Am I a fool in thinking we can keep them safe?" I asked Zarris softly. "Hundreds every flare, and they have a solar-run to choose?"

"Why must they stay at the station to choose? If each species will be allotted a predetermined number, send that number to the home world. The conservators can visit and will know if they've bonded or not. Those who wish to leave can travel with the conservators until they find a home elsewhere."

"Many will protest," I said.

"Protest what? The opportunity to persuade a female in Oebri care to live on their planet? Write the suggestion well, and there will be no opposition. If a female here and there bonds to an Oebri in transit, it is a fair trade for the opportunities provided."

"He's not wrong," Stacy said, pausing their conversation with a glance back at me. "No one wants so many females on the station that it attracts the wrong kind of attention. Just be blunt about the reasons they can only stay there for a limited time unless they're bonded to a staff member or they're a staff member themselves."

"That should go for all races," Adriana added. "Not just humans. It'll keep them from forming an endless waiting line."

It was the perfect solution to the potential issues in having such a large number of females on the station. Sending them out in the systems would strengthen the alliances with the contract races, free the Senwar system from unnecessary ships, and prevent any outbreaks of sickness on the trade station.

"Thank you," I said, glancing at Zarris.

"I've watched how the Oebri truly treat females. Whether on the station or your ships, they will be cared for."

"We will add those points after our rest cycles," I said.

Until then, I wanted to focus on the meal and showing Stacy the new suite of rooms we would be sharing. I couldn't deny how much I was looking forward to holding Stacy in my arms again.

The younglings were just sitting with their food when we

entered the galley. They spoke excitedly of the new room in their entertainment space and the learning devices they'd been given.

"Baynol is already writing his ABCs," Nicky said, looking at Stacy. "He's really smart."

Baynol, the "smart" male, motioned to the plate he'd already prepared for Stacy.

"They are all safe foods," he said.

Knowing that he wouldn't make the mistake of feeding her something that would harm her, I went to select my own meal.

"I heard she is recovered from her injuries," Foyen, Raaln's assistant chef, said. "Has she responded to anyone yet?"

"I'm not certain all humans will respond," I said, answering evasively. "Adriana responded to me from the start. Very subtly, though. Nothing like the Anrothe and many other races. Stacy did not."

"At all? Is she bonded?" His questioning gaze shifted to her.

"I asked that too and don't believe so. I believe some humans may have a stronger resistance to us."

Considering the strength of Adriana's resistance, that was significant, and Foyen slowly smiled.

"Then their responses will be genuine."

I nodded.

"I must speak with her."

I caught his arm when he started to move toward her.

"When she is with her youngling, she asked not to be approached."

"Ah, yes. I remember. Apologies." He let out a heavy breath. "Perhaps before she leaves with you, then?"

"I intend to show her and her youngling their new accommodations—a family unit—as soon as they finish."

Foyen gave me a considering look. "She will either be with her youngling or with you until the contract with Earth is signed."

"Correct. She witnessed Quinoll's recent surge, and although she was not moved as one might hope, she was moved with human compassion. Her wish to have the contract fully prepared prior to Earth's agreement is so we can obtain females as quickly as possible." I hoped the information would be enough to keep him from protesting how I was monopolizing her time.

Foyen glanced at her again. "Lose our chance at one in return for the hope of gaining many. I can accept that. Win her over, Alernon. Don't let another female go to the wardens. It's unpalatable."

I chuckled and left him to join the others. The younglings were still talking about their day. I listened, entertained by their enthusiasm and enchanted by their feedback regarding the learning center.

"I shall ensure you have adequate supplies tomorrow," I promised as they finished their meals. "Would you like to go see your new sleep bay now?"

"New sleep bay?" Adriana asked. "Where? Why?"

"Oh, sorry," Stacy said, placing her hand on my arm. It silenced my forthcoming explanation and almost distracted me to the point that I didn't hear hers.

"That's my fault," she continued. "I don't want to split Nicky and Lil apart when they feel safe sleeping together. But I've missed Nicky like crazy, and it doesn't feel right sleeping so far away from him. So I asked for new rooms."

"It's a family suite of rooms where two sleep bays are connected by a common living space for the family," I said.

Adriana looked from Stacy to Nicky and Lil. "Yeah. I guess that makes sense. Do you mind if we tag along so we know where to find you?"

I sensed Nicky's distress and noted the way his lower lip began to tremble. Lil, ever the perceptive female, saw, and tears began to gather in her eyes as well.

"Of course," Stacy said quickly. "I'm not taking the kids away from anyone. Baynol? Peltear? You'll come too, right? I'm sure the kids want to show you their room."

The wardens nodded, but no one looked pleased by the upcoming change. I needed to salvage the situation, or I knew Stacy wouldn't obtain what she'd asked for.

"Stacy's request came at a very opportune time. We now have the perfect opportunity to test our standard accommodations to ensure they will meet a human family's needs. Just as you younglings are testing the learning center and letting me know what needs adjustments, you'll also be testing this new space."

Everyone looked less upset after hearing that.

"We can use what we learn to build better accommodations on the trade station for the humans who will live there. We need to ensure everything feels welcoming for when the new f—"

"Friends," Stacy said.

"Yes. Of course. For when our new friends arrive."

She nodded encouragingly at the younglings. Nicky looked at Baynol. The man set his hand on top of the youngling's head.

"Sleeping in a different room changes nothing. I will never leave you."

Stacy frowned at the words and glanced at me. Did she understand what she'd done? That she'd looked to me for guidance in a situation she didn't like?

I smoothed my hand down her back to ease her concern as Adriana stood.

"He's right," Adriana said. "We're on a ship. It's not like we can really get away from one another. Let's go check out these new digs of yours."

Stacy used my supporting hand to stand and didn't pull away when I wrapped it around my arm to escort her.

The walk wasn't as far from the galley, which seemed to relieve the group. And when the wall opened to show the new space, everyone's reservations seemed to disappear.

"No way!" Nicky said, running in.

His head pivoted on his little shoulders as he tried to see everything all at once. I had to admit the space was impressive for the time I'd allotted the crew to complete it. Many of the colorful decorations were from my quarters, collected over the decades as I traveled the systems.

A softly woven blanket's vibrant yellow stood out pleasantly from the dusky rose central lounge. Paintings of my home world's luminous blue and orange skylines decorated the perimeter, giving the space life and comfort. The light brown tones of the low gathering table for family eating warmed the area between the lounge and the food prep area.

The items on the table—color sticks and data pads—caught the younglings' attention.

They raced forward, looking at the items.

"Their sleep bay is over here," I said, moving to the left.

Stacy walked into an equally decorated space. I'd glanced at the images from Earth that adorned the walls and knew the younglings would find comfort in them. After researching what Earth younglings enjoyed, I'd also provided them with a unique array of imitation taxidermy for creatures from the systems, including the rather impressive kerflur from Anrothe.

Beneath the small mountain of creatures, each bed had a color-shifting blanket from my home world that indicated the occupants' comfort level. The expensive and highly prized items were typically only given to expecting females. But to help ensure Stacy's permanent agreement, I spared nothing.

"Wow," Adriana said, looking in with Stacy.

The younglings weaved their way around us and ran into the room. They stopped when they saw their taxidermy.

I began to worry I'd selected poorly until Nicky's cry of delight filled the room, and he jumped onto the creatures.

"These are awesome," he cried.

I smiled, watching his antics until I felt Stacy's gaze.

"You did a great job," she said, setting her hand on my arm. "Thank you."

"It's beautiful," Adriana agreed. "And here I thought the Oebri hated decorations."

"Not at all. The paintings on the walls in the common area are originals from my home world, but the replicators on this ship can recreate anything for you. That's what the paintings in here are."

"Replications from Earth?" she asked.

"Yes."

"That's incredible. Be ready for a list tomorrow," she said. Then she covered her mouth and yawned. "I swear thinking is more exhausting than running up a mountain."

Zarris made a soft sound, and she grinned at him.

"Okay, fine. Running up the mountain was exhausting for you. But I'm still tired." She pulled Stacy in for a hug, taking her from my side. "I'll see you in the morning."

Stacy nodded, hugging her back before releasing her.

"We will return as well," Baynol said with a nod before leaving with Peltear.

I glanced at the younglings, who were still sorting through their taxidermy.

"Would you mind showing me how to pull up a book on the datapad before you leave?" Stacy asked, drawing my attention and freezing my heart.

"What?" I asked, following her across the space.

"I want to read them a story before bed once they're done playing," she said.

She bent at the waist, picking up one of the devices and giving me a very pleasant view of her backside. The urge to slide the silky material up and over her waist so I could see her tempting—

"Alernon," she said, straightening. "Focus."

I shook my head slightly.

"Apologies. I believe we misunderstood one another."

"I don't think so. You painted a pretty clear picture just now."

"Not that. Regarding your request for this space and the permission you granted me to care for you. I wish to remain with you and the younglings."

I felt the rush of panic my words caused her, and when her lips parted, I knew it was to deliver a firm denial.

"By observing how you use this space as you prepare to put the younglings to sleep, I will be able to make any necessary adjustments."

Was I a flecker for misleading her? Absolutely not. Stacy did not oppose my presence. And she had agreed to allow my care *after* allowing a kiss. Her denial was due to her previous mistreatment. She didn't trust that my care did not mean sex if I stayed with them. She needed proof, and I would give it to her.

"Oh. Um, that wasn't—I mean." She cleared her throat. "Okay."

I took the datapad from her hand and opened a translated book from my home world. One my mother had read to me countless times.

"I believe they will find this one entertaining."

The younglings were briefly disappointed when they realized the others had left, but Stacy expertly diverted them with a story then invited them to explore the suite with her.

I explained every item and its purpose, from the paintings to the private cleansing unit. Stacy stopped me from explaining how to use the food dispensers, saying they were off-limits to the younglings. Considering her recent sickness, I understood her reasoning.

While they jumped on the responsive lounge, I opened the door to our sleeping bay. More paintings decorated the walls while the one through which we entered showed a holographic image of one of my world's many oceans.

Like the younglings' beds, ours also had a comfort blanket. Only no taxidermy partially hid it from view.

"This is incredible," she said, running her hand over the material. It shifted colors under her fingertips, leaving behind a fading trail of pink and blue.

"I'm relieved it pleases you. Rest well. I will return to check on your well-being. Do you object to me observing your morning routine?"

"Not at all."

I closed the distance between us and pressed my lips to her forehead before she could object. Then, I left the suite of rooms. I didn't go far, watching the feeds from the comfort blankets on my wrist display. The younglings succumbed to sleep first.

Stacy took much longer. But once I knew she was deeply sleeping, I joined her.

She didn't rouse as I wrapped my arms around her and held her close.

"You are safe with me," I said softly.

# CHAPTER TWENTY-THREE

## STACY

I DIDN'T WANT TO WAKE UP EVEN THOUGH I KNEW I NEEDED TO. WE were in a new place, and I didn't want the kids freaking out or getting into anything they shouldn't. But I'd easily just had one of the best nights of sleep in my life, and the bed was so damn comfortable I didn't want to open my eyes.

The low murmur of a voice reached my ears, and I bolted upright in my bed.

The "live" wall sparkled with the nautical twilight view of foamy green water lapping at a white-pink sandy shore, broken by the door opening. Through it, I saw Lil dart toward the cleansing unit.

A clink followed another indistinct low murmur.

I flailed out of bed and rushed into the living space to find Nicky sitting at the low table and Alernon moving around the kitchen.

"Good morning, Mom," Nicky chirped. "Alernon is making pancakes for us here. He told us not to wake you up."

"I appreciate that you were so quiet. What are you doing?" I asked, going to him and kissing the top of his head.

"Alernon read these books when he was my age."

I looked down at the image of a naked woman wrapped in chains giving a little boy a hug.

"Eeeh-no," I said, plucking it from his hands.

"Do you believe Nicky has a brighter future in the systems or on Earth?" Alernon calmly asked as he set a plate of pancakes on the table.

I looked at him, trying to understand why he was asking and why he was showing my son pictures of Oebri women.

"Even if you believe that he will return to Earth once he is grown, he will still experience much of the cultural diversity of the systems when living on the station. Educating him on what is normal for each species will protect him. He will be able to identify suspicious behavior and avoid situations that might endanger him."

I wrinkled my nose at Alernon and sighed.

"Fine. You're right. He should know what he's facing. But it's my job to introduce information to him, not yours. You had no right to make that decision on your own."

Alernon glanced at Nicky, whose gaze was bouncing between us. When his gaze locked with mine, it gave no hint of what he was thinking or feeling.

"My experience with younglings is limited to my own upbringing and the time I've spent with these two. Please forgive my ignorance of human culture. In the systems, younglings are rarely raised by a single adult. The responsibility is shared by many, allowing the younglings access to a diverse knowledge pool."

"I'm ready to throw a pancake at your head, Alernon. You just apologized and politely scolded me in one breath."

"It actually took several," he said with a slow smile.

I threw a pancake, and he caught it without looking away.

Nicky busted out laughing, and Alernon's sexy smile turned into a grin as he took a bite out of the pancake.

"Throw one at me," Nicky demanded.

"Me too!" Lil shouted, racing back toward the table.

"I live in a zoo," I said. "You're all animals. Sit down, and let's eat like civilized people."

Even before Pin, breakfast with Nicky had never been a sit-down affair. I'd always been rushing to get ready for work. Now, listening to the kids' plans for the day while we ate filled in a piece that I hadn't realized was missing.

Once we finished, I was able to walk the pair of them to their entertainment space. I felt like one of those stay-at-home moms I'd always envied. The ones who got to walk their kids to school and stand there and wave as they went in instead of in the tuck-and-roll drop-off line.

I loved being present. Finally.

But at what cost? Would living on the station like I'd planned lead to a better life?

Alernon's wrist thingy chimed, and someone's voice echoed into the hallway.

"You're needed in the nav center."

"Understood," Alernon said. He turned toward me, stealing my hand for an old-fashioned kiss before I knew what he was doing.

"I will meet you in the comms center shortly," he said.

"Take your time."

As soon as he turned the corner, I headed for Zarris and Adriana's room. He answered a few seconds after I requested entry.

"Late start?" I asked.

"Sorry," Adriana called from within the room. "We're ready. Are the kids starving?"

She appeared in the doorway and still had sleep lines on her face.

"They're actually fed and already in the entertainment area

227

with Baynol and Peltear." I glanced at Zarris. "Any chance you'd be willing to go say hi to them so I can have a few minutes alone with Sleeping Beauty here?"

Zarris glanced at Adriana.

"Back on Earth, it's normal for women to want to spend time together without their husbands or boyfriends around," she said.

"And it doesn't mean there's anything wrong," I added. "Sometimes we just miss spending time with our friends."

He nodded, kissed Adriana on the lips, then left.

"Get in here," she said, tugging my arm. "If I have extra time, I'm showering."

Her room wasn't the sterile canvas of white mine had been.

"Nice, right? After I saw your place, I put in a few requests," she said.

"Is that a Van Gogh?" I asked.

"Not a real one, but it looks like it, right? A replica Persian carpet and a Chinese folding screen."

"That was fast."

"Not really. Zarris said they just dropped it all off before I woke up. Their replicators were working on it all night. I felt really bad when I heard about that." She stepped behind the traditionally painted folding screen. "Zarris was curious how they were made and started asking questions. It sounds like getting the real deal from Earth would be a lot easier and conserve their replication materials."

Her dress came sailing over the top of the screen, and the water turned on.

"Are you ever worried you're going to regret it?" I asked. "Not going back to Earth?"

"Regret being looked down on? Alone? Financially overwhelmed? Wishing for a better life? Nope. Not even a little.

"When I was taken, I was worried about surviving and getting the kids back to Earth. And, honestly, I was mad at you."

I sat at her small table and looked up at the painting above it.

"I don't blame you," I said. "I did you dirty."

"No, you didn't. I didn't know that then though. I thought you were being a crackhead like my mom, and I was determined to go back and shake some sense into you. You can imagine how guilty I felt when I realized what you'd been dealing with."

The water stopped, and the air started.

"But even before all of that, I thought our lives were both borderline shitty. What are you worried you're going to miss out on?" she asked.

"Not me. Nicky. I just don't know what's going to give him a better future."

"Knowledge is power, and he's going to learn way more with the Oebri than he would on Earth. And who says living on the station is irreversible? Especially with the agreement we're cooking up? Maybe he learns so much about Oebri technology that he becomes some high-paid consultant on Earth. You see how they treat the kids. Those two will not be lacking in any way."

"You're right," I said with a sigh. "It just feels like everything is moving so fast."

"I hope it moves faster. Earth needs to get on board with protecting its people. Plus, I'm dying to eat a real burger again. Grilled, not pan-fried." She moaned like she was really thinking about it.

"I threw a pancake at Alernon this morning. It was pretty good."

"The throw or the pancake?" she asked as the air turned off.

"Both?"

She laughed at my uncertain answer as the clean dress disappeared from view.

"I might have to try both then," she said,

I smiled, feeling better for having talked to her about my fears.

She emerged dressed and without face creases.

"Come on. Let's see what we can grab on the go from the galley before we head to the comms center."

We reached the comms center at the same time as Zarris. Alernon stood in the center of the room while five other members of his crew read rapidly moving feeds.

"What's going on?" I asked.

"There was a ship detected at the outskirts of this system. We attempted to make contact with the ship, and it fled. We sent the information to the world leaders, warning them of the ship's brief presence. Their reactions are varied."

"You kicked the hornet's nest, didn't you?" Adriana said.

"Honestly, you would have been better off letting it approach Earth so they could see it for themselves," I said. "They won't believe you otherwise."

"And risk people being taken?" Adriana asked. "No way."

"This gives us more reason to continue our work," Alernon said. "I doubt that ship will return until it knows the purpose behind our presence here."

"I will let you know if there are any inquiries," Quinoll said.

Alernon nodded at the man and gestured for us to go to our private conference room.

"Inquiries from who?" I asked.

"Anyone," Alernon said, closing the door. "As species learn of our presence here, they will begin to question what we are doing, and Earth will attract more attention than it will want."

"Can you just not tell anyone?" I asked.

"We cannot hide our purpose here without looking like we are doing something wrong. We are as accountable for our actions as any other species."

"So, it's only a matter of time now," Adriana said, sitting. "We better get to work."

There were so many points to add to the agreement. By what we considered mid-day on the ship, I was ready for a break. Eating a meal in the galley with the kids was a good reset to tackle the second half of the day. But by the evening, I wanted nothing more than to retreat to our new suite and just spend time with the kids.

Like the day before, Alernon stayed with us until it was time for bed. I was out as fast as the kids.

OUR DAYS FELL into a pattern after that. Wake up to Alernon making us breakfast. Walk the kids to "school." Then work, sleep, and repeat. The best parts were meal breaks with the kids and my dreams at night.

While my dreams were never of the same thing, they did have a common theme. Walks through a weird forest while holding someone's hand. Standing by the ocean with someone's arms wrapped around me from behind. Walking through the ship's hall and almost running into someone so the collision turned into a hug.

I never saw who it was, but he always felt the same. It wasn't a past boyfriend. I was sure of that.

Everything that happened before back on Earth began to feel like a dream too. Or a distant memory.

Within a week, we finished the full contract proposal and created a key point version to share with Annah Bergen.

*In exchange for protecting Earth from any form of aggression or resource theft, Earth will provide two thousand females of breedable age every Earth week. This is the only resource of interest.*

*Earth is a rare planet with flourishing sentient life numbers. However, the planet is on the cusp of unsustainability. Removing the number proposed should help preserve the precious ecosystem and, in time, restabilize it.*

*To preserve Earth's most precious resource, no export of any other resources, such as dirt or minerals, can be allowed. Other races would strip the planet bare so Earth's females, the true resource, would be forced to relocate to other worlds.*

*Also, to protect Earth's most precious resource, no other species can be allowed to inhabit Earth.*

*Enclosed is our proposed contract, along with an appendix to clarify the purpose and thought process behind the listed conditions.*

"I think that's everything," Adriana said, having read through it one final time. "What are the chances that they'll accept it as soon as they see it?"

Alernon laughed. "Very small. We have not encountered a people yet who did not attempt to negotiate, which is why I insisted on stating two thousand instead of one thousand."

I bit my lip and considered what would happen if Earth did sign quickly.

"We're not even close to being ready yet," I said. "You have eighty-nine rooms on this ship and ninety-three on the other. I know you're not going to turn away females if Earth decides to start sending them to you tomorrow. Shouldn't we have some kind of welcome program in place, and—"

Alernon's hand settled on my shoulder. Before I knew what he intended, he turned me to hug me.

It felt so familiar.

"There's no need to worry yet. This isn't our first time."

His words echoed in my head for a second before everything clicked into place.

My eyes rounded.

This *wasn't* our first time. Alernon had hugged me before. Many times over the past week, in fact.

In my dreams.

# CHAPTER TWENTY-FOUR

## ALERNON

STACY STIFFENED IN MY ARMS, AND I KNEW I'D MADE A MISTAKE IN thinking she might finally allow me to comfort her when she was awake. How many rest cycles had I held her in her sleep now? Seven? Eight? She'd pressed her cheek against my chest each time, welcoming my embrace. But never when she was awake. What would it take for her to see I only wanted to be present for her—a shelter whenever she needed one? Would she ever seek my embrace like I sought hers?

She eased from my hold with her face averted. The need for her to tip her head back and look at me with even a hint of fondness surged through me. She gave no indication that she felt it.

"You may have experience dealing with other races," she said without meeting my gaze, "but Adriana and I know humans, and I think it's better to be safe than sorry. Now that the agreement's drafted, we should focus on what will need to be done once they sign."

Her apparent detachment speared my heart. But I followed her lead and focused on work rather than how badly I wanted to hold her.

"Quinoll has drafted plans for the station if you'd like to look at those," I said.

"Let's get this sent off first," Adriana said. "Annah Bergen's reaction will give us an idea of how long we might be waiting. And I wouldn't mind a quick nap before we start again."

"A break sounds good," Stacy said. "Actually, let's just plan to meet up tomorrow. I think we've made enough progress for today, and I could use some time to myself."

She stood quickly and started for the door without saying anything else. I wanted to go after her but forced myself to stay where I was.

Adriana arched a brow at me. "I didn't think you two were to the hugging stage yet. Seems like Stacy agrees."

"Yes, it would seem so," I said.

Adriana reached across the table to pat my hand.

"Focus on the agreement and getting more females here. Not every female is going to choose someone. That's why we built in all those clauses, right?"

"Of course," I said, trying to ignore the dead weight filling my chest.

After Zarris and Adriana left, I sent the message to Annah Bergen and told Quinoll to let me know as soon as there was any response.

I left the comms center and made my way to the younglings' entertainment center, determined to speak to Stacy. However, she wasn't there like I'd thought she would be. The younglings were taking a break from their learning and playing on the equipment. When they saw me, they ran toward me, stories of their day tumbling from their lips.

Lil took my hand and led me to their education room as Nicky ran and jumped ahead of us, excitedly telling me that I needed to see what they had done. Their small table within the room was covered with colored drawings that they proudly showed me, one at a time.

I praised their talents and encouraged them to spread their work throughout the ship so everyone could enjoy them. When they heard that, they grabbed several pieces and raced out of the room with Peltear a few steps behind them.

"If you're ever willing to share this experience, I know many of my crew would enjoy a flare with the younglings," I said quietly to Baynol.

Baynol nodded slowly, watching Nicky help Lil onto the balance beam while she clutched her drawing.

"On Anrothe, we work together to train the younglings entrusted into our care. It should be no different here," he said. "But we won't leave the younglings in anyone else's care until they're comfortable."

"I understand," I said, clapping him on the shoulder. "We want the younglings to feel safe too. I'll notify the crew and provide a schedule for your approval."

"Zarris mentioned your plan to build a station. Do you believe the humans will agree?"

"I do. There are too many of them. They will see how unprotected their planet is eventually. It will be good for the younglings to interact with others on this ship before we move to a larger station."

Leaving the entertainment area, I headed for our suite of rooms.

Stacy paused her pacing in the living area as I entered. Her gaze remained locked on me as the opening behind me closed. Uncertain of her state of mind, I remained where I was and waited for her to speak first.

"You've been sleeping with me every night, haven't you?"

"I have," I said.

"Why?"

"You have troubled dreams when I'm not holding you."

She frowned slightly. "Why do you think that?"

"You make sounds. Whimpers. And your expression is often pained."

"I don't remember any bad dreams. Only ones where someone is hugging me or holding my hand. That was you, wasn't it? You were messing with my head while I was sleeping."

"I only wanted you to feel safe."

"Well, I don't feel safe. I feel violated and lied to."

I nodded slowly. "You feel lied to because I kept information from you. I understand the feeling well. It's similar to how I felt when I discovered you could feel my surges after all."

"Are you saying you did this to get even?"

"Certainly not. However, if you wish to do the same to get even with me, you may."

She snorted. "You'd like it too much."

She turned her back on me, and I thought she meant to go to our room. However, she suddenly pivoted to face me and strode in my direction, her expression angry.

"What is your game, Alernon?" she demanded when she stood in front of me. "You said you wanted to care for me. Sneaking into my room at night isn't caring. It's creepy. Why are you doing this?" The edge of panic in her voice made me itch to wrap my arms around her.

"You care for Nicky by providing what he needs to be healthy, happy, and safe. If he's upset, you don't turn your back on him. You hold him and speak softly. You tell him how much you love him. I've heard you do this. How is what you do not creepy, but I am after you've given me permission to care for you?"

Her arms slowly fell to her sides.

"I didn't understand what I was giving permission to. If I ask you to stop sleeping next to me, would you?"

It felt like she was ripping a hole through me.

"Please don't," I said, my voice rough.

She exhaled and briefly closed her eyes. "I need some time to think. Please just go."

I clasped her arms and pressed my lips to her forehead.

"I will return," I said before leaving.

Quinoll glanced at me when I entered the comms center.

"Impeccable timing. Annah just forwarded the contract to another supporter after a lengthy phone call to another agency that monitors the world's climate. I believe they are taking our warning seriously."

"Good," I said, moving toward a private comms room. "I'll update homeworld. Let me know if anything else develops."

I closed myself into the room and sat down to send a message to my mother and my birther, asking for advice. Then, I sent a detailed message to our home world with the latest news along with our plans for the trade station.

"We cannot wait for the agreement to move forward. Although sending the requested supplies will put a strain on the people of Oebrion, it's only temporary, and what we will gain is worth enduring any hardships this would create. I await your response," I said in conclusion.

Once the message was transmitted, I left the room and watched the feeds with Quinoll for a while.

"There," I said, expanding the notification thread. The files Annah Bergen received from the World Climate Agency contained data related to the earth's atmosphere from the past twenty solar-runs. It showed the gradual changes and gave projections for things like air quality and crop viability in relation to the population's current growth curve.

"They know," Quinoll said.

"They're too advanced not to," I said.

"They are very calm knowing their end is imminent."

"I believe they are treating it like they did our existence. An equal number will deny it as accept its truth."

The person to whom Annah Bergen sent the message had also responded with a request to meet with me. I took up a datapad and started corresponding with the pair.

Quinoll said nothing as I made the arrangements and left for the transference bay.

It was completely dark when I materialized on the surface. The orbs with me spread out and illuminated the area as two other beams appeared.

"It's good to see you again, Alernon," Annah said. "Thank you for agreeing to meet with us. This is David Renolds, an associate of mine."

"It is my pleasure to greet both of you. Are you well, Annah?"

"Thanks to you. Early detection means I have more options. Much like our current situation. We are a bit surprised by your resource request. We'd honestly thought you were interested in our freshwater supply."

"Fortunately, there are abundant water sources in the systems, and we have the technology necessary to purify and conserve what we have. We understand that Earth is suffering from water shortages as well and will be happy to help with those problems once we address the root issue."

"Yes. About that," David said. "It's not going to work. People aren't going to willingly give up their families and friends just to save themselves."

"Two already have," I said. "Stacy and Adriana have already affirmed they do not intend to return to Earth regardless of the outcome of our negotiations."

"I understand neither of them had people here," he said.

"Are you saying the females here will not want to give up their families and friends or that their families and friends will not allow them to leave their planet regardless of their choice?"

"A little of both," Annah said.

I nodded and considered what to say. Realizing my words would hold little weight, I asked Quinoll to play the recording I'd archived.

The image of the private comms room appeared between Annah, David, and me.

*Stacy nudged Adriana under the table to draw her attention. Zarris and I looked at the pair as Stacy said, "Does this feel weird? Talking about the volunteers like this?"*

*"A little, especially now that we've acknowledged they won't all be volunteers," Adriana said. "But it's necessary. Even if the Oebri would be generous enough to offer to protect Earth for nothing, they wouldn't be enough. There's a whole planet to watch over. That's going to take a lot of cooperation, and those other races aren't going to spend all their time and resources helping without compensation. They'll just take what they want. So, either way, females will be leaving Earth. Only, this way, it can be on their terms. Or at least on terms that are more favorable to them."*

*"And after the way Alernon removed the delegates from their meeting, I don't think the humans will need much convincing to understand how powerless they will be against being taken," Zarris said.*

The image faded, and I met Annah's gaze.

"This was recorded several flares ago while Adriana and Stacy helped create the draft of the contract we sent you. This is why neither female wishes to return to Earth. A single ship was already detected since our arrival. How much longer until more appear? Your people will be indiscriminately taken, just as Adriana, Nicky, Lil, and countless others were taken. And they will likely suffer similar cruelties."

"So we should give them to you rather than have them be taken by force?" David said with a shake of his head.

"I must admit, neither option sounds good," Annah said.

"You were aboard our ship. You saw how Stacy, Adriana, and

the younglings were treated. Do you truly believe one option is not better than the other?"

"It's not what David or I believe. It's the impossibility of convincing the rest of the assembly."

"If you do not sign and word about Earth's resources spreads throughout the systems, every ship that appears in your orbit will fill their cargo bays. They will take more than your people. They will take your creatures and your water and your minerals."

"You said there's plenty of water."

"Yes, on active trading planets protected by the conservators, my people. Without an agreement with Earth, we have no right to interfere with any interactions between your people and any other species. Your only recourse will be to file an unfair trade complaint with the nearest Helix station. The complaint would then need to be reviewed by the Prime Assembly, which could take up to a lunar. Imagine what would be left of your world after thirty flares of non-stop raiding.

"Some of your people might have means to hide, but when they emerge, there will be no food, no water, no way to live."

"So the only way to save ourselves is to let you raid us instead?" David asked.

"The only way for you to save yourselves is to *negotiate* with us. Adriana and Stacy already heavily negotiated on Earth's behalf, adding sections to the contract to ensure the safety of the females who volunteer."

"And the lottery?" Annah asked. "Whose idea was that?"

"Also theirs," I said. "Adriana realized quickly that many would think like David and be unwilling to leave family and friends. And to prevent people from being forced into volunteering, she proposed a randomized drawing controlled by the Oebri to ensure females cannot be excluded based on their Earth connections or money."

I focused on Annah's gaze.

"My people want your people and your planet to thrive. We do not want to unnecessarily remove females from your planet and jeopardize your unique ecosystem. But that system is failing, regardless of the threat of being discovered by other races. Let us help you restore your planet's balance.

"To prove our intentions, I would like to invite a select number of guests to live aboard our ships for however long they wish. These guests have illnesses already identified by your doctors. With your permission, we would like to cure them."

# CHAPTER TWENTY-FIVE

## STACY

EVEN AFTER AN HOUR OF ANGRY PACING, I STILL COULD NOT BELIEVE Alernon's audacity. How could he think for even a second that what he was doing was okay? I didn't care if I hugged Nicky all the time and tucked him into bed. That hadn't been what I'd given Alernon permission to do when I said he could care for me. Even though he'd said I should say yes to find out what it meant, I'd thought he'd been offering the same as what he'd already been providing—a place to stay and good food to eat.

Pausing my pacing, I reflected on how selfish that made me sound and rubbed my temple where a headache was starting.

I didn't need this level of drama in my life. I was already living in a spaceship on the dark side of the moon. Wasn't that enough?

With a sigh, I collapsed into the huge pillow lounge thingy in the middle of the room and pulled the yellow throw blanket over me. Thoughts of home and the jobs I'd given up months ago filled my head. Waitressing and a grocery stocker. Two jobs and I still had barely managed to pay my bills.

I looked around the room, noting all the small luxuries he'd obtained within hours of my request for a new space.

Frustration boiled over, along with a single thought whispered in the back of my mind.

*Why hadn't Alernon come to rescue me sooner?*

Stunned, I thought back to everything he'd done for us. For me.

He'd found me and saved me right when I'd needed him. He made sure we had everything we needed, including the kids. And he held me while I slept.

Was I really mad about that, or was I just scared that it was all an act and he would turn out to be exactly like Pin?

My stomach twisted with guilt and fragile hope at the honest answer.

"Command Alernon," I said softly. "Locate Alernon."

"Alernon is located on the Earth country known as Tanzania."

I sat up.

"What?"

"Alernon is located on the Earth country known as Tanzania," the ship repeated.

I scrambled off the pillow and flew out the door. No one stopped me on my way to the comms center where I arrived breathless to shock the hell out of Quinoll at my sudden appearance.

"What's happening?" I asked.

"Happening?" he echoed.

"Why is Alernon on the surface?"

"He's not. He's in transference bay two."

I left the comms center as quickly as I'd entered and took the left hall toward the transference bays.

Alernon emerged from the bay just before I reached it, and I attempted to backpedal to avoid colliding with him. He caught me in his arms, turning with my momentum and spinning us around as he pulled me close to his chest.

"What's wrong?" he asked. "Why are you running?"

I could hear the threat in his voice and felt the tension in his arms.

But on my behalf or directed at me?

I pulled back...or tried to. He dipped his head and breathed in along my neck.

"Tell me what's wrong, Stacy," he said.

The need to tell him everything, to cling to him and allow him to comfort me, filled my mind and crawled under my skin.

Ignoring it, I turned my head so my nose brushed his jaw.

He stilled, and the need I'd felt disappeared completely.

"Pin wanted me to need him, too," I said. "And once I was completely dependent on him, he—"

Alernon's lips skimmed over the side of my throat.

"I am not a fool like Pin. I see the rare treasure you are and know how to give you the gentle care you deserve."

I tipped my head further to the side, giving him more access. He was teasing the side of my neck in a way that was sending bolts of "hell yes" straight between my legs.

How long had it been since I wanted to have sex? Since I wanted to feel good?

So long. I needed this. Badly.

But would this end with more heartbreak?

Lost and unsure what to do, I tried not to feel what his mouth was doing to me as I clutched his shoulders to hold him to me.

He made a frustrated sound and set his forehead to mine.

"Are you fighting my feelings or your own? Please tell me you're fighting yourself and not me."

"I am. I can't feel anything from you right now."

His silver eyes held mine, and in them, I saw his devotion and desire. For me. Just me.

He cupped the back of my head. The intensity of his hunger and the way he crowded me without letting go stalled my thoughts, so there was only him and this moment. His gaze swept over my face, and whatever he saw there had him groaning.

Deliberately, he closed the distance between us until his lips feathered over mine. He gently teased them like he had my neck until I felt the brush of his tongue.

On a sigh, I let him in.

He kissed me slowly. Reverently. I lost myself in the feel of him.

When he finally pulled away, we were both breathing hard. My hand had slipped from his shoulder to his chest, just over his heart. His pulse beat rapidly under my palm.

"Please tell me that was you," he said, studying me.

I could feel his anguish and his desperate need for me to say I was still myself and that his emotions hadn't influenced me. I knew only one way to reassure him.

"Please tell me you'll stop sneaking into my bed once I'm asleep."

He looked at me as if I'd just kicked his puppy, and he closed his eyes. His dejection and acceptance felt like my own, but neither evoked pity. Only feverish hope I wasn't making another mistake as I tapped his chest.

"If you want to sleep next to me," I said, "ask me when I'm still awake."

A second later, he had my back against the wall with his arms caging me in.

"You'll allow me to sleep beside you?" he demanded.

I wanted to say it wasn't as if I had a choice, but deep down, I knew that wasn't true. I'd felt what he had when I'd said to stop sneaking in. He would have done what I'd asked.

"I like the dreams," I said instead of giving some kind of smartass answer. "I feel safe."

He pulled me into his arms again, holding me close.

"You are safe," he murmured.

"Mom!"

The shout echoed down the hallway, and I pushed out of Alernon's arms in a panic. He released me quickly but looped an arm around my waist as I turned to face Nicky.

Face lit with a huge smile, Nicky ran toward us with a piece of paper fluttering in each of his hands. Lil was only a few steps behind him with her own colored papers.

"What are you two up to?" I asked, glancing at Baynol and Peltear, who trailed behind the pair.

"Alernon said we should hang up our art so everyone can see it," Nicky said. His gaze flicked to the arm Alernon had around my waist then to the man beside me.

Nicky frowned and grabbed my hand.

"You should help us, Mom. Come on."

I stepped away from Alernon, willingly going with Nicky.

"How many have you already hung up?" I asked.

"Lots. And everyone loves them."

"Yeah," Lil chirped excitedly. "One man asked me to draw another Mommy and Daddy picture just for him."

She held up a stick figure picture of two larger people holding three-fingered hands with a much smaller person.

"I can see why it's popular," I said.

Nicky started towing me down the hall, chattering about the pictures they'd already distributed.

I fought the pressing urge to look back at Alernon, afraid to give him more than I already had.

Realizing I was touching my lips, I quickly dropped my hand and tried to focus on Nicky as he took me on a tour of where they'd already hung their art. My thoughts kept wandering back to Alernon, though. And it wasn't until I was in the entertainment space with the kids that I realized I'd never found out why Alernon had been in Africa.

"Hey, Mom?" Nicky asked, demanding my attention. "Can

Baynol make us breakfast tomorrow instead of Alernon? I don't want to eat pancakes again."

"Sure," I said, smoothing my hand over his hair. Nicky's whoop of joy sent up a red flag. "You know what? I think I have an even better idea. Let's all go to the galley and see if we can set up some cooking lessons so Lil and Nicky can be the cooks for the grownups."

They were so excited by the idea that Nicky didn't even realize I'd sabotaged his matchmaking efforts.

Foyen, the chef on duty, was delighted by my request and fawned over everything the kids did. The fact that they trashed his workspace and more ingredients landed on the floor than in the dishes didn't even faze him.

I stood back with Baynol and Peltear and just observed.

"Are you going to take one for the team?" I asked Baynol quietly.

He gave me a questioning look.

"I already threw up on alien food once and don't want to repeat the experience. But those kids are going to want someone to try their creations."

Baynol chuckled. "Peltear and I will eat what they prepare."

My forethought paid off when I witnessed the way both big men paused after their first bites.

"Nicky. Lil. You should make a plate for Alernon and Zarris, too," I said.

As soon as the kids' backs were turned, I motioned for the guys to spit out their food. They discreetly disposed of their portions under Foyen's knowing smirk and left with the kids to torment Alernon and Zarris.

"I would give all my chit to watch what's about to happen," Foyen said.

"How much do you think they'd choke down before someone distracts the kids?"

"All of it," Foyen said. "The wardens didn't eat it because you didn't want them to. Otherwise, they would have eaten every bite as well."

I cringed.

"Would you mind teaching me to make a few dishes that are actually edible?"

I spent the next hour with Foyen. If he slipped and I saw what he was thinking or felt his need, I didn't mention it. However, it firmed my resolve to work harder on setting up what was needed to have a successful adjustment and integration system on the station.

By the time we finished, the kids returned to the galley with the empty plates. Adriana was grinning from ear to ear as she followed the pair with the three Anrothians and Alernon trailing behind.

"It looks like we might have two mini-chefs on our hands," she said. "Zarris couldn't stop eating."

"Can we make them some more?" Nicky and Lil asked.

Zarris smiled slightly, and I glanced at Alernon.

He watched me steadily as the image of me laying over his lap while he rubbed a palm slowly over my bare ass burned into my mind. Understanding the threat well enough, I blinked at him. After what I'd gone through, I didn't find it funny at all.

However, before I could react, the image immediately changed. I was no longer on Alernon's lap but was the one sitting while he lay over mine and my palm skimmed over his sculpted, smooth ass.

"Whaa!" I squealed as I stumbled back a step.

Everyone stilled. Everyone except Alernon, who grinned wickedly at me.

I definitely didn't feel threatened anymore. At least, not in the scary way the first image had leaned.

Since the kids were watching me, waiting for a clue regarding my reaction, I cleared my throat and focused on them.

"Actually, I just finished helping Foyen clean up. Maybe we can eat the dinner I helped make tonight, and tomorrow you can take another turn?"

They nodded and ran to the table where I had the dishes waiting.

Alernon wrapped his arms around me from behind, hugging me to his chest and dipping his head to brush his lips against my neck.

"Forgive me," he whispered. "I will take more care when attempting to tease you." His lips brushed my skin again. "I would never do anything to cause you physical distress."

I elbowed him lightly to distract us both from what he was trying to do.

"What about emotional distress? I'm pretty sure I'm going to need therapy after that last image."

He chuckled low, and the purely seductive sound wrapped around me.

"Come now, don't tell me you weren't intrigued."

"By what part?"

"Everything all right over there?" Adriana called.

# CHAPTER TWENTY-SIX

## ALERNON

STACY'S SMALL, SHARP ELBOW DUG MORE AGGRESSIVELY INTO MY SIDE, and I reluctantly released her.

"Everything's fine," she said, hurrying away from me. "Let's eat."

I watched her walk away yet again and reminded myself to have patience. She'd openly invited me to her bed. It was a *small* step in the direction I wished but still a step.

She took the place next to her youngling, leaving the one across from her open. I studied her flushed face as she spoke to Nicky and Lil, explaining the nutri-paste she'd made. Color had flooded her skin when we'd kissed in the hallway too.

Nicky took a bite of his meal and made an unhappy face.

"What are the chances we can get human food up here soon?" Stacy asked. "Oh, and what was up with your trip to Africa? Who did you meet?"

"You went to Africa?" Adriana asked.

"Did you get to see a lion?" Lil asked. "I went to the zoo and saw a lion. They come from Africa too." She frowned a little. "That's where they're supposed to come from. The lion I saw was from Pittsburgh."

Adriana started to choke.

"Pat her on the back," Stacy said to Zarris while Lil watched me expectantly. "She'll be fine."

"I did not see a lion," I said to Lil, "but now I wish to."

I glanced at Adriana, who was catching her breath, before focusing on Stacy.

"I went to Africa to meet with Annah and her associate David, regarding the agreement. They were predictably against the resources we requested despite having privately acknowledged to each other the need to reduce the number of resources currently occupying your planet for the health of the ecosystem. To prove our goodwill and the level of care any friends we acquire would receive, I let them know we planned to extend an invitation to heal a certain number of ill."

"Oh, wow," Stacy said. "You moved faster than I thought. Does that mean we'll be having company soon?"

"Yes. While the younglings were creating their delightful meals for us, Quinoll and I were sending inquiries to the applicable parties. I anticipate we will begin receiving replies before this rest cycle."

"How many did you invite?" Adriana asked.

"Did you invite kids?" Lil asked excitedly.

"Over fifty," I said, answering Adriana first. "I anticipate not all will accept initially. A few of them were younger, but no younglings close to your age." I nodded toward Lil.

She made a sad face then perked up. "Did you invite Aunt Grace?"

As much as I wished to gain another female's willing presence on the ship to distract my crew from Stacy, I wouldn't risk being accused of an abduction. Everything indicated that Grace was living peacefully under the watchful eye of her country's government, and we had no reason to intervene.

"Not yet, but I intend to as soon as I have permission from Earth's leaders."

The youngling accepted the answer and took a bite of her meal.

My gaze lingered on the confusing female across from me as we ate. When I'd left Stacy, she'd been angry. Yet, when I'd returned from the meeting with Annah, Stacy had met me with a kiss.

I ached for the upcoming rest cycle and the chance to test her response to me. She hadn't spoken to me in the hallway like someone mindlessly under the thrall of my desires. She'd reprimanded me and pushed away from me when the younglings had discovered us. Nothing an enraptured female would do.

The need inside me built at the knowledge that the kiss had been real…that every sweet sound and touch had been her own.

"What's wrong?" she asked, nodding toward my bowl. "Too full?"

I smiled slightly and ate a bite of the meal she'd prepared. She made a small amused sound.

"Baynol can still cook us breakfast, right?" Nicky said beside her.

Stacy glanced at the youngling, Baynol, then me.

"I think, after all the hard work you put into your creations today, it's only fair to let Baynol have a chance," she said.

Nicky lit up and turned to the warden.

"Be there early."

I didn't miss the way the younglings glanced at me after he said it and almost smiled. He was worried I would arrive before Baynol and make the meal instead of his preferred suitor for his mother. I had no intention of interfering with Baynol's meal prep duties, however. If the systems were aligned, I would still be holding the youngling's mother in my arms when the warden was preparing our feast.

As soon as the younglings finished, they begged for more time to play in the entertainment area and ran off with their guardians.

"So, what exactly are the plans once you start bringing sick people on board?" Adriana asked before I could suggest Stacy and I follow the younglings.

"We will scan them and treat them. Most will need several treatments, so they will be assigned a sleep bay to rest."

Both females watched me expectantly for several beats before Stacy said, "That's it?"

"What more should there be?" I asked, curious.

"A tour of the ship? Give them something to eat? Show them the view from the observation bay? Anything to help them feel more comfortable about being here."

"Ah. I understand. However, the first patients likely to agree will be those who are very seriously ill. Rest will benefit them the most in the beginning."

"Can one of us at least be there when they arrive?" Adriana asked. "They're coming alone, right?"

"Yes, the invitation is only for those who are ill. And you may certainly be present for their arrival. I will notify you both as soon as I receive word."

Foyen approached the table.

"How did you find Stacy's cooking?" he asked.

"Much better than the younglings," Zarris said.

Stacy grinned, and Foyen focused on her. I fought not to scowl at him for what I knew was coming.

"If you have nothing planned after this rest cycle, I can teach you more meal preparation options," he said.

I wanted to remind her that she'd agreed to look at the station plans, but in reality, the work could start on the station even without finalized plans. The core systems wouldn't need to be changed, only the finishes and how to use the spaces. So I maintained my silence and waited for Stacy's answer.

"I think today proved that it's best to leave the cooking to the pros. Thank you for giving us lessons, though."

"Allowing the younglings time with the other members of the crew was something I previously mentioned to Baynol," I said before Foyen could attempt another route to coax her away. "If you wish the younglings to live on the station once it's complete, it would be wise to help them integrate with the crew now to grow their circle of trust."

Stacy nodded slowly.

"How much bigger will the station be compared to this ship?" she asked.

"Much larger. Stations have their own gravity, a network of integrated grow bays within the living spaces to assist with air purification, and their own water sources. They have their own ecosystems."

"So, like a mini-planet?" Stacy asked.

"Yes."

"I'd love to see the plans."

"Me too," Adriana said.

"Of course. I can show you now if you'd like," I said.

"Tomorrow's good," Adriana said, rising. "I'm ready for bed. It feels like the days up here are a lot longer."

"That's actually something that might help people feel more at home," Stacy said, also standing. "Clocks set to their local time zones in their rooms. And maybe suggest that they bring their own comfort foods, too."

"Thank you for the recommendations. I will see that the sleep bays display their local times. Do you wish that for your rooms too?"

Adriana shook her head. "It might mess with my head to know it's actually noon or something like that when I'm ready for bed now."

"Same," Stacy said. "Although it might be easier to wrangle the kids into bed."

The pair of them started for the door, and with a nod to Foyen, I followed.

Zarris glanced at me, a knowing smirk on his face, but didn't comment.

I had no regrets about welcoming Zarris and his companions aboard. Although I knew all the Anrothians were as equally starved for a female of their own, they weren't confrontational about it. They understood as well as my people did that it was the female's choice, not ours.

"Would the wardens be willing to assist with the new arrivals?" I asked.

He nodded without asking how or why.

"Thank you. It will allow the crew to continue working on station plans."

"What are they working on?" Stacy asked, glancing back at us. "I thought we'd be involved in the planning."

"The basic systems planning is standard for all stations. The final architectural design has room for changes, though. We can meet in the comms room first thing, and I will go over everything with you."

She nodded and said farewell to Adriana and Zarris when they parted ways to return to their sleep bay.

Stacy didn't look at me again as we made our way to the entertainment space. I couldn't stop looking at her, though. The way the material caressed her body mesmerized me. I imagined my fingers dancing over her skin instead of the fine cloth.

She scowled at me. "Cut it out."

"Apologies. I'm struggling to maintain my focus."

"I can tell."

I caught her arm and stopped her in the corridor.

"Did you mean what you said earlier?" I asked.

"What part?"

"That the kiss we shared was because you wanted it too, not simply because I wanted it. That you want me in your bed."

She held my gaze, and I could feel her worry and guilt.

"I just realized you understand how I feel," she said.

"Only when the emotions are strong."

She laughed suddenly, confusing me.

"That wasn't what I meant." Her smile faded. "I doubt everything you do, Alernon. I look for hidden motives and meanings, waiting for the moment you turn into a monster pretending to be a beautiful, kind man. It's the same way you're doubting that I'm a woman who sees you for you and that I'm not under the influence of your very persuasive imagination."

She carefully removed my light hold on her arm and twined her fingers through mine.

"I don't want to start over with you," she said. "The thought of that is too exhausting. But I'd like to move forward with mutual understanding.

"My time with Pin has left me with some serious mental and emotional scars. I can't promise that I won't stop doubting you, but I can promise that everything I do and say to you will be my own thoughts and feelings, not a projection of yours."

I itched to dig my fingers into her hair and kiss her as I had previously.

She smiled slightly.

"My promise doesn't mean I'm oblivious to the thoughts you're throwing at me, though. So, please, try to tone it down a little. It's not easy picturing you petting my ass when I'm walking next to Adriana."

Stunned, I stared at Stacy.

"You can see what I'm picturing?"

"Yes. Am I not supposed to?"

"As I said, every species reacts to our unique abilities a little differently. Most feel the emotions we feel to a degree. Our lust.

SAGE ALDER

Our need. It can translate into actions. I haven't encountered many species that can read an Oebri mind."

"I don't think I'm reading your mind," Stacy said. "It's more like you're pushing your thoughts into mine."

Something I would consider very invasive. Yet, she watched me with concern as if I were the one who might be upset by this revelation.

"Humans are truly a wonder," I murmured.

"We'll see if you're still awestruck when you have to explain to my son why I'm not willing to jump into bed with his chosen hero." She frowned. "Wait. No. I don't want you to explain anything. You're way too open with information."

I chuckled and tucked her hand around my arm.

"I would prefer the younglings and my crew understand your choice as soon as possible."

"And what choice is that exactly?" she asked with a thread of suspicion.

"That you have started to show a preference for me," I said.

"Is that what I'm doing?"

"Is it not?" I asked.

My wrist comm chimed before she could answer.

"We have received the first reply," Quinoll said. "The male is ready for transfer at our earliest convenience. He is dying, Alernon."

The teasing light left Stacy's gaze, and I felt her compassion for a human she'd never met.

"I understand," I said back. "Has a sys-unit been set up in the transference bay?"

"Everything is ready," Quinoll said.

"Do you still wish to join me?" I asked.

"Please."

Her pace was quicker as we turned back toward the

transference bay. When we entered, I saw the sys-unit waiting, along with two wardens and over a dozen floating orbs.

"Thank you for joining us," I said. "The male is terminally ill by Earth standards and lost consciousness three days ago. We are transferring him from his care facility on Earth and will need to move him from his bed to his unit as soon as he appears. Will you help with that?"

Both males nodded.

"He may regain consciousness and be disoriented. If he wakes, allow Stacy to speak with him and reassure him."

I looked at Stacy. "If his behavior becomes erratic or threatening to you in any way, the wardens and I will prioritize your well-being over his. For the sake of your younglings, you will not risk yourself, Stacy. Please." It was a command and a plea all wrapped into one.

"I'll be careful. I promise."

Transference energy illuminated the area near the sys-unit. I moved forward as the male and his hospital bed solidified. His guardian was the one who I had thought was most likely to respond immediately. The male was also the one most likely to die.

We'd gathered a great deal of data regarding human illnesses since arriving. More since discovering Annah's reproductive growth. Human cell degeneration and cancers were within our means to heal. However, the process would not be easy, and if the patient did not want to live, he wouldn't likely survive.

The man I'd selected had much reason to live, though. A wife and two female younglings.

"Lift him onto the sys-unit," I said.

Stacy moved to clasp one of his hands as I started the scan.

I looked at her as she watched him and felt her compassion. I wasn't foolish enough to wish she felt that for me. The dying man could have her compassion. I wanted her love and devotion. Her loyalty and even her anger.

After approving the sys-unit's recommendations, we waited for the first round of treatment to complete. He didn't regain consciousness.

"What's his name?" Stacy asked as the sys-unit arm moved away from his torso.

"Tebo Jaylaani."

"Will someone sit with him until he wakes up?"

"We have found it's more conducive to the healing process if they do not wake with an alien species present."

She slowly turned her head to look at me. "I can't tell if you're being serious or trying to be funny."

"I assure you that his reaction will not be entertaining if he wakes with one of us present."

"Maybe one of you, but I doubt seeing me will send him into a panic."

My gaze swept over the material encasing her body and hinting at the treasure beneath.

"He most certainly will not panic," I agreed. "However, I would prefer you spend the night with me as you promised."

She frowned at me. "Don't you want this to go well for the sake of the treaty? Wouldn't it make more sense for me to be here?"

"Of course. But if he didn't wake for this scan and repair, he is unlikely to wake before the next is needed. We will monitor him from a distance while he rests. When he shows signs that he might wake, we can summon you or Adriana to greet him."

# CHAPTER TWENTY-SEVEN

## STACY

Nicky yawned and fought to keep his eyes open as I read the story. He gave in to sleep a minute later. I tucked both of them in and brushed their brows with kisses before making my way to the cleansing unit, glad I finally had a few minutes to myself.

I had a lot to think about, and thankfully, Alernon was giving me time to do that. After collecting the kids from the entertainment space with me and saying goodnight, he'd left to check on Tebo and send reports to all the people who wanted them.

As the cleansing water ran over me, I thought about the kiss Alernon and I had shared and the decision I'd made to try having a relationship with him. It hadn't been lightly made. Nicky and I were adrift in space, both literally and metaphorically, and dependent on Alernon. Whether I wanted to admit it or not, Alernon controlled our future. However, he never abused that control.

I knew how much he and every other single male on the ship wanted me. I saw it played out in images in my mind. Yet, Alernon hadn't done any macho chest-beating bullshit to keep them away from me. He'd told me he wanted to stake a claim and then let me choose.

The way he'd felt when I'd chosen had humbled me. Rather than feeling triumph or anything even remotely like winning ownership of me, he'd been awed and grateful.

Horny too.

Which didn't bother me like it probably should have. At least, not after that last kiss.

But that didn't mean I was ready to have sex with him. Nope. Not happening.

My libido laughed at my lies, and I made a face as I turned on the warm air. Fine, I was attracted to Alernon. The man was sexy. There was no denying that.

And I'd meant every word I'd said when we were in the hall. Kissing him had been all me. But seeing the things he wanted to do to me had fueled my desire. I liked knowing what he wanted to do. Even the spanking bit. While his sense of humor was unique, I still appreciated the glimpse of it that he'd given me.

Alernon seemed real, and that scared the hell out of me. What if I was falling into another lie? What if he turned out to be like Pin? What if—

The door opened, and I spun around to look at Alernon. His worried gaze met mine. He didn't look anywhere else but my eyes as he opened his arms for me.

"You have nothing to fear anymore, Stacy. I won't let anything hurt you."

The comfort he offered lured me closer, one step at a time, until I was wrapped in his embrace.

"Your fear and uncertainty undo me," he said softly into my hair. "Tell me how to comfort you. What do you need?"

I tipped my head back to look at him.

"I need you to be real." Without waiting for his answer, I rose to my toes and brushed my lips against his.

He made a pained sound and kissed me in return. Images flashed in his head. His hands gripping my ass so I could wrap my legs around his waist. Me tearing off his clothes and forbidding him from wearing any type of covering again. My mouth gently suctioning the crown of his shaft. His face buried between my legs.

I tore my mouth from his, panting as my hands smoothed over his chest.

"Bedroom," I said.

That single word set loose a storm of desperate need. It flooded me. Consuming my thoughts. My hands stroked down his stomach until my fingers closed over his hard length.

"Alernon," I breathed.

"Yes," he groaned. "My beauty. My life. I am yours."

"Stop."

The need immediately cut off, and he looked at me with horror as I released him.

And at that moment, I had my answer.

Alernon wasn't Pin.

I smiled and gently touched his cheek.

"I'm still me," I said. "I just wanted to feel my own feelings. Yours were a little too loud."

He stared at me, and I could see his doubt.

"Even if you begged right now, I wouldn't spank you. Does that help?" I asked, gently stroking a finger along his handsome jaw. "But if you need more convincing, let's hold off on sex for another night and just snuggle tonight."

I could feel the war of his emotions. The relief and the denial both made me smile.

"Or…if you ask really, really nicely, I'll let you do that last thing you imagined."

In my mind, I saw him from where I lay, sprawled on the bed. He slowly stalked forward, maintaining eye contact the whole time, almost challenging me to stop him from what he was about to do. My legs opened wider in invitation, and I started telling him exactly how I wanted him to pleasure me.

"I never hear words," I said. "I just understand what I see. Is that supposed to happen?"

"You are the first of your kind that I've met, Stacy. I have no idea what's supposed to happen, but I'd like to discover that together."

He lifted his hand between us, offering it to me. I slipped my fingers over his palm.

"The image you painted? I liked it. A lot."

He led me without a stitch of covering from the cleansing unit. When I glanced at the kids' room, he tugged playfully at my fingers.

"They are deeply sleeping. My comms will alert us the halo-flash that changes."

The door to our sleeping space closed behind us, showing a clear view of the living room. Alernon caught the direction of my attention.

"From the other side, this room is not visible."

I nodded and let him lead me to the bed where he kissed me senseless then slowly started kissing his way down my torso.

"Will you welcome me?" he asked, his breath tickling my stomach.

My answer was just what he'd imagined. I parted my legs for him.

He growled and kissed his way to my inner thigh.

"Tell me what pleases you," he said.

"I think we'll need to figure that out together, too," I said. "No one's taken the time to do this for me."

His gaze held mine as he dipped down to gently kiss my clit. A quiet breath escaped me, and his lips curved in a knowing smile. When his tongue came out to play, I lost myself to the sensation of being loved.

My fingers found their way to his hair as erotic images flipped through my mind one by one. None of them were overwhelming like in the cleansing unit, but each added to the heat building inside of me.

"I need more," I panted, using my fingers to show him what I meant.

His throaty chuckle as his fingers replaced mine at my entrance might have embarrassed me if he wasn't sending images of him slowly thrusting into me instead of the two long digits he was using.

The build to my release wrapped around me tighter and tighter until the wave of tension broke free, and I melted in a state of relaxed bliss.

Alernon's fingers slowed inside of me, and he placed a gentle kiss on my thigh.

"You are a wonder, Stacy," he said. "Thank you for sharing your pleasure with me."

He kissed my other thigh and lightly licked my folds. The image of him slowly coaxing me into allowing him to do that again filled my mind, followed by an image of me sleeping draped over his naked, sweaty body.

"Let's go straight to option B," I murmured.

He chuckled and reached up to untangle my fingers from his hair.

"That option is how I picture us after a very long breeding session."

I almost snorted. Sometimes he said the weirdest things.

"I suppose I could be convinced to partake in a breeding session if you give me a minute to catch my breath."

The wave of hunger I felt from him didn't help me catch anything other than his hair as he kissed his way up my body.

"Tell me what you want," Alernon said before his mouth closed over one peak.

"That's pretty good," I said, arching my hips into his.

He made a pleased sound and switched to the other side. I

hummed my enjoyment. His fingers skimmed over my ribs...the three that Pin had broken.

Alernon abandoned my nipple to kiss me there while caressing the thigh that had been bruised.

"My body will be your shield for the rest of my life," he said. "I vow you will never again suffer at the hands of any male. Only pleasure."

He kissed his way up my neck and held my face so I met his gaze.

"You honor me, Stacy. Thank you."

I wasn't sure why he was thanking me. He'd been the one to rock my world and just offered me his life. But I wasn't in the mood to nitpick details. I pulled him down for a kiss, tasting myself on his lips.

He moaned into my mouth as his thick, hot length slicked through my folds. More images flashed in my mind too quickly to register, and then it vanished.

Alernon's lips left mine as he reached between us. His fingers teased over my sensitive clit.

"I've watched many videos documenting human mating. Many were not pleasant. I do not wish to hurt you. If this causes discomfort, will you tell me?"

I nodded as he positioned himself at my entrance. "Just go slow."

My eyes almost rolled back into my head at his unhurried entry. I felt each stretching inch in the best possible way. And just when it started to get a little uncomfortable, he withdrew and glided a little farther in.

"Yes," I breathed. "Yes. Like that."

He continued until there wasn't any more space in me that he could fill. We may have both made some unintelligible sounds when he began a careful, shallow thrusting rhythm. I relaxed around him, growing wetter. The sounds were indecent and only had me clinging harder to his impressive shoulders.

Then his hips started to meet mine.

"Find your pleasure for me, Stacy. Show me you want this."

I writhed under him, the hunger in his words becoming my hunger. His need for my release became mine. I embraced it all, climbing higher and higher until I found what we were both looking for.

The intensity of my orgasm lifted my hips from the bed. He growled and swore as I clenched around him. He gripped my hip firmly, pinning me into place as he thrust into me a few more times. Then I felt the intense heat of his release filling me.

Breathing heavily, he rolled us so he was on his back and I was sprawled over him. His semi-hard length twitched inside of me.

"Will you stay like this?" he asked softly, petting my hair.

"Until you move me," I said, knowing there was no way I'd have the energy to move myself.

THE WAVES LAPPED at the shore as I stood safely within the circle of Alernon's arms and watched the sunrise.

Something chimed.

Alernon nuzzled my neck, brushing a kiss there. It felt so real and loving. I sighed and leaned more firmly against him, never wanting the dream to end.

Another chime rang out.

Alernon gently caught my earlobe between his teeth. The sensation pulled me from the dream enough to understand the next chime I heard was coming from his wrist comm.

"What time is it?" I asked sleepily.

"Time for you to sample the meal Baynol is preparing for you with the younglings' help."

More awake, I twisted around to frown at Alernon.

After a brief nap the night before, he'd coaxed me into the cleansing unit where he'd proved his strength by taking me against the wall. Then he'd washed me tenderly and dried my hair while holding me. No one had ever cared for me after sex like Alernon had last night. He'd even gotten me a clean gown to put on because he understood I wasn't comfortable being naked if the kids needed something in the middle of the night.

Now, knowing that Baynol was already here and the kids were awake, I was grateful for Alernon's consideration. And for the pants he wore.

My gaze dipped to his bare chest, which had been pressed against my exposed back all night. I hadn't realized how starved for skin-to-skin snuggling I'd been.

"If you continue to stare at me like that, the younglings will be disappointed."

I lifted my gaze. "What do you mean?"

"They will see you hunger more for me than for the food they made."

I rolled my eyes at him and flipped back the cover. He groaned and did a pretend grab for me, provoking my grin.

"You're not going to behave today, are you?" I asked as I smoothed back my hair.

Instead of answering, he stood and stretched, not looking away from me as my gaze swept over him, lingering at the obscene outline of his semi-hard cock in his silken sleep pants.

"You can't wear those around the kids."

"Your view of nudity will not help you or the younglings assimilate to living on a station. What I'm wearing is more than acceptable."

I made a face as I mentally compared his pants to his mom's chain "dress." In comparison, his pants were modest.

"Fine. You're right."

I turned to the door and realized I was about to leave my bedroom with a man. Panic and doubt hit me like a baseball bat.

What was I doing? I'd always been careful about introducing Nicky to the men I dated, never wanting him to get attached to someone who might not make the cut. But he had gotten attached. Baynol was a great guy, and I could see Nicky loved him a lot.

"Tell me why you're filled with fear and doubt," Alernon said as he hugged me from behind. "Allow me to help you."

"What's going to happen when I walk out that door with you? Nicky's not dumb. He's going to understand that I like you instead of Baynol, and it's going to break my son's heart. After everything he's been through because of my shitty choices, I can't do this to him."

Alernon held me even tighter and kissed my temple.

"This, too, is something that the younglings will come to learn…family units in the systems are not only the birther and the donor. It takes many to raise younglings safely. Choosing me as your bonded mate does not mean Baynol is not part of Nicky's family."

I turned to look at Alernon.

"So if Nicky wants Baynol to make him breakfast every day?"

"Then Baynol will learn to make Nicky many foods and teach Nicky how to make them himself as he grows. And I will teach Nicky about the systems. And Terrabak will teach him about grow bays. And Zarris will train him how to fight. And—"

"Okay. I get it. We're all family."

Alernon's happy smile melted my insides.

# CHAPTER TWENTY-EIGHT

## ALERNON

I COULD FEEL THE SHIFT IN OUR BOND THROUGH THE SWELL OF HER affection as she turned in my arms and brushed her lips against my chin.

"Thank you," she said. "That does make me feel better about this."

I wanted to coax her back to the bed but knew another breeding wouldn't finish winning her heart and mind. Both those would need to be won without the use of my cock. Unfortunately.

"Come. The younglings will follow your lead. If you greet everyone naturally, they will see nothing wrong with me sleeping in your bed."

She nodded and held my hand as we left the room.

Baynol didn't notice us as he placed another flower on Stacy's plate. Nicky did, though. His gaze shifted between his mother and me before settling on our hands.

"Good morning," Stacy said. "It smells amazing in here. What did you three make for everyone?"

Baynol looked up from his creation. The disappointment in his gaze was brief as he nodded at me.

My wrist comm chimed again.

"What does it mean when it does that?" Stacy asked.

"It's a non-urgent request for my presence." Prior to returning to Stacy, I'd made Quinoll aware that she'd invited me to her bed. He understood what that meant and was attempting not to intrude. However, the fact that he'd sent repeated requests likely meant the issue wasn't non-urgent.

Stacy seemed to think the same.

"You should check in with whoever is sending that," she said.

I glanced at the younglings as I accepted the comms request.

"You asked that I alert you when Tebo shows signs of waking," Quinoll said. "Do you want me to comm Adriana?"

"No," Stacy said quickly. "I can go."

"Thank you, Quinoll," I said before ending the comm and lifting Stacy's hand to kiss the back of it. "Allow Baynol to serve you breakfast first. We can check on Tebo after you've eaten."

"Who's Tebo?" Nicky asked.

"He's a man from Earth," Stacy said. "He's very sick, and Alernon is trying to help him to get better."

She released my hand and sat across from Nicky.

"Remember how afraid you were when you woke up on that ship? Tebo will probably feel that way too. That's why I want to be there when he wakes up. So he's not afraid."

Nicky nodded and held Lil's hand, proving he was a very caring youngling.

"You should hurry up and eat, Mom."

Baynol set her plate in front of her. He hadn't removed the flowers. Nicky's gaze shifted to me, and I smiled slightly at the youngling's keen perception of the situation.

"Since Baynol prepared this meal, does that mean you'll prepare another meal for us?" I asked the youngling as I went to serve myself a portion of the meal Baynol had made.

"Can I?" he asked, looking at Stacy.

I could feel her hesitation and chuckled.

"Your first attempt was adequate, but I believe you can do much better with more practice. Perhaps you'd like to spend some more time with Raaln learning about the different foods in the systems and what's safe for humans."

Nicky looked at Baynol.

"It's a good idea," Baynol said. "I will join you."

"While you do that, would it be all right if I stay with Tebo?" Stacy asked.

The younglings quickly agreed, and I sat beside Lil, enjoying the novelty of eating as a family unit.

Too soon, we all finished and parted ways.

Stacy walked beside me, casting glances at my chest.

"Are you purposely attempting to distract me?" I asked. "I assure you, it is working well."

Her gaze dipped lower before it flew to my face.

"You need better pants."

I grinned at the flood of wanton need I felt from her and nodded to a passing crew member who'd paused when he'd felt the same.

"I believe these pants are serving their purpose."

"Barely," she mumbled, staring straight ahead now.

My wrist comm chimed.

"Alernon, Tebo is awake."

Stacy started to jog, and I found myself very distracted by her chest as I kept pace beside her. Once we reached the door, she held up her hand to stop me from opening it.

"I've got this. You go check in with Quinoll."

"Stacy, this male has no idea where he is or what's happened to him. He could have an adverse reaction—"

"Alernon. I need you to trust that I'm capable of speaking to the people who board this ship, or I have no place in your life."

The complete determination I felt paired with her words surprised me.

"Of course you're capable. I'm simply worried about your safety."

"I'll be fine. I doubt a man who's been in a coma for several days is going to jump out of bed. Go. Talk to Quinoll. I know how to send a message to you if I need you."

With reluctance, I nodded and made my way to the comms center.

Quinoll stopped his pacing when I entered.

"Tebo's second scan and treatment were completed during your rest cycle. I sent the result to the appropriate Earth contacts as you asked. Since then, we've received fifteen more responses to our invitation. Several are urgently requesting a reply."

I spent the next several arcs corresponding with Earth to coordinate the arrival of additional patients. The promising results of Tebo's treatment made the others eager, and I arranged for Adriana to be present for the transference of the second patient.

Tired and eager for Stacy's presence, I sought her out in the entertainment room where she sat at a low table with the younglings, Baynol, and Peltear.

"These are perfect," she said, looking at the drawings the younglings were working on. "Tebo's going to love them."

Her compassion for Tebo and love for the younglings teased me. Needing to feel an emotion that was just for me, I imagined quietly closing the distance between us and kissing her bare shoulder blade as my fingers toyed with her breasts.

I felt a surge of amusement and desire as she glanced over her shoulder at me.

"The children are making some art to hang in Tebo's room. He's resting now, but I thought seeing the kids and their pretty pictures would help him acclimate as they share stories about the ship."

I looked at the art and saw it wasn't Earth pictures but images from their time on Anrothe. Nicky had drawn an impressive likeness of a cravnar and another of one of the native aquatic species. Lil had drawn a picture of a warden carrying a youngling.

"I'm sure Tebo will be as enchanted with your inspiring drawings as my crew has been."

"I'll be right back." Stacy patted each of the younglings' heads and rose to join me at the door.

"Tebo was pretty out of it when he woke up and closed his eyes after I explained he was being treated on a ship," she said softly. "I don't think he believed me."

"You are likely correct. Many don't believe it's real even after seeing an Oebri."

She smiled slightly. "Yeah, I was the same. It took a bit of convincing. But rather than trying to do that, I thought we could just focus on helping him feel safe and comfortable first so maybe the shock when he realizes where he is won't be that bad."

"It's a good idea. Will the younglings be willing to make more pictures?"

"Absolutely. They already know that a woman's come aboard, too. Lil asked about Grace again. I told her soon, hopefully."

"It will be difficult to win Earth's trust. Tebo's progress has spurred others to accept. However, there has already been correspondence suggesting a patient switch with military personnel to gain information about our location and intent."

Stacy's expression filled with worry.

"What will we do if that happens?"

I chuckled. "It won't happen unless I allow it. Allowing a species to believe it can trick us only increases its hostility. It is better if they learn now that we cannot be tricked and that such attempts will not stop us from providing treatment to those who need it."

Stacy nodded. "Setting boundaries is smart. What is it going to take to earn their trust enough so they start signing the agreement? I really want to ask for Grace. She's the only family Lil has left."

"Every race is different. I believe proving ourselves indispensable to humanity is our best course."

"Which is going to take time," she said, repeating my early words with a hint of disappointment in her tone.

"Have you and the younglings eaten your second meal yet?"

"We just finished."

"Send me a comm when you're ready for the third meal so I can join you."

"I will. And send me a comm when the next person is ready to transfer." She set her hands on my chest and rose up on her toes to brush her lips against mine. I experienced her tender affection physically and mentally. The fondness she felt for me was just as potent as her lips against mine.

My need for her surged. Breeding wouldn't be enough. I needed her in my life and at my side. Always.

I lifted my arms, ready to deepen the kiss, but she twirled away with a laugh before I had the chance.

"Try not to broadcast what you want to do next time," she called over her shoulder as she strode away.

I stared after her swaying backside, and my thoughts drifted to the pleasure we had shared.

"Not happening, Alernon. Get back to work."

Grinning to myself, I watched her disappear down the next hall and returned to the comms center where I struggled to maintain focus on gaining Earth's trust. My thoughts continued to drift to Stacy until Quinoll set down his datapad and left the comms center without a word. I reined in my passion and joy for Stacy and commed Vegori to take over for Quinoll.

The crew needed Earth to sign quickly. Even though I knew none of my crew would resent me for tempting Stacy to my side, I understood how much they needed a chance at females of their own as well.

I couldn't lose focus on the importance of gaining Earth's agreement.

However, I'd made little progress before Stacy commed me for the third meal. The leaders were openly grateful for our support and help to heal the few sick who'd come aboard while also subtly questioning why only sick and why only the few we selected. Meanwhile, in communications they believed to be secret, many were hostile toward the terms of the contract we'd created. Despite the data we'd given to prove that their home world could not continue to support their numbers, they were unwilling to part with a single female.

"That doesn't look like a happy face," Stacy said.

I looked up from where I'd focused on the guiding line on the floor and found my beautiful female waiting for me in the hall just outside the galley. The frustration I'd felt melted away as she stepped forward and slipped her arms around my waist.

"Something happen?" she asked as she hugged me.

"Earth's leaders are a source of frustration. But this helps remind me why I must endure."

She laughed lightly, the sound filling my heart. It soothed away the last few hours completely.

"Humans can be extremely stubborn," she said. "But I think they'll come around to our way of thinking."

She withdrew and threaded her fingers through mine.

"Tebo is doing better after his third scan. I think he'll be ready to get up and walk the halls soon. If you think that's safe."

"Tebo is still weak and recovering. I have no concern that he walks the hallways so long as one of the wardens accompanies him. It will not help negotiations if a human collapses aboard our ship."

She gave my hand a squeeze and led me into the galley where the younglings were already eating with the wardens and Adriana.

"The kids have been working on their art all afternoon," she said. "They have pictures ready for any new friends who come aboard. They've also spent some time with Raaln, helping him figure out a palatable version of the nutri-paste that our new sick friends can stomach. They've come up with three options they both liked."

We'd reached the table, and the younglings excitedly began telling me about their day. I sat and smiled as Nicky called Raaln over with samples for me to try. While I would prefer the foods from my home world—and many others—over the nutria-paste options they'd helped create, I agreed all three were much better than the original.

"You've worked hard today," I said to the pair. "Thank you for your efforts. Perhaps tomorrow you would like to help in the grow bays and see how the sweet roots you've chosen grow."

Both cheered and quickly agreed.

Adriana smiled at the pair and encouraged them to finish their meals so they could play some more.

"I'll take a turn in the entertainment room if you want to do the rounds," she said to Stacy.

"It's a deal," Stacy said before looking at me. "Should I comm you when we're done for the night?"

"Without hesitation," I said, already thinking of the night ahead.

She shook her head at me and leaned in to kiss my cheek. Nicky made a distressed sound.

"Mom," he said. "Gross."

"Oh yeah?" Adriana said. "What about this?" She grabbed Zarris's face and started placing small kisses all over it. The male grinned at the display of affection while Peltear and Baynol looked on with longing.

Stacy laughed. "See? There's nothing wrong with kisses from the people who love you. Come here." She stood and reached for

Nicky. He scrambled from his seat and started to run from her. Baynol laughed.

"When you are older, you will not run," he said.

"Kiss me!" Lil said, lifting her face to Stacy.

Stacy kissed the youngling's forehead and cheeks with enthusiasm. Lil's delighted laughter filled the galley, and I felt Raaln's surge of longing.

We needed more females and younglings on this ship.

"I should go," I said. "Thank you for the meal."

The younglings waved their farewells as I left the galley and returned to the comms center.

"Has there been an update from the engineers?" I asked Vegori.

"Yes. The core systems will be ready in another flare. When do you anticipate agreement?"

"From Earth? Not for many more flares."

"If we're caught preparing—"

I held up my hand.

"Stacy and Adriana are certain that Earth will contract with us. I will not delay what I know we will need by a single arc when I know how desperately we need females, and I believe the Prime Assembly would agree."

Vegori nodded, but I could see his doubt.

"I will take full responsibility," I said.

He nodded and brought up the building plans for the station, showing which of the pieces were already underway in the largest storage holds of our ship.

"In another two flares, they can begin replicating the pathways needed for the airflow. Water pathways for the grow bays will take another five flares."

I nodded. "I will arrange for more transfers of Earth's sick. Tebo is doing well and expressed interest in leaving his room. I estimate he will need three more scans before he will be fully healed. It would be wise to convince him that we are real and of

Earth's need to reduce its numbers before he leaves. He has the ear of one of the delegates from Earth's African continent."

"I'll ensure the crew knows," Vegori said before an alert started to ping.

We both looked at the light that indicated an incoming message from our home world. Likely a response to my request for materials.

"I'll take it in the comms room," I said.

Seated alone, I started the message and felt sad joy at the sight of my mother's beautiful face.

"I greet you with my heart, Alernon. I've missed you greatly, and your message filled me with joy. A human female? I have too many questions to ask and very little patience for answers.

"Which is why I've meddled, my sweet son. I and every female on homeworld petitioned for your request for materials to be approved. While the Prime Assembly cannot condone building a trade station without Earth's consent, they have approved the temporary creation of a comms station. Complete it as quickly as possible, Alernon. I wish to speak to this female who has confused you.

"Since this message has likely taken several flares to reach you, I hope that you were able to discover the answer to your question yourself. But if you weren't...*ask* her, Alernon. If there is ever anything you need to know...*ask her*. Females across the systems tend to be more emotionally based than males. We want to be asked. But we will only answer truthfully when we can trust the male to listen without judgment and with understanding. Establish that first, then ask."

# CHAPTER TWENTY-NINE

## STACY

I SMOTHERED ANOTHER YAWN WITH MY HAND AND TURNED DOWN THE lights in the kids' room. Adriana had to be right. The days felt longer on the ship. But I couldn't imagine shorter days. There was so much to do now.

Tebo's next scan would happen overnight. He was doing great, though. As were the other patients who'd come aboard during the last twenty-four hours.

The door to our suite opened. I turned away from the kids' room and watched Alernon walk in. He looked just as tired.

"Long day?" I asked.

He smiled slightly and hugged me.

"Without you? Yes."

I could feel how much he wanted to hold me and kiss me and talk to me. It was the talk to me that really twisted my insides and made me feel needed on a whole new level.

"If we shower together, will you be able to stay focused enough to tell me about your day?"

His gaze heated as he looked down at me.

"Yes."

I had my doubts but let him lead me to the cleansing unit.

While he eased the gown off my shoulders and placed light kisses on my skin, he told me about the continued split in Earth's response to the proposed protection agreement, the progress they'd made on the core systems for the trade station, and how Quinoll had walked out of the comms center because Alernon had been daydreaming about what he was currently doing.

And what he was currently doing was distracting enough that I could barely focus on his words. Especially when his mouth closed over my breast for several seconds.

"We received word from our home world too," he said, switching sides. The heat of his mouth was going straight between my thighs, which was where I wanted his mouth to go next.

I threaded my fingers in his hair, my thoughts already heading south.

"It was from my mother," he said when his lips left my nipple.

It was like a bucket of cold water dumped over me.

"What?" I asked, pulling him back by his hair.

His shock was plain on his face as he gently pried my hold loose.

"I've upset you," he said. "How?"

"Um…" I blinked at him and considered grabbing my gown off the floor. Then I realized what I was doing and thinking and took a calming breath.

"Talking about your mom while doing what you were doing is unsettling. I'd prefer clothes on while talking about your mom."

His slow, amused smile melted away some of my skittishness.

"She would like to speak with you soon. And she likely will be wearing a systems dress. You do see why I'm amused, don't you?"

I rolled my eyes at him.

"Yes. I do. But you can understand my reaction too, right? I'm from a culture that likes to cover up."

He let out a dramatically sad sigh. "I'm well aware of that misfortune."

"What's the message from your mom?" I asked, swatting his shoulder.

"She is delighted that I've captured the interest of a female and would like to speak with you. She also said to expect the supplies I'd requested. I have the support of homeworld to build a comm station immediately."

"Is that good?" I asked.

"It is. A comm station can easily be turned into a trade station."

"Which means you can begin building prior to Earth's agreement."

"Exactly."

I ran my fingers through his hair. "How does the crew feel about it?"

"Driven. They see the joy that you and Adriana bring and want the same. They know the station is the key to acquiring females."

"I thought the agreement was the key," I said.

"The agreement is the key to the trade station, and the trade station is the key to exporting females. Earth having access to send messages into the systems is another benefit to signing the agreement."

"You're stacking the deck, then. I like it."

"Does this mean I can continue kissing you?"

"As long as you don't bring up your mom again until you're done," I said.

He grinned and brushed a kiss over the skin between my breasts.

For the next several minutes, he didn't talk at all. His mouth was too busy. Mine wasn't, though. I said all sorts of things. "Yes." "Right there." "Harder." "If you don't stop teasing me, I'm going to pull out your hair."

I came apart on his mouth and fingers then wrapped my legs around him as he took me against the wall and made me babble nonsensically a second time.

He didn't release his hold on me as he started the cleansing water. Still impaled, I rested my head against his shoulder and let him wash whatever he could reach. When I came around enough to kiss his shoulder, he let me down and finished washing me.

Like the night before, Alernon had only been getting started in the cleansing unit. He had so many dirty ideas in his head, and it only took seeing a few for me to rouse and ask for more. By the time he was finished with me, I couldn't keep my eyes open.

He carried me to the shower a second time to wash me then helped me into a clean gown.

"It is a very good thing the younglings sleep deeply," Alernon said as he snuggled me from behind. "Your screaming is quite loud."

I elbowed him lightly and smiled at his laugh before drifting off to sleep.

I WOKE ALONE IN BED. The door to the main living space was open, and I could hear the low murmur of hushed conversation.

Smiling to myself, I rolled onto my back and stared up at the ceiling. My life on Earth seemed so distant just then. Here, on the ship, my life was just as busy, but I was able to spend as much time as I wanted with Nicky and didn't have to worry about bills or some asshole hurting my son. Every male on this ship adored the kids. Especially Baynol and Peltear who were their almost constant, protective shadows.

Alernon's words about how "younglings" were raised by many filled my head. It had sounded terrifying at first. Now it just made sense. Living on this ship made sense. Alernon made… God, he made me orgasm so many times that I thought I was going to lose my damn mind.

My chest ached with what I felt for Alernon.

Frowning, I sat up and rubbed the questionable organ. How dumb was I to feel this much for a guy I barely knew?

But did I barely know him?

He was the kind of guy who would choke down an awful meal to make a kid happy. He was the kind of guy who followed the rules but knew when to break them to save the people he cared about. He was the kind of guy who spoke about his mom with love and reverence. Sure, it was a slightly weird reverence but one I was starting to understand.

I knew more about Alernon in the time I'd been on the ship than I'd known about Pin after the months I'd spent with him. So why shouldn't I feel something for Alernon? Why shouldn't I let myself love him?

A jolt of fear filled me at the thought of that, but I pushed it away. I refused to give Pin more control over me than I already had. And letting fear dictate my actions absolutely was control.

Alernon appeared in the doorway, his expression filled with concern.

We watched each other for a long moment as I continued to tell myself I was okay and that Alernon was safe.

"I'm trying," I said softly.

"Trying to do what?"

"To stop being so afraid to love you."

The images that stormed my mind had me grinning like an idiot. Alernon wanted to smother my face in kisses. He wanted to pick me up and carry me around the ship to tell everyone I loved him. He wanted to close the door and have his way with me again until I kicked him in the face because it was too much.

"You're really weird," I said.

His grin widened, and he crossed the room to give me a single kiss on the forehead.

"I believe the human definition of alien means different. So calling me weird is logical. Come eat what Baynol and the younglings have prepared."

We ate a nice breakfast together then dropped the kids off at the entertainment room. After kissing the daylights out of Alernon in the hallways, I went to check on Tebo.

He was sitting at the table in his room. His closely cut dark hair looked a bit fuller than it had when he was in bed. Maybe it was due to the way he was running his hand over it as he sipped water from a cup.

"Good morning," I said.

He jumped a little as he turned to look at me.

"How are you feeling?" I asked.

"A lot better, actually. It's real, isn't it? Everything you said."

"It is. Would you like to take a walk and look around the ship?"

"Can I?"

"Alernon said that only you can decide if you're up to it or not. But he'd like someone stronger than me along just in case you need help."

Tebo looked at his glass, which wasn't really glass but a glass-like substance that reflected light like a prism.

"By someone else, you mean an alien?" he asked.

"Yep. Nothing scary. I promise."

He gave a dry laugh and nodded. Five minutes later, the kids, Baynol, Peltear, and I took Tebo on a very slow tour. Having the kids there helped make it not tense or weird. And because of their time with the crew, they actually had answers to most of Tebo's questions.

We didn't make it to the observation deck, but we were able to show him a grow bay and the galley before he said he needed to go back to rest. We checked on the next patient and visited with her for almost an hour before Alernon commed that there was another transfer.

This patient was awake on arrival and threw up during the

scan. I held the girl's hand and assured her she was safe as she quietly cried. She had some kind of blood cancer. I hadn't even known that was possible. Once the scan and the stims were done, one of the Anrothe carried her to her room.

I sat with her and explained how I'd come to be on the ship and why they were helping people like her. She closed her eyes.

"I didn't believe my parents. I'd pretended to because I thought they were in denial." She turned her head to look at me. "I'm so tired. Dying doesn't sound bad, you know?"

I held her hand tighter. "Alernon told me that the treatments work, but it's up to the will of the patient. Don't give up. Not yet. There's a view I want to show you. Promise me that you'll wake up to see it with me, okay?"

She smiled slightly and nodded without opening her eyes.

I left the room and hurried to the comms center. Alernon was standing before the feeds, watching them.

"I'm worried about the new patient," I said. "I think she's giving up. Who's your youngest crew member?"

Alernon turned to look at me with a slight frown.

"Why?"

"Because he's going to sit his butt next to her bed and be responsible for giving her the best, most hopeful dreams of her life."

"Why the youngest, though?" Quinoll asked.

"Because she's young, and waking up to someone around their thirties sitting next to her would be creepy."

Alernon tilted his head as he studied me.

"How old do you believe I am, Stacy?"

Just the way he said it was enough for my eyes to go wide. While drafting the agreement, he'd mentioned technology to prolong a lifetime. Adriana and I had been against adding it for various reasons. I hadn't considered what having that technology might mean regarding Alernon's age, though.

"No…" I breathed.

"Not every species ages the same or uses a solar-run to count the passing time," he said. "However, if I were to age myself by Earth's standards, I would have experienced one hundred and seventy-three rotations."

I stared at him for several mind-numbing seconds.

"This is another one of those things I'm just going to need to get used to," I said finally. "Send whoever you think is best for the role then. But make sure that person knows they aren't trying to win a mate. They're just trying to give her the will to live, okay?"

Alernon nodded just as an alarm started to sound. It wasn't the first time I'd heard the piercing sound.

"Ship detected in Senwar system," the ship said.

"Display the ship's location relative to ours," Alernon said.

I gasped when I saw it on the other side of the Earth.

"Command Alernon, identify the ship," Alernon said.

"The ship is of Quanl origin."

"Send a comm request," Alernon said.

"Comm request denied."

Quinoll closed his eyes as if in pain.

"Command Alernon, send an emergency message to Earth's leaders with the location of the ship and the following voice clip," Alernon said. "A ship with stealth capabilities has appeared in your orbit. Our attempt to communicate with them was denied. According to the laws of the systems, we cannot intercede on your behalf. Know that the humans you have entrusted into our care are safe. End message."

"What is it doing?" I asked, even though I knew.

"It's a smaller ship," Alernon said. "Its hold capacity would be similar to the ship that took Adriana."

I watched the screen.

"Call Annah Bergen," I said.

She answered within a minute of Alernon opening a comm to her cell phone.

"Hello?" I heard her ask, sounding confused.

"Annah, it's me, Stacy. There's another ship in Earth's orbit. Alernon just sent an emergency message. Did you get it?"

I heard movement. "Yes. I see it. Another Oebri ship?"

"No. It's the same kind of ship that took Adriana and the kids. The Oebri can't do anything but watch because there's no agreement, Annah. If they did try to help, they'd start a war with other races in the systems. And guess where that war would be fought?"

Annah's exhale told me she understood.

"People are going to be taken because Earth's leaders refused to acknowledge the truth. Kids, like Nicky and Lil. Annah, please," I begged. "A female living with the Oebri is safer than anyone forcefully taken from the planet. We need help. It's not too late to accept it. Please."

"I have calls to make," Annah said. "I will be in touch soon."

The call disconnected, and I looked at Alernon.

# CHAPTER THIRTY

## ALERNON

THE NEED TO SOOTHE AWAY STACY'S DISTRESS CAUSED A SURGE. IT wasn't filled with breeding need, though. It was filled with gentle peace. I watched her take a calming breath then another.

"Send a message to Baynol and Peltear so they can reassure Nicky and Lil," she said. "Is there a way to tell if the ship is already taking people?"

I pulled Stacy into my arms, hugging her and kissing her temple.

"We will monitor the situation closely. Perhaps you can—"

Adriana entered the comms center. Her gaze immediately went to the ship on the screen. The creamy color left her cheeks, and her lips parted.

"It's them," she said.

Her eyes rolled back in her head, and she started to collapse. Zarris moved quickly, catching her in his arms.

Stacy pulled free of my hold and went to Adriana, lightly tapping her cheek and calling her name.

"We should take her to a med bay," I said. I glanced at Quinoll, who nodded.

"Go," he said. "I will comm you as soon as I hear anything."

I strode out the door, heading for the nearest med bay where Zarris carefully set Adriana on the sys-unit's bed.

"Prepare for species type: human," I said. "Scan for health abnormalities and compare to the previous scan."

Stacy held one of Adriana's hands while Zarris held the other as the scan beam swept over Adriana. She roused with a sigh and a confused opening of her eyes.

"What happened?" she asked, looking at Zarris and Stacy.

"You fainted. How are you feeling?"

Adriana's confusion cleared, and she paled again. "A little queasy. Was that really the same ship that took me?"

"The ship that took you was destroyed," I said. "It is the same species, though."

She shuddered as the beam swept up her torso. "Lizard people."

Stacy patted her hand, and I could feel the well of her compassion. "It must have been bad for you to faint like that. Thank you so much for protecting Nicky."

I moved to wrap my arms around Stacy from behind, hating the tears she shed.

"Honestly, I'm not a fainter," Adriana said as the scan finished. "Not sure why I did."

"No injuries detected," the ship said. "Vitamin and mineral levels are normal. Dual Anrothe life detected and recorded. No abnormalities detected. Vitamin and mineral levels are normal. Scan complete."

Stunned, I stared at the female on the table.

"Wait, what did it just say?" she asked, looking at me. "What does dual Anrothe life mean?

"You are carrying Anrothe young. Dual young."

"Twins?" Adriana said.

Stacy let out a little squeak and leaned closer to Adriana.

"Are you happy? Cuz if you are, then I'm happy."

Adriana looked at Zarris, who was grinning like a man who'd been told his female carried dual life.

"I'm happy," Adriana said, glancing at Stacy then me. "I guess that explains why I've been so damn tired."

"Alernon," Quinoll's voice cut in through the room. "You're needed in the comms center."

"No more stress for you," Stacy said to Adriana. "You're on light patient visitation duty until further notice."

Stacy took my hand. "Leave communicating with Earth to us for now."

"I'll only agree if you add the kids to my duty roster until this unwelcome ship issue is resolved."

"Deal," Stacy said, pulling me from the room.

"They're going to want some alone time," she said after the door closed behind us. She stared at the smooth expanse of wall for a moment.

"She's going to be okay, right? Having alien babies won't kill her, will it?"

"She will be well. I vow it," I said, giving her a hug.

We hurried back to the comms center where Quinoll was pacing.

"They've begun taking humans," he said without preamble. "Communications from Earth continue to be conflicted. Annah is rallying for support of the agreement. An emergency meeting is set to start within the arc."

I looked at Stacy.

"My voice has done little to persuade them. Are you willing to try?"

"Yes."

We went to a comms room where she took a few prexels to organize her thoughts. Then, looking into an orb, she began to record a message for Earth's leaders.

"News of Earth's existence is spreading in the systems. The

ship in Earth's orbit will be the first of many. It is taking people—not water or plants or dirt but *people*—right now because we've stubbornly refused to listen to a race that has experience with what happens to newly discovered species.

"Have you looked at the data on the orbs? At the species that exist out there? The ones that will want to use us for breeding? I have. Some of them are terrifying.

"The people being taken aren't going to have a choice about which species they end up with or how they'll be used.

"I know what it's like to have no choice. What it's like to lie there and pretend that what's happening is enjoyable just to spare myself pain."

Anguish filled me at her admission, and I struggled to remain silent.

"We need to get smarter before everything else the Oebri predicted comes true. You view sending two thousand females to the Oebri every week as lives lost. They're not. They're lives saved from a fate worse than death. With the Oebri, they can't be taken. Ever.

"The contract that Adriana and I helped draft will give the women of Earth a real choice. You say people won't like this? I think it's time to ask them which is better. Abduction that results in forced breeding or worse? Or having time to say goodbye to the people we love and having a choice?

"Stop hesitating. Decide before you lose someone you love too."

She looked at me.

"I don't know what else to say. Maybe if we give the ship the coordinates for the next meeting and a few delegates are taken, those asshats would start listening."

"Some of them are listening, Stacy. Give them time."

"And what about the people already on the ship? What do you

think they'd have to say about giving the delegates more time to decide what's safest for the human people?"

I ended the recording and sent it from the room with a few taps on my datapad.

"Come. Let us see what the delegates think of asking the public how they feel about abduction."

Three arcs later, seventy-five humans had been taken, and we finally received a counteroffer. Water in exchange for protection and the immediate assistance with the ship in their orbit.

Stacy was so angry that Quinoll continued to send her nervous glances.

"They know damn well you don't need water." She pointed at one of the messages on the feed. "Just because they're giving up something they think is precious doesn't make it precious. We warned them," she said. "It's time to broadcast this live. Get me a list of names."

Once she had the names of those already reported missing, she recorded another message for the public.

"Several weeks ago, Adriana Wilston broadcasted that aliens were real. While the public debated whether or not her message was a hoax, Earth's governments attempted to determine the location of the alien ship. Our leaders *believed* her. Yet, even after speaking to the Oebri in person on multiple occasions, our leaders continue to ignore the warning the Oebri came here to deliver...that there are hundreds of other alien species in the systems, and Earth has resources they want.

"No," she said, correcting herself. "We have resources they need so badly they will be willing to start a war to get them."

"Our leaders were warned by the Oebri that, without contracted protection, our planet would be open to invasion and that, once the ships appear in our orbit, the Oebri cannot intervene on Earth's behalf. And since that warning, our leaders have made no progress toward an agreement to protect us.

"Right now, there is a ship in Earth's orbit quietly taking resources."

She began to read each name she'd been given and where they'd been taken from and when.

"People are the resources they need. And while our leaders are shouting 'impossible' over what the Oebri are asking in return for protection, another species is already here, taking what they need.

"The problem is simple. Many of the races in the systems are dying due to fertility issues. Issues humans don't have. That's why these people are being abducted. They'll be taken to planets and used for breeding without any say in the matter.

"If we want any choice in who our partners are, we need to negotiate. We *will* be used for breeding. That's a non-negotiable fact. How we're used can still be up to us.

"You have a voice. Use it. Help us save the people who were taken. Please."

I ended the video there and released it along with the proposed agreement to the public.

"You did well, my beauty," I said, coming around the table to hold her. "If your passionate appeal cannot convince them—"

"Then hundreds of thousands of people will go missing," she said sadly, rubbing her face against my skin. I held her, allowing her to seek whatever comfort she needed from me. When she'd had enough, she pulled back and met my gaze.

"If that video doesn't convince them, I think we should start sending videos of shirtless Oebri and Anrothe doing general tasks like cooking, cleaning, lifting heavy things. Maybe some handstand pushups. You'll have women ready to come aboard without any agreement needed."

"We would have no shortage of volunteers for those videos," I said.

She grinned at me then opened the door to the comms center.

Quinoll and Vegori were both present and feverishly tapping on their datapads.

"The most recent video has incited mass response. Many are talking about protests. Some have already started gathering at various global locations. The world leaders know, and they are reacting swiftly in an attempt to calm their people.

"However, another ship appeared while you were broadcasting. I sent the information to world leaders, but their systems were able to detect the ship as well. It's a much older trader ship. The people on the planet noticed. There are pictures already circulating, which has added credibility to Stacy's message."

"There's a new message from Earth," Vegori said. "One female for each ship destroyed."

"Unbelievable," Stacy said. "Nicky listens better than they do."

"Annah Bergen is asking if she can sign the contract as it is on her country's behalf. She believes protecting one piece of the planet at a time is the best way to convince other countries."

"Tell her we agree," I said. "And ask if she would be willing to sign aboard our ship and visit the recovering humans afterward."

Taking Stacy's hand, I started for the hallway. "We'll be waiting in the first transference bay."

As soon as we were in the hallway, I swung Stacy into my arms, startling a yip from her.

"Why are we running?" she asked.

"She will agree, and when other leaders see that she was welcomed aboard the ship to sign, we will see more willingness."

The next several arcs passed in a blur, and Stacy stood beside me through it all. We had collected over a dozen signatures and provided an equal number of tours for delegates.

Stacy began to yawn in earnest, and I knew she wanted to return to the younglings, though she said nothing.

"Go," I said when another agreement came in.

SAGE ALDER

She shook her head and took my hand.

"I'll sleep when you sleep."

I kissed her forehead and looked at Quinoll. He smiled slightly and nodded.

"Go. I can accept signatures and provide tours while you rest."

The younglings were already asleep in their beds with Baynol resting comfortably on the family lounge when we entered.

"Were they scared when they went to bed?" Stacy asked.

"No," Baynol said, rising. "They know they are safe on Alernon's ship. They saw you walking with a delegate twice and wanted to call your name. I suggested they allow you to speak privately. I hope that was okay."

"That's fine," Stacy said. "I think they would have been more anxious if they'd been included in anything today."

Baynol nodded and started for the door. "I'll return to make the morning meal in a few arcs. Rest well, Lady."

"Thank you, Baynol."

As soon as he left, I turned her and kissed her hungrily.

"How tired are you?" I asked against her lips.

"Not that tired," she said, tugging me toward our room.

I loved her responsiveness and hunger for me. It felt like it equaled my own, but knowing it was all her made it more delicious.

When she reached the bedroom, she pushed me back onto the bed.

"I've been thinking of this all day," she said, lifting her skirt and straddling my hips. Tugging down my pants, she slowly impaled herself. "Imagine sitting in a chair and doing this? Or better yet, on one of the conference tables. No underwear opens up a world of possibilities."

And I imagined every single one as she rode me. My release tingled up the base of my spine, demanding that I grip her hips and arch into her. She mewled little sounds as she dug her fingernails into my chest and ground her wet breeding slit against me.

When I reached between us and gently tugged her clit, she came with a scream.

An emotion wrapped around me, burrowing deep and deeper still as she trembled, until it touched my heart.

Everything went silent as I stared up at the woman who had just bound herself to me; mind, body, and heart.

# CHAPTER THIRTY-ONE

## STACY

Panting and barely keeping myself upright, I smiled down at Alernon and reveled in the pulsing aftershocks of my release. Sex with him was off-the-charts amazing, and I didn't care if I had to commit to living on an alien space station for the rest of my life to keep it. He was worth it. I wasn't letting go. He was mine, and I was his. But I'd be even more his if he flipped me like a pancake and aggressively—

He rolled us so he was on top and started moving within me again. The long, firm strokes had me shivering and gasping. It was everything I'd wanted.

*Shit. Could he read my mind now too?*

"I'm humbled and overjoyed by what you've given me. Allow me to give you more."

Sweet heaven, did he give it. Again and again.

Exhausted, I lay with my head on his shoulder while I caught my breath.

"My beauty. My life," he murmured, stroking his hand up and down my arm. "My hunger for you will never fade."

My nethers gasped in fear, and I made a face.

"It needs to fade until tomorrow," I said. "I need sleep."

He chuckled and hugged me closer.

"Then rest, my love."

My heart gave a painful thump hearing those words. His love? Me?

"No," he said softly. "There is no room for fear now. Not here, safely in my arms. I will never do anything to hurt you. Close your eyes. Calm your mind. Rest."

As he spoke, a sense of complete calm washed over me. I closed my eyes and exhaled heavily.

WHEN I WOKE, I was clean, dressed, and alone in bed. Through the open door, I heard the kids quietly laughing and the low echoing rumble of masculine laughter.

I also heard the unmistakable chime of Alernon's comm and his sigh.

"Tell your mother I wanted to wait for her to wake but that Quinoll needed me."

"Okay," Nicky said.

I scrambled out of the bed and raced out of the bedroom.

"Mom!" Nicky said when he saw me.

Alernon paused before the main door and looked back at me. The heat in his gaze sent chills through me as I hurried to his side and hugged him. He returned the hold without question.

"Thank you," I whispered.

He pulled back to look at me in confusion.

"I'm clean and dressed," I said.

His slow smile added to the heat I felt.

"It was my pleasure." He kissed my forehead. "Baynol made an exceptional breakfast this morning. Eat. Join me whenever you are ready."

With one last kiss and smile, he released me and left.

I turned toward Baynol and the kids, marveling at my new reality. My lover was encouraging me to eat the breakfast the guy who'd been trying to win me over had made.

When Baynol handed me my plate, and I saw all the flowers decorating the heart-shaped pancake, I amended that thought to "still trying to win me over." Oddly, it didn't make me feel even a little uncomfortable. I thanked him for the meal, sat with the kids, and had a relaxed breakfast, knowing that Baynol was just happy to be a part of our lives. That all of the Anrothe and Oebri were.

If only the people on Earth would see that.

After kissing both the kids on the cheek, I left them with Baynol and Peltear and went to join Alernon.

The comms center was completely silent when I entered. Quinoll stood beside Alernon, watching the feeds. Just to the side, another two Oebri read their feeds. Their absolute focus drove my attention to what they were reading.

Earth leaders were addressing the public, doing their best to stop protests and riots before they started. And in doing so, they'd acknowledged the truth of my message. They'd been talking to aliens. And the abductions were real. They also plainly stated what the Oebri were asking for in return for helping retrieve the abducted people and how they'd refused because they couldn't in good conscience commit to giving away people they had no right to give.

"We need to address this before the media spins it like you're the bad people here," I said from behind them.

Alernon turned to face me.

"How? What more can we say or do to prove our intentions?"

"I think it's time for some reality TV," I said. "Start broadcasting everything. Show the work on the comms station. Visit Tebo and talk to him about his story and how he's feeling. Get Adriana in a med bay and do a scan on the babies again. Show the world how over the moon everyone on this ship is."

"If you believe it will help, then that is what we'll do."

I stayed next to him through it all. We didn't just do what I'd suggested. We did so much more.

We showed the kids playing and new patients coming aboard for scans. We showed the grow bays and our view of the moon. And the orb caught every single loving glance Alernon threw my way and how he asked if I was tired or hungry in between everything we did together.

When it came time for Adriana's scan, it caught Alernon's tears as he stared at the two tiny 3D projected blips.

"How long until your fancy machine can detect gender?" I asked.

Adriana's gaze swung to Zarris. "Do we want to know the gender?"

I snorted. "You're carrying two hybrid babies. Do you honestly want any kind of surprise?"

She shot me a dirty look. "They're Anrothe like Zarris and human, not some weird elephant-human mashup. There's not going to be a whole lot of surprise." Her gaze shifted to Alernon. "Right?"

"You have nothing to fear, Adriana," he said. "I vow it." Then to the ship, he said, "Provide detailed analysis on new life forms."

"New life forms detected. Anrothe genetics eighty-five percent. Human genetics fifteen percent. Vitamins and nutrient levels normal for Anrothe genetics. Size below average for Anrothe genetics for single births. No data for dual births. Size above average for human dual births."

Adriana made a face and looked at Zarris.

"That means my belly's going to get huge and be covered with stretch marks."

"You will be beautiful carrying these younglings," he said, full of love and adoration.

I wanted to look at the orb so badly and yell, "See? This is what you're missing out on," but I refrained.

"Reproductive organs match Anrothe and human females," the ship said. "End report."

"Twin girls?" I asked, looking at Alernon.

He looked like he'd been hit with a brick. Zarris leaned on the table while staring at Adriana's middle with an open mouth.

"Two females?" he echoed, lifting his gaze to Adriana.

"Happy?" she asked with tears in her eyes.

He picked her up off the table and left the room without a backward glance. Grinning, I looked at Alernon.

"Ready to tell the crew that bit of news? I'm betting Quinoll faints."

That jarred a laugh from Alernon as he took my hand.

"News of a dual female Anrothe birth will spread quickly," he said as the orbs hovered in front of us. "The systems are aware of the Anrothe low female birth rate. That a human could help produce two will attract the attention of many."

We slowly started toward the comms center.

"Can we keep it secret for a while?" I asked.

Alernon gave me a compassionate look. "I can gain more support and protection for Earth if I report this news to my home world and the Prime Assembly. Earth will need the support, Stacy. The ship in orbit likely already has a full hold and is watching our broadcast even now. They will understand the importance of the humans they've taken and will be less likely to sell them as a food source when their value as breeders would be much higher."

Quinoll was facing the door when we entered, the images from the orbs were playing in 3D behind him.

"The ship is moving to leave Earth's orbit," he said.

My hold on Alernon's hand tightened. "What do we do?"

"We continue to wait for Earth to negotiate mutually beneficial terms for protection. Once they understand that the contract you

SAGE ALDER

and Adriana sent is not exclusive to the Anrothe and Oebri but to all technologically advanced species, I hope they will see our wisdom in requesting two thousand female volunteers a week. That number is far fewer than what would be taken if the contract is denied."

I knew he was speaking for the viewers' benefit rather than mine and played along.

"Can't you ...I don't know. Park in front of their ship or something so they can't leave yet? Anything to buy Earth some more time?"

Alernon shook his head and brought my hand to his lips to kiss me tenderly.

"I cannot. To do so would start a war right at Earth's doorstep. Thousands of ships would fill this space, attempting to destroy one another for the right to plunder your planet at will. Humans would be taken, and your planet would be destroyed. That is something neither of us wants."

I turned toward Quinoll. "Show me the ship."

The image of us changed to an image of the ship slowly leaving Earth's atmosphere. The tears that gathered in my eyes weren't fake as I imagined the people on that ship. Their fear. Their helplessness.

"Whatever you are, if you're watching this broadcast, please, please, return the people you've taken. They have families. Friends. People who will miss them. Please."

The ship began to blur.

"What's happening?" I asked.

"It's preparing to jump," Quinoll said.

We all watched in silence as the ship disappeared.

"It's outside of the broadcast range now," Quinoll said. "We've tracked its first jump, but there's no way for us to know if they jumped again until we pursue them."

I glanced at the feeds, seeing the frantic correspondences and

314

news updates from my planet, and hoped the leaders wouldn't take too long to decide.

"I'm going to put the kids to bed," I said. "Join me when you can." Then I stood on my toes, intending to give Alernon a sweet parting kiss.

He took it to another level that left me panting and dizzy when we finally parted.

"I will join you soon," he said roughly. "I vow it."

I nodded, and it took some effort to force myself from his arms and out the door.

The kids looked like they were ready to collapse when I showed up at the entertainment room.

"It's been a long day, hasn't it?" I asked. They both nodded, and I looked at Peltear and Baynol. "Would you mind carrying them to our rooms?"

Lil immediately lifted her arms for Peltear.

"I can walk," Nicky said stubbornly.

I could see the impending meltdown, though. "Of course you can. But how many more chances will Baynol get to carry the boy he thinks of as his son?"

The rebellion vanished from Nicky's gaze as he looked up at Baynol. The big guy didn't say anything to Nicky, letting the petulant child decide for himself.

"Fine," Nicky said with a sigh. "You can carry me."

Nicky fell asleep on Baynol's shoulder before we reached our rooms. Lil had been out first, though.

"They're at the age where they just stopped taking afternoon naps," I said. "Which means they're more likely to get overtired by the end of the day and act out. Crying. Tantrums. Things like that. Let me know if that ever happens."

Baynol nodded as I opened the door for them.

I watched them tuck the kids into bed then walked them to the door.

"Thank you for today," I said.

"Did showing Earth what life is like on the ship help?" Peltear asked. He'd been the one to do handstands for the kids while the orbs were recording.

"I think so," I said, hoping I was right.

We were all ready to start the next phase, and I desperately hoped that the leaders would think of the people on the ship that had just left orbit.

Alernon didn't return to our rooms before I fell asleep alone. But he made it up to me by waking me in the best possible way. Spasming around him and reveling in the hot wash of his release, I caught my breath underneath him then leisurely kissed him.

"Good morning," I whispered when I pulled away.

"A very good rising," he agreed, tenderly kissing my brow. "The younglings are already awake and eating with Baynol, and Earth has agreed to your terms."

I pushed his head away from my neck.

"What?"

He chuckled. "The leaders have unanimously agreed and have begun signing the contract in earnest. Tebo has had his last treatment and is ready to return to his home as well."

Stunned, I looked up at him.

"Are you serious?"

He slowly smiled, and I felt a wash of amusement from him. It stirred my own smile.

"I know we've been waiting for this, but I'm still surprised they've finally agreed. What does that mean for us? How soon are they going to start sending women? When will the station be done? We will need to finalize those plans and figure out where—"

He stopped me with a toe-curling kiss.

"Live in the present moment," he said, moving inside of me. "I will ensure it's pleasurable for you."

He delivered on that promise twice before his wrist comm started to ping.

Thanks to Baynol, we were able to sneak into the shower and clean up before facing the kids. They agreed to go with us to say goodbye to Tebo before heading to the entertainment room. Tebo promised to tell everyone about his time on the ship and the second chance at life he was given. And Alernon promised to monitor him after Adriana voiced her worry about Tebo being taken for questioning.

"We are past that phase," Alernon said. "Now that Earth has agreed, they have no reason to mistreat anyone who has been on the ship."

Adriana and I shared a doubtful look but didn't say anything else as we watched the kids leave again with Baynol and Peltear.

"Baynol said they are going to watch the engineers float the core systems," Zarris said. "He wasn't sure what that meant, though."

"The engineers will begin building the trade station outside of the ship," Alernon said. "When the primary hub is finished, they will then move it to its permanent home."

"Which will be where?" I asked.

"Near one of Jupiter's moons," Alernon said. "It's the most defensible location. Come. It's time to look at the station plans."

# CHAPTER THIRTY-TWO

## ALERNON

I READ THE UPDATE REGARDING THE COORDINATED SEARCH FOR THE missing humans and felt a surge of frustration. After almost seven flares, we'd been unable to locate them. Earth's leaders were equally frustrated. However, due to the new agreement, three more Oebri ships had arrived and successfully prevented another abduction.

The official report sent to the Prime Assembly had been received and acknowledged. Flagships from the prime races were already en route to Earth, eager to join the protection agreement. Meanwhile, Earth's separate governments were setting up volunteer registration centers. There were already over ten thousand names.

Excitement and anticipation radiated from Adriana and Stacy as they entered the comms center.

"Okay, we think we have it," Stacy said, offering the datapad the pair had been using to finalize their "intake" plan for all new females.

I took the device from her, ignoring it momentarily in favor of a kiss. Her desire stirred at the first touch of our lips, and I reveled in it even as she pulled away and told me to behave.

"Tell me your plan," I said while looking at the datapad she'd given me.

"Earth's getting you the female volunteers for your Alien Bride program—that's what we're calling it. We are not calling it a Human Breeding program." She aimed a narrow-eyed stare at Quinoll, who looked away quickly.

"What we need," Adriana continued, "are volunteers to help with the intake. They'd be outside the scope of the two thousand volunteers we accept weekly because they wouldn't be sent away to live anywhere else. Station only work, once it's complete."

"We want to ask Grace to join us," Stacy said. "If she's here, we wouldn't need to separate Lil and Nicky."

"And at least five more volunteers," Adriana said. "But you have to stress it's not about hooking up. We need them to become comfortable with the ship, the Oebri, and Anrothe, and they have to be friendly and empathetic."

"Problem solvers and a calm influence," Stacy added.

"We want you to contact Annah with our proposal."

I continued to read what they'd written. It was impartial and fair to all parties. And while it stressed that the females who volunteered were not coming here for the purpose of breeding, it also stated they had the right to change their minds and accept a partner if they chose.

"I'll contact Annah now."

Immediately after signing the protection agreement, I'd sent a similar request for Grace's presence, which had been ignored. Understanding that Earth's leaders were dealing with coordinating a very large change that impacted all of its people, I hadn't pressed for an answer. But waiting longer wasn't sensible for the sake of sweet Lil or her birther's sister.

Stacy and Adriana waited as I sent the comm request to Earth. Annah responded a few prexels later.

"Good morning, Alernon," she said with a smile. "How can I assist you today?"

The pleasant female at the end of her breeding years had proven to be an invaluable ally.

"My request to the US delegate to speak with Lil's aunt has gone unanswered. Can you relay to all the delegates that I will transfer to the surface to speak to Grace in person about their reunion? Since I did not receive prior approval, I will record the visit."

"I'm sure that will be fine," Annah said.

"Adriana and Stacy also have another request. With the trade station progressing swiftly, they would like to recruit volunteers to help with the intake process. I will send you the proposal."

"I look forward to receiving it. The medical team was extremely impressed with the information you sent regarding the latest patients you scanned. They are very interested in acquiring a sys-unit for use on Earth."

Stacy set her hand on my arm before I could answer.

"That's actually something Adriana and I are working on...free sys-unit scans for all volunteers and family members. We will have that proposal to you next."

I hadn't been aware but was impressed with the direction of her thinking. It would continue to encourage volunteers and eliminate unnecessary, preventable deaths of breedable females.

"I look forward to that proposal too, then. Please let me know how your visit with Grace Adley goes."

I nodded and ended the comm, turning toward Stacy.

"You are as intelligent as you are beautiful," I said.

She smiled at me. "After the public reaction to Tebo's recovery story, Adriana and I figured Earth was going to ask for sys-units. But we were worried they'd privatize them and make it financially impossible for everyone to use them. Making them free and putting them in volunteer centers is the best way to keep them from being privatized and keep them widely available. Saying it's open to volunteers and their families creates opportunity. We won't care if it's a cousin two times removed or not. It'll help keep relations between the public and the trade station positive."

I kissed her forehead.

"Brilliant. Truly."

"How soon are you going to talk to Grace?" Adriana asked. "Should we get the kids?"

I turned to look at Quinoll.

"I'll verify she is still in her home and prepare the transference bay," he said.

"Now?" Stacy said. "I should go with you. The invitation will be a little more believable coming from me."

"I would prefer you stay here," I said. "You are safer here, and there is still widespread unrest in—"

"Alernon." Quinol's tone cut through what I was about to say.

Turning, I looked at the screen. Grace's house was taped off with yellow ribbon.

Stacy's distress hit me, and I immediately sent her a calming wave.

"That's police tape," Adriana said. "What happened?"

Quinoll tapped on his datapad, and a list of correspondence related to Grace's disappearance over a week ago appeared on the feed.

"With the abductions, the protection agreement, and the trade station build, we missed this," he said. His anger and devastation were plain to see.

"It's impossible to catch everything," I said. "Go back to the day she went missing. Scan for any recent surveillance showing her likeness."

I stroked my hand up and down Stacy's arm as he did as I asked.

"It could take flares," I said. "I'll contact Annah and let her know what—"

"Grace Adley located."

Several images popped up. Grace looked terrified in each one, and beside her was a face I would never forget.

"Pin," Stacy gasped. Her fear swelled as she looked at me. "He thought it was all a prank. He was watching the news when Adriana said Nicky's name and mentioned Lil's Aunt. He thought we were running some kind of scam for money. If he took her a week ago…"

She trailed off and looked at the images showing the inside of the same trade center she'd visited when the ship had first detected her.

"Pin took her back to his house."

"How dumb can he be?" Adriana asked. "He would have let her go after the peace agreement, wouldn't he?"

Stacy slowly shook her head. "You're assuming he's logical."

I read through the feeds and saw that the US delegate had been made aware of the kidnapping shortly after my original inquiry. She'd requested discreet effort to locate the woman, assuming she'd left to look for her niece herself.

"Prepare for transference," I said.

Stacy's grip on me tightened. "He's crazy, not stupid. He'll know you're real now."

"He cannot hurt me."

"Don't be overconfident," she said, angrily poking me in the ribs.

"I vow to be the most cautious bonded mate."

She tilted her head at me. "Bonded mate?"

"Did you not accept me into your heart, mind, and body?"

"Don't even try lying about the body part," Adriana said. "Baynol said he walked in when Alernon had you bent over the couch."

The absolute horror on Stacy's face promised it would take much coaxing to repeat that very enjoyable experience.

"Once Baynol realized we were occupied, he left," I said.

"You knew?" she said in a very high pitch.

I glanced at Adriana, needing guidance to understand Stacy's expression.

"Hey, I think it's only fair," Adriana said. "Alernon walked in on Zarris and me."

"This is why I want to know how to lock doors," Stacy said.

Adriana laughed and bumped into Stacy. "If they can't do the deed themselves, it helps to know that someone else at least is. Don't be mad. I think it made Baynol's lifetime."

Some of the distress left Stacy.

"Next time, we lock the door," she said, narrowing her eyes at me.

Relieved there would be a next time, I nodded.

"Allow me to retrieve Grace, and I will show you how to lock the door once I return."

Stacy wrapped her arms around me.

"Be careful. Please."

I kissed her again and left the comms center. The orbs were waiting when I entered the transference bay and told Quinoll I was ready.

Once again, I appeared on Earth's surface as the sun set. Not pausing to look at the colorful sky, I strode to the house. Instead of knocking, I kicked the primitive lock free.

The wooden portal banged against the wall with the force of my entry, and a flurry of noise sounded inside. I watched Pin scramble from his chair. It fell to the floor behind him as he reached for his gun.

"Where is she?" I asked.

He fired at me, which the orbs' barrier absorbed.

"We have surveillance showing Grace Adley was with you seven days ago. Where is she?" I repeated.

Pin withdrew something else from the back of his pants. Two probes shot toward me only to fall to the floor when they met the orbs' shielding.

"You want her? Give me Nicky and Stacy," Pin said before launching himself at me.

Knowing that what happened here would be watched by many, I did not give into my urge to break his neck when I caught him by the throat and lifted him off his feet.

"Detain lifeform human for further questioning," I said.

The orb to my right shot him with a stun jolt. Pin arched in pain, and his eyes rolled back into his head. I dropped him on the floor and went to check the rest of the house.

Grace was in the bedroom, tied to a bed. When she saw me, she started to cry.

"Be at peace, Grace. I am Alernon. Your niece, Lil, has been living on my ship. May I untie you so we can speak?"

She nodded frantically, and I quickly untied the cloth from her mouth.

"Thank you," she rasped. "I thought I was going to die here. That guy is a nut job. He went crazy when he saw Stacy kissing you on the TV."

She surprised me by wrapping her arms around me as soon as they were free. Shaking, she sobbed and held onto me. I glanced at the orbs, knowing that Stacy was watching this, and hoped she would not think I was showing preference to another female.

"My apologies that our actions caused you distress," I said. "Allow me to finish untying you."

Crying, she nodded and released her hold on me. I finished removing her bindings and helped her stand. She was shorter than Stacy by a hand's width but had more roundness.

Her soft terra-colored eyes were puffy and red from her tears as she brushed her chin-length brown hair back from her face.

"Where's Lil?" she asked. "Is she still on your ship? Can I see her? Please?"

"Of course. I will take you to her." I lead Grace out of the bedroom. She hesitated when she saw Pin on the floor of the living room.

"Is he dead?" she asked.

"No. He is simply immobilized."

"What's going to happen to him?"

"He violated a prime system law, punishable by death, when he abused Stacy and her youngling, Nicky. Taking you and confining you as he did is also a violation of prime system law. Did he hurt you, Grace?" I asked when she continued to stare at him.

She tore her gaze from him to look at me.

"If you're asking me if I was beaten or raped, the answer is no. However, he forgot to feed me, gave me water by pouring it on my face, and I'm wearing clothes I've peed in."

Despite everything that she suffered, she met my gaze steadily, and I didn't feel a hint of fear from her.

"Forgive us for not coming for you sooner. We requested permission from your government to contact you seven days ago. Instead of telling us that you were missing, they ignored our request and attempted to locate you on their own."

"Don't worry. No hard feelings," she said. "To you and your people, anyway."

I wasn't entirely certain what she meant by that, but she offered me a small smile, which I hoped meant she was assuring me she wasn't angry.

"Since Pin's crimes are against females under Oebri protection, it is within our rights to hold him until the Prime Assembly can examine his actions. I'll take him back to the ship with us to await his examination. Will you be able to follow me without assistance?"

"I'll stick to you like glue. Promise."

Odd speech, I thought as she nodded in agreement.

I picked up Pin and slung him over my shoulder. After checking to make sure Grace was following, I led the way out the door.

She laughed when I asked her to step into the light but willingly walked into the transference beam. The ship's bay solidified around us. Near where we stood, Lil waited with Adriana.

Grace let out a cry and ran toward the little girl, picking her up and hugging her through her tears.

"I've got this," Adriana said. "You go take care of that and find Stacy. She's with Nicky. She didn't want him to be anywhere near Pin."

"I understand," I said.

Leaving her with Grace, I exited the bay and headed down another hall. Quinoll already waited for me.

Without a word, he opened the door to a much smaller holding bay with bromin barrier cells. I tossed the human male on the floor of one. The bromin barrier engaged, and I waited for the stun effects to wear off. It took several more prexels.

Pin groaned and sat up. He studied his cell then me.

"Do you think this scares me?" he said with a laugh. "I've been watching the news. You can't do anything to me. Hurting a human will upset all your precious negotiations." He stood and stalked toward the bromin barrier. "You took me by force. What do you think is going to happen when people find out? They're going to demand my release. And if you want me to keep quiet about the way you treated me, you're going to return my family with me."

A disbelieving laugh escaped me.

"Humans are unique in so many ways," I said. "Your ability to self-delude is exceptional. I believe your people will not ask for your return.

"They are interested in gaining access to our healing technology, and I want you to be held accountable for your crimes against Stacy, Nicky, and Grace. I believe we will be able to come to an agreement.

"And I don't fear showing your world what you did to Stacy to warrant your capture and inevitable punishment. It will help the people of your planet understand how precious your females are to the systems.

"Stone Pinchas, your death will not be kind."

I turned my back on his yelled threats and left the holding bay with Quinoll. The orb that had followed me stayed there to monitor the male's behavior.

"The Prime Assembly representatives can't get here soon enough," Quinoll said.

I silently agreed.

# CHAPTER THIRTY-THREE

## STACY

While I watched Nicky play, my emotions wavered between disbelief and worry. I hated that Pin had taken Lil's aunt because of me, and I was so glad Alernon was able to rescue her and bring her back to the ship. I was even happier he was able to do all of that without a scratch on him. But why did he have to bring Pin back onto this ship? What if Pin escaped?

I wouldn't be able to sleep until I knew Pin was off this ship again. Why couldn't Alernon just leave Pin on Earth?

Nicky glanced at me then the door. Baynol drew his attention with another handstand demonstration. Both Baynol and Peltear were doing a great job distracting Nicky from the fact Lil wasn't with him.

How they and the rest of the crew treated us was part of the reason I'd decided to give life on the trade station with Alernon a try. They were all amazing, and I couldn't imagine Nicky ever being happy to go back to Earth's standard curriculum after everything he'd experienced on Alernon's ship.

And honestly, I wouldn't have been happy to go back either. I loved life on the ship. I loved life with Alernon. The only problem now was the fact Alernon had brought the man who had mentally, emotionally, and physically abused me onto the same ship that my son and I were on.

Couldn't Alernon understand that I—

Alernon walked through the door. His gaze swept the space, searching for me. And once it locked on me, it didn't waver as he closed the distance between us.

Everything else in the room faded into non-existence as I stared at his beautiful face.

He didn't stop moving until I was in his arms with my head resting against his chest. I was so desperately relieved. With him, I felt safe. The worry fell away even though I still didn't like the situation.

"It's over now," he said.

"Is it? He's on this ship, Alernon. Why this ship? There are three others."

"I'll have him transferred immediately," Alernon said without hesitation. "Forgive me."

I let out a breath and tipped my head back to look at him. His beautiful pale eyes met mine.

"You saved me. You protected my son, and you caught the man who hurt us. I feel safe and loved every second of every day now. There's nothing to forgive, and I'm sorry I sounded like I was complaining. I wasn't. I just don't want him anywhere near Nicky again."

Alernon kissed my forehead and cheeks, touching me soothingly in a way that showed just how much he loved me.

"I understand," he said. "My apology is for not anticipating how you would feel."

I snorted and grinned at him. "You are the most amazing man I have ever met, and I'm so grateful you persistently pursued me until I gave in."

He smiled in return and would have kissed me if Nicky hadn't called his name just then.

"When is Lil coming back?" Nicky called.

Alernon glanced at me in question.

"I didn't tell him what was going on," I said softly. "Only that you needed to see Lil for a few minutes. I wasn't sure if Grace was going to agree to stay or not."

"Nicky is smart. It's better for him to know the truth of the situation than to hide it from him."

I knew Alernon was right, but I also didn't want Nicky to freak out about a separation that might not happen.

Facing my son, I debated how much to tell him.

"Alernon was able to find Lil's Aunt Grace. He brought her onto the ship so she could see where Lil's been living."

Nicky's expression shifted between fear and desperation.

"Auntie Rin and I are going to ask Lil's Aunt Grace to live here with us. So we're going to do our best to show her how fun and comfortable it is here and how much the Oebri and Anrothe really need our help. If you can help us do that without outright begging her to live here, you can come with us to talk to her if you want."

As Alernon said, Nicky was smart. I watched him take a few calming breaths then nod.

Turning, I gave Alernon a quick hug. "We'll see you at dinner then?"

"Of course."

I watched him walk away and felt a sense of real contentment. Whether Grace decided to join us or not, I felt I'd absolutely made the right choice for Nicky and me. I only hoped Grace would make the same choice to stay. It would break everyone's hearts to see Lil leave.

"Would you two mind staying behind?" I asked Baynol and Peltear. "Adriana and I want to talk to Grace first before we start slowly introducing her to everyone. The Anrothe will be before the Oebri to help ease her into what it'll mean to live on the ship. If she even agrees to stay, that is."

"Of course, Lady," Baynol said with an incline of his head.

"Try really, really hard not to call her lady when you do meet her, too, okay? Although I know it's respectful to you, it's odd to us, and I want you to make the best first impression possible."

They both nodded in understanding, and I held my hand out to Nicky.

"Ready to go say hello?"

As Nicky and I walked the quiet halls, my mind went over what Adriana and I planned to say. For now, Adriana was giving Lil and her aunt time to reunite. Once I arrived, the plan was to find out how much Grace knew about current events and what happened to Adriana, Nicky, and Lil before sending the kids away and explaining the situation Earth women would be facing.

"What happens if she doesn't want to live on the ship?" Nicky asked. "Will we go back too?"

I paused in the hall and kneeled so we were eye-to-eye.

"Do you want to go back if Lil does?"

Nicky's bottom lip trembled, and I pulled him into a hug.

"I don't want to leave either, Nicky," I said. "But I know how much you love Lil." I pulled back to wipe the tears from his eyes. "Do you know why I left you with Auntie Rin?"

He nodded. "Uncle Pin wasn't nice, and you didn't want him to trip me anymore."

My heart broke that he'd understood so much.

"It hurt so much to send you away with a smile that day, but I knew I had to do it because it was the best thing for you. If Lil's aunt decides living on Earth is the best thing for Lil, then we'll smile and say goodbye. But it won't be like when I had to say goodbye to you. We'll be able to call Lil and talk to her anytime.

And I bet Alernon would invite them to visit as often as they'd like, okay?"

Nicky sniffled and hugged me again. After he calmed down enough, we continued walking toward the transference bay.

Lil's eyes were as red as Nicky's when we entered. And the little girl took one look at him and ran to him. He opened his arms for her and caught her in a hug.

"It's okay," he said, patting her back. "I'm here."

I glanced from the kids to Grace. Her eyes were tearing up as she watched them, and in her gaze, I saw she understood how much Nicky meant to Lil. I hoped it meant she wouldn't need much convincing to stay.

"Why don't you two go to the galley and ask Raaln for a special snack, okay?" I said, looking at the kids. "I think we still have some of that ice cream Annah brought with her on her last visit."

Nicky took Lil's hand, and they raced from the transference bay.

"They're safe here. I promise," I said to Grace.

She nodded, and her gaze swept over me.

"You must be Stacy," she said. "I heard a lot about you. None of it was flattering, but considering the source, I didn't pay much attention to it."

My heart hurt for her. "I'm so sorry about what happened to you," I said. "Pin—"

She held up her hand and shook her head.

"Pin isn't your fault," she said. "I was with him long enough to understand he was completely crazy. I'm so grateful someone found me and got me out of there and that Pin won't be a problem for anyone anymore." She looked between Adriana and me. "Was the guy who saved me serious when he said Pin would die?"

"He was," Adriana said.

She and I shared a glance, and I changed the subject quickly.

"Are there any family or friends you want to contact to let them know you're okay?"

She shook her head. "My parents passed the year after Lil was born. A drunk driver." She shrugged slightly. "Other than my sister and my book club, I stayed to myself."

Her stomach rumbled loudly. "Any chance I can get in on that ice cream and maybe a change of clothes before we get serious?"

She saw our confusion and smiled. "I'm assuming we have something to discuss since you sent the kids away."

"We do," Adriana said, indicating we should start walking. "How up to speed are you on what's been happening with the aliens?"

"They're real. They're here. And they want two thousand women a week indefinitely in exchange for keeping the Earth safe," she said.

"It sounds a little disturbing when you say it like that," I said. "But you don't seem upset by it."

She laughed a little. "I saw parts of your 'reality with aliens' broadcast and the way they all looked at you and treated you. Although they're saying they want females, they're not being all grabby hands about it. I guess it helps that I was kidnapped, tied to a bed, and left to pee myself."

"Uh, what?" Adriana said.

I knew Adriana wasn't questioning the pee part. I could smell it as I walked beside Grace.

"I mean, being kidnapped by Pin helped put things in perspective," she said. "Would I rather be kidnapped by aliens who want to stare at me adoringly or by a psycho human? I'd rather have this reality."

"To be clear, you haven't been kidnapped," Adriana said quickly. "You can go back to Earth at any time."

"But we're really hoping you'll want to stay," I said.

"As an alien babymaker?" Her gaze swung to Adriana. "I saw

you're pregnant. The men you were with seemed pretty excited about it."

"No, not as a babymaker," I said quickly. "We could use your help getting everything ready for when the trade station is finished and all the female volunteers start coming up."

She nodded slowly, her gaze studying the empty hallway.

"What's the catch other than having to wear matching dresses?" she asked.

I really liked Grace. She was a few years older than us and so practical and calm. Exactly what we needed.

"Well, you'd be working with aliens, obviously, which might be a little nerve-wracking. Especially the Oebri. They can influence your emotions in a way that makes it feel like you're going to want to jump their bones to make babies with them," Adriana said.

"But it's not so overwhelming that you can't resist," I said. "Especially when you know in advance what you're feeling might not be your own emotions. It's kind of hard to explain until you experience it. And that's why we want your help. We need at least a dozen women who are used to the Oebri, Anrothe, and whatever other aliens come our way before we start accepting the volunteers."

"I'm twenty-nine and single," Grace said matter-of-factly. "My favorite pastime is reading romance novels and gardening. Having sexual fantasies about hot men without turning into a sex-starved maniac is my MO, so I don't think there will be any problems."

Adriana snorted a laugh.

"Does that mean you're interested in staying?" I asked.

She smiled slightly and looked at me.

"I have eyes. I saw how much your son meant to my niece. According to the news report I watched, my sister and brother-in-law are dead, right?"

At Adriana's remorseful nod, Grace's eyes watered a little before she took a deep calming breath.

"I think Lil has suffered enough loss for a while, don't you think? It's better to stay where she's happy. And if things change, I can always take her back to Earth, right?"

"Absolutely," I said.

I breathed a little easier knowing Lil and Nicky wouldn't be separated, and I couldn't wait to share the news with Alernon.

# EPILOGUE

## STACY

WE STOOD ON THE OBSERVATION DECK AND WATCHED MORE components for the trade station float away from our ship.

"We'll need to move soon," Alernon said from behind me, nuzzling my neck.

"Do you mean us or the ship?" I asked.

He chuckled. "Us. The ship will need to remain in Earth's orbit for protection."

I turned my head to meet his lips and enjoyed his tender kiss for a few moments before I heard, "Mom!" echoing down the hallway.

Alernon lifted his head and released me with a smile so we could face Nicky. He came tearing around the corner at a run, joy lighting his face.

"Guess what?" he shouted. "I was in the comms center helping Quinoll read the feeds, and a live comm came in."

He reached us, out of breath, and grabbed Alernon's hand, tugging on it slightly. It was the first time I saw Nicky treat Alernon like this, and it made me so happy I could cry.

"I got to talk to Grandma. She said she'll be here in a few days with presents for us."

Nicky continued to jump around, holding Alernon's hand, completely missing my confused look. Nicky didn't have a grandma.

"A few days?" Alernon said, scooping Nicky up. "Did she say what kind of gifts she would be bringing?"

"She said she's bringing your brother, Cobay, so I have someone to play with, and I told her about Lil, and she was really happy, and she said she has a gift for Lil too and that maybe she'll stay long enough to make sure she has a room next to ours on the station so that Cobay, Lil, and I have more time to play together, and she wants to meet you too, Mom."

Nicky looked at me, his outpouring of information complete. It'd done its job, though. I finally understood that Grandma was, in fact, Alernon's birth mom.

"Wow," I said. "That's super exciting. Have you told anyone else yet?"

He shook his head and did the "let me down" wiggling, which Alernon promptly respected.

"Quinoll said that I had to tell you first." Nicky grabbed Alernon's hand and tapped the comm on his wrist. "Command Alernon, let Quinoll know that I told Papa Alernon. I'm going to tell Papa Baynol now."

During one of the many long talks I'd had with Nicky while we waited for news of Grace, I'd explained how the systems view fathers. That it wasn't about who helped make Nicky but who loved him and helped guide him as he grew up. He'd been the one to ask if he could have more than one dad. Since Alernon had said it took many people to raise a "youngling," I'd said sure.

So far, Nicky had bestowed the Papa title on Alernon, Baynol, Peltear, and Quinoll. Since Raaln was close to perfecting a copycat vanilla ice cream recipe, he probably wasn't far behind.

Nicky took off before I could say anything else. I stared after him with a sigh.

"Sometimes it feels like he's turning feral," I said.

"With so many fathers, that would be impossible," Alernon said.

I laughed lightly and leaned into Alernon.

"I can't wait to see what the future brings."

He kissed me tenderly.

"With you by my side, it will bring untold joy."

Smiling to myself, I took his hand and slowly followed in Nicky's wake.

THANK you for reading *The Fey*, the second book in the **Alien Bride: First Conquest** trilogy. Don't miss **The Defender**, the final origin book in the Alien Bride universe. Check out the author's note to learn more!

# AUTHOR'S NOTE

Thank you so much for falling into this brand-new world filled with limitless untapped potential. So many things are happening. Building a trade station, making arrangements to accept all those new women, more aliens on the way...

How can the next book be the end, right?

It's not. It's the end to the *origin* of the Alien Bride universe, not the *end*-end.

I have so many more books planned. The systems are filled with *hundreds* of different alien species, and things are just getting started.

You can help shape the direction of this new world by leaving a review and telling me what you did or didn't like. Want more spice? Tell me! Want dubcon or rags-to-riches or aliens with extra fun-bits? Let me know. I'm always up for a challenge.

Just like Alernon.

That man had his work cut out for him. He knew when to push Stacy's boundaries to prove that he wasn't an asshole (even when those pushes might have made him seem like it) and he knew when to give her space.

And I hope I wrote Stacy's physical, emotional, and mental

recovery in a mostly believable and satisfying way. Healing takes time. We all know that. However, for the sake of the world-building, I had to hustle things along.

After all, more aliens are now on the way. ☺

Be sure to sign up for my newsletter at https://mjhaag. melissahaag.com/subscribe-sage-alder/ for all the upcoming alien news.

I'll be introducing several more species in Baynol's book, *The Defender*. But don't worry...the Oebri and Anrothe will still be around.

Until next time, happy reading!

Sage (aka Melissa)

# TERMS

**Arc** - An Hour

**Flare** - A Day

**Halo-flash** - Second

**Lunar rev** - One Month

**Prexel** - Minute

**Revolution** - how long it takes to go around a given sun - varies by system.

**Grow bay** - The room used for growing, like a greenhouse/solarium.

**Med bay** - The room with the sys-unit.

**Sys-unit** - A machine that can patch people up

**Fabrication unit** (aka fabricator) - a machine like a 3D printer that can make just about anything

**Jump** - hyperspace jump

**Standard** – Systems standard language

**Terra** - soil/earth

**Tuber** - the equivalent of a bastard

**Nutri-paste** – a food/paste that is nutritionally packed, but doesn't taste the best.

**Psy-surge** - This is what happens when the Oebri lose control of their emotions/shield.

**Birther** - the female who gave birth; "mother" is the one who raises the child

**Donor** - The sperm donor; "father" is the one who raises the child

# THE DEFENDER

## ALIEN BRIDES: FIRST CONQUEST, BOOK 3

### GRACE

The hot water felt like heaven on my skin as I scrubbed every inch of my body with vengeance, determined to wash away the stench of my captivity. Too bad it couldn't remove the crap in my mind too.

Closing my eyes, I tipped my head back to wash my face. A memory immediately bloomed.

*The news anchor's voice drifted in from the living room. Earth's leaders had accepted the aliens' terms, and the negotiations were over. My time was up.*

*A shadow filled the doorway of the bedroom. The ropes tying me to the bed bit into my skin painfully. A whimper escaped me.*

*"Blame that bitch, Stacy, for this, Grace," the man said. "She's why you're here."*

*He crossed the room and grabbed my face.*

*"If they don't come soon, you're not going to like what happens to you next."*

*Cold dread settled into my stomach with the certainty that he would kill me.*

"Fucking tool," I said, scrubbing my face and the memory away.

I wasn't in that psycho's home anymore, and in the last hour, my life had yet again been irrevocably changed.

*Be sure to check out The Defender, book 3 in the Alien Brides: First Conquest series!*

Did you know that Sage Alder also writes Paranormal Romance under M.J. Haag?

Be sure to check out her other titles!

FAIRY TALE TRILOGIES

(SAME WORLD)

### *Beastly Tales*

Depravity

Deceit

Devastation

### *Tales of Cinder*

Disowned (Prequel)

Defiant

Disdain

Damnation

RESURRECTION CHRONICLES

*(zombies and hottie demons!)*

Demon Ember

Demon Flames

Demon Ash

Demon Escape

Demon Deception

Demon Night

Demon Dawn

Demon Disgrace

Demon Design (novella)

Demon Discord (novella)

Demon Fall

Demon Kept

Demon Defeat: Part 1

Demon Blind (novella)

Demon Defeat: Part 2

*Connect with the author*

Website: MJHaag.melissahaag.com/

Newsletter: MJHaag.melissahaag.com/subscribe